QUEEN CROW

# All Hail

# J BREE

# Prologue

## THE JACKAL'S LAIR

"**B**eaumont. Don't be an idiot, just fucking stab me."

I squeeze my eyes shut a little tighter. I'm not one to attempt to block things out normally, I face everything head on but this? This situation I would do just about anything to get out of.

There's a knock at the door and I can't help but look as the Jackal steps up to answer it. The thick tattooed lines on his face are stark against the olive complexion of his skin. Objectively, he's an attractive man but the sadistic light behind his eyes makes it impossible to find him anything but disturbing.

He looks exactly like the deranged psychopath Lips has described to me dozens of times.

No wonder she's always been so scared of him.

"I told you I didn't want to be interrupted."

I can't hear the answer to his snarl, my heart is beating

too loudly in my own ears. My feet hurt in a way that I've never had to feel before. Sheltered. I've lived in a house with Joseph Beaumont Sr. my entire life and yet I've never had to feel pain like this before.

Ash felt it all for me.

"Listen to me, Beaumont. If he offers you the knife again you need to take it. There's no way I'm walking out of this room unharmed and you covered in blood and wounds. Just take the fucking knife."

I turn to look at Aodhan. The only marks on him are the ones he's done to himself, straining against the ropes and handcuffs. His wrists are a mess, blood dripping down his hands and onto the ground, pooling there slowly.

He looks nothing like the cousin we share.

I keep my mouth sealed firmly shut. I can't answer him because there's no way I could stab him, not even to save myself the pain. Dancing is an outlet to me and something I love doing but it's not everything to me. It's not more important than my morals or my friends and this man killed half his family as a gift to Harley. He's paid penance for actions his blood took that he never once condoned.

I know Lips and the guys will be raising hell to find me.

I just need to hold out until then.

"Avery… listen to me, I'm not going to let you die for me. There's no fucking way that I'm letting a girl like you

die for the likes of me."

The Jackal steps out of the room and shuts the door behind him. I try to distract myself from the pain and say, "And what type of girl is that, O'Cronin? Some delicate little rich bitch? I'll die how I want to, thank you, and if I decide that my death happens here then it does. You don't get a say on how that happens."

He leans back in his seat, easing the pressure off of his wrists finally and rolling his shoulders the small amount that he can. "I think you're too fucking good to die here for me. I think you waged war for your family from the moment you took a breath on this Earth and I think that you'll do it to the end. I think that you saved Harley when the rest of us were too fucking scared to try. I think that I'm not worth the life of someone like that and if anything happens to you… fuck, just stab me. Either I die for you or I die after you, either way I'm dead."

The air in my lungs seizes up and stays trapped in my chest until I think I'm going to pass out. "I'm not… I'm not like that."

He shakes his head and leans forward towards me again. "You're ruthless and you're fierce. You're unstoppable and you're so fucking loyal that you won the Wolf's friendship. The Jackal doesn't fucking know who he's messing with."

The door opens again and the Jackal steps back in, his eyes manic and frenzied as he looks around. I squeeze my

eyes shut for a second.

"We don't have time for you two to be fucking flirting, are you dying Beaumont or are you killing O'Cronin?"

I open my eyes and stare into the deep forest green of Aodhan's eyes. He stares back at me without reproach or any sort of hesitation. He's already chosen to die here for me, whether I'm dead or alive.

I take the knife.

# One

Beaumont Manor is in a highly exclusive *and* reclusive estate about three hours away from the ranch that I bought and renovated to be the perfect house from my family. The Manor is everything the ranch isn't. Cold, formal, and full of the dead bodies of hundreds of girls my father and oldest brother murdered for their own sick pleasure.

There's a reason I hate the place I was forced to grow up in.

"It's so fucking ugly."

I roll my eyes at Blaise's comment and Harley elbows him in the ribs sharply. "Yeah, I don't think we're burning it to the fucking ground because the building looks like a mausoleum, dickhead."

Ash slings a careful arm around my shoulders and leans down to whisper, "Are you sure you're ready to do this, Floss? We can just hire someone to knock it down… or leave it here and pretend it doesn't exist."

I give my twin a sharp look. "Mom and Lips both died in there. Even if the rest of the horrors didn't happen, I need to destroy it for them."

My Mounty doesn't look at all phased as she steps out of the building, Illi chuckling and jogging down the stairs with her. He looks extra… joyful today.

I'm not sure what to make of it.

Lips nudges him with her shoulder and then stalks over to me, a half smile on her face. "It's all ready, you guys just have to light the matches."

I grab her hand and tug her over to where we'll be safe, behind the fence, and leaving the boys to light it up.

"You okay?" Lips murmurs, and I nod.

"I will be once this is gone."

She nods and looks back out at the ugly building. It's not really that ugly but I can't look at it without seeing all of the terrible things that happened in there, the things that I can't ever put into words because they're nothing but festering scars on my soul.

All of the girls my father and brother both tortured inside those walls.

The memories of my mom live inside me. They're not tied to a place, they're tied to Ash's grin and to the angle of Harley's cheekbones. They're all the little memories that only mean something to Ash and me because no one else lived through it all.

No one else survived it all.

"Do you want to stick around and watch it burn?"

I glance over at Lips but she's still staring at the Manor. She's good at that, at respecting your space when the situation isn't the best. No one knows better than her what it feels like to be breaking open with an audience waiting to pounce on any weakness you might show.

I shake my head. "I'm done here. I never want to come back again."

Lips gives me a sharp nod and links her arm with mine, steering me back over to my car. We'd come out here together, leaving the guys to ride over in the Cadillac that was packed with all of the supplies necessary to burn the Manor down.

The Phantom drives like a dream and every time I slide in behind the wheel I question why it is that I let the guys drive me around so much. When I slide my phone out of my pocket and find thirty notifications that answers the question for me, travel time is too valuable to spend behind the wheel.

I very rarely drive myself anywhere.

It's not that I don't enjoy driving, I'm far better behind the wheel than Blaise or Lips are, but being around Harley and Ash means I always let them get behind the wheel. Driving is nothing more than operating a luxury piece of machinery to me but for the guys it's like a shot of ecstasy

straight to the blood.

Lips slides into the passenger seat without any hesitation, her hair down and fanning across her shoulders. Her nail polish is chipped and I've been meaning to try out a new color with her but time has run out for that.

She's leaving in the morning.

They all are.

I refuse to let the panic bubbling in my chest show on my face. They're going to go out and enjoy their lives together for a few months, they deserve that at the very least.

Lips deserves that and so much more after what she sacrificed for us all.

She tried to die for us… succeeded too, only to have her brother save her. The Devil himself and possibly the most unlikely choice for a secret sibling, none of us were expecting the heads arriving to our doorstep to be from the criminal underworlds most feared and notorious killer.

None of us were expecting him to be such a caring brother either.

I can't think about their budding friendship, or the fact that Lips adjusted to having a true psychopath for a brother with such ease, so I distract myself the best way I know how.

Digging for information and sharing intel with my bestie. "Why was Illi so happy? I thought he'd be sulking

about you leaving him on babysitting duty."

Lips grins and huffs under his breath. "Well, about that… he needs a little practice at babysitting… to prepare him."

It clicks before she finishes the sentence. "Johnny 'The Butcher' Illium with a baby? That sounds… well, I was going to say strange but he's probably the most qualified out of all of us to be a father."

Lips laughs and rubs a hand over her face. "I honestly can't believe he waited so long. He's been ready for kids since he first saw Odie."

I lose myself in the traffic for a moment, categorizing information and planning out what I need to do next. It's easy to zone out in the Phantom though I do need to do better about driving myself in Ash's sports cars a little more often so I don't get rusty at driving a stick shift. He's not a fan of letting the guys touch his cars but he's accommodating to Lips and I.

Probably because I bought more than half of the cars in his garage, all of them gifts because there's no one that I enjoy spoiling more than my brother. He always appreciates his cars so much that it's soothing to me, like a weird sort of ritual like my cleaning and obsessive need for perfection.

Lips clears her throat and pulls me out of my own thoughts. "Can we talk about my… the other Graves kids

for a second? I think we need to have a plan here."

I nod slowly, thoughtfully because all I've done since the Boar told us about them is think about them and what they mean for our family. "Do you want to meet them? Do you want me to arrange something with them?"

She's nervous about it.

I know her well enough to see her tells, all of the little ways she fusses with her clothing and picks at her nails, so even though she barely twitches I can see the nerves in her. I don't blame her for them either.

Siblings are a touchy subject in our house.

Just because you share blood with someone doesn't mean that they're going to turn out anything like you. Ash and Joey couldn't have been more different as brothers, and finding our older brother's head in that cardboard box back in junior year was one of the biggest reliefs of our lives. Knowing that his life was no longer in our hands, but that he was gone from ever touching either of us again, was like a weight was lifted from us both, no matter the consequences from Senior.

Blaire is another touchy sibling issue. Blaise's baby brother is now nearly two and he's only seen him twice in his life despite desperately wanting to know him.

Lips and I have both discussed it often.

There's no question that Blaine Morrison's days are numbered, we just need to make sure that his company will

be under our control when he's gone. One way or another, Blaise will get what he deserves even if he says he doesn't want it.

"I don't want to meet them… yet. Can we just get all of their details and the dirty on them for now? I don't really know if I want to know them all yet."

I hum under my breath and tap my chin while we wait in traffic. Ash, Harley, and Blaise are in the car behind us, the music blaring and I can see Blaise laughing like an idiot in the mirror. They all just look so… relaxed now. These past few years of fighting to be together and alive and whole really was like a boulder sitting on our chests and now we're free.

Except I don't really feel free.

I feel lost and tired and traumatized.

I feel terrified of what's going to happen next, of who is going to be hiding in the shadows to kill us all next, of what the consequences of the Jackal and Senior's deaths are going to be. Nothing ever happens without the ripples affecting everything, the Twelve can't lose two members the way they did without repercussions.

I can't think about what happened in the vault in the Jackal's lair.

I cook a three course meal for our last dinner together.

I don't tell anyone that it's supposed to be eaten separately because then they'd all know that I'm not coping as well as I'm pretending to be. Lips watches me a little too closely so I already know that she's suspicious but the guys all miss it.

They always have.

Not that I'm upset by that at all. As the only girl in our family for years, it was always good to know that I could hide my feelings from them all if I needed to… which was most of the time. Ash and Harley are both too protective and Blaise would tattle to them both without a seconds thought.

The thing that makes Lips the perfect best friend is that she knows all of this without me saying a word and not once has she tried to convince me to go with them on tour. The relief of knowing she trusts me to get through this my own way is overwhelming.

This is why she's my family.

"I'm packing your bags for you. I'm not leaving here without you."

Ash, on the other hand, will not leave me alone about coming with them.

I roll my eyes at the sound of his voice but I manage to keep my face calm and serene as he stalks into the kitchen wearing one of Blaise's band tees and a pair of Harley's sweatpants. You'd almost think their relationship was

a true poly-style orgy at the way they've all become so codependent but Ash is as straight as they come.

I hand him a platter of roast vegetables and a jug of gravy, ignoring the huff he gives me but when I move to grab another platter of food he snaps at me to leave it for him to carry like it's somehow too heavy for my delicate hands.

Ash Beaumont is chivalry in the most arrogant and snarling package.

I adore him.

That doesn't mean I'm going to live under his ridiculous rules just to ensure nothing could ever possibly happen to me again. He'd smother me in under a week and I might have complied while we were at Hannaford but things have changed.

We're supposed to be free.

"You're going to be too busy getting drunk and high to even notice I'm not there. Please don't ruin our last night together."

Ash's eyes narrow at me and I shrug at him. "It's true. I don't just want this for me, you need to go and have fun with your girlfriend. Act your age for a few weeks and just forget about everything that happened. Illi will be here if anything happens but *nothing* will happen. You're whole life can't be about keeping me safe, Ash. You need to figure out exactly what you want to do now school is over."

I follow him into the dining room and we find Harley snarking at Blaise while he pours out drinks for everyone. My Mounty is tucked under Blaise's arm at the table with an AirPod in one ear as she hums along to a Vanth song, working on my trauma before they're on tour. I already know about her plans to surprise him and she's working hard to make it happen.

Nothing about Ash's appearance or facial expressions changes but I know him better than I know myself.

He's desperate for the time away.

I don't blame him for it.

He waits until we've placed the tray on the table and headed back to the kitchen for the last of the food before he says, "Illi is going to be busy with Odie."

I should have known Lips would tell them all. I roll my eyes at him. "She's pregnant, not terminal, she won't need all that much from him on a daily basis. You better hope none of you knock Lips up while you're away if pregnancy is that foreign a concept to you."

He huffs at me and snaps, "Like I'd ever risk our bloodline being passed down."

I sigh as he stalks back into the dining room. I almost feel sorry for them all for having to deal with his sour mood while they're gone… almost, but not quite because I'm sure he'll cheer up the moment they all fall into bed together. Gross.

I take a seat next to Lips and shoot Harley a glare when he grumbles at me over it. Lips shoots a little smile at him and he calms down a little. She wears that smile so hesitantly still, like she doesn't really want to admit just how happy she is. Like maybe if she admits it everything will fall apart.

I know the feeling well.

Ash huffs as he sits down and knocks back the entire glass of bourbon Blaise poured for him in one go. I roll my eyes.

The dramatics are about to start.

He opens his mouth and Lips cuts him off. "I can't eat if you're going to argue. If you want me to finish my plate then you'll have to leave it off for tomorrow."

Blaise snickers at the end of the table. "Way to shut him down, Star."

Ash shoots a glare at him but Harley elbows him. "Just leave it. You've been fucking ranting for weeks about it, Floss is fine. She's a big girl, she can make her own choices."

Ash doesn't look at all like he's going to back down but then Blaise distracts him with some stupid plan for their trip and Lips piles on with plans for picking up her little sister Posey from Mississippi.

I need to have a full background check on Poe's entire MC family before they make it there. If there's anything

that flags we'll need to get her out of there. Now, I know that chances are the Devil himself will have been thorough about where he allows his beloved sister to live but it can't hurt to look into it myself.

I'm not very fond of bikers.

The Boar is very firmly on my shitlist for lying to Lips about their relation for so long. They were both members of the Twelve for years and not once did he bother to mention to her that not only did he know who her father was but that he was actually her uncle.

He might have helped take down the Jackal but he's still not someone I will ever trust.

Once dinner is over I scrub the kitchen down and deep clean the oven. Lips hangs around with me for a while before Ash drags her off to bed, still pissed off at the world and probably wanting to hate-fuck his angry right out.

Thank God for the sound-proofing I thought to put into this place.

There's things a girl doesn't need to hear her brother doing and my bestie is one of those things.

When everything is finally shining to my standards and the chaos in my head has settled a little, I park myself on the couch with my phone to work through some leads I'm already chasing on the Graves siblings. I get the TV going in the background with something that won't draw in my attention at all and none of my old favorites that are sure to

make me spiral into a self pity party.

I leave that to Blaise.

It's quiet for over an hour and I assume I'm the only one awake so when Harley creeps into the living room and sits down next to me I hold in a sigh.

I knew he was too accommodating at dinner.

I toe my slippers off and then prop my feet up in his lap because if I'm going to be forced to listen to whatever he's going to throw at me then I should get a foot rub in.

He huffs at me like he always does but gets to work anyway, his thumbs pressing into the arch of my feet just the way I like it. I'd won a bet against him for free foot rubs in freshman year and I've never been so happy with being right.

I knew he'd fall for the Mounty girl, I just didn't realize at the time that we all would.

"I need to know that you're not going to do anything stupid while we're gone."

I side-eye him. "Since when do I do stupid things? That's your job."

He huffs at me again and keeps his eyes on the reality show on the TV. He looks so much younger and calmer than the guy I've spent the last four years of high school with. He looks happy.

Still, I desperately want to feel the same way.

"Floss, you haven't been… right since the Jackal took

you. I don't know what happened in there and Aodhan has promised me that he was with you the whole time but I know something happened. I know you. I know something hurt you too deep for you to talk about it and Lips told me to leave you alone about it but I'm not sure I can wait you out."

The soft and sincere tones cut right through me.

I don't want to cry and I can't afford to slip into pity for myself or worse. I can't think about what really happened in that room.

I blink away tears and clear my throat until the lump shifts a little. "The Jackal is dead. The hurt is all that's left to worry about and I need some quiet to heal from that. I promise, if there was something you could… kill or avenge for me, I'd tell you. There's nothing left to do but get through this."

He nods and shifts to put my feet back down on the ground before he tugs me into a hug. "Ash isn't the only one who breathes for you, Floss. I'd level fucking cities for you, any of us would. If you need some quiet then it's yours, just… just don't drown in it."

# Two

The bus arrives in the early afternoon, empty but with a driver who barely bats an eyelid at Blaise and Harley snarking at each other. Lips looks a little wary of him but when he ignores the rampant PDA she's getting from all three of her guys she relaxes a little.

The bus is packed and ready to go in no time and I start to go about hugging them all goodbye. Blaise is the quickest and easiest, I swear he's still half convinced that if he hugs me for longer than a second Ash will assume we're secretly in love and kill him which is utterly ridiculous considering they're *both* dating my best friend.

Harley's hugs always feel as though he's trying to break my heart in half because I feel every inch of the sadness and loneliness in him that I did the very first time we hugged after we got him out of juvie. Maybe it's just in my head, maybe he really is whole now that he's found his place in the world, but still I feel gutted when I finally let him go to pull Lips into my arms.

She hugs me without hesitation now, clinging to me just as fiercely as I cling to her.

I might be the one pushing for this time apart but that doesn't mean I'm not going to miss her so badly my heart is hurting in my chest. I have to focus on my breathing to keep it even, to stop the panic from clawing at my throat and stealing the ability to speak to her.

I'm not just saying goodbye to my brother.

I'm saying goodbye to the last four years of living and breathing my family, these four people who have occupied every second of my time and energy.

It's six months away from each other. Six tiny months but it might as well be all of eternity, my heart breaks the same way.

"Call me. All the fucking time, just text me for no reason at all. I'm really going to miss you. Is it too late to run away together? The Caribbean is still an option."

I snort at her and blink quickly to stop any tears from falling. "I think Harley would duel me for your hand. Ash would throw the biggest tantrum about it too, I couldn't deal with it without bleeding him out."

Lips chuckles and pats the knife strapped to my hip. "You could too. I'd pay to see you use it."

And then there's Ash.

He hugs me like he's scared I'll disappear the second he lets go.

I hug him back the exact same way.

It doesn't matter how much our lives change, we came into this world together and from our first breaths we've been at each other's sides through all of the hell we've been put through. Even these six months apart might just be too much but I have to try.

I have to get some space to work through what was done to me.

There's the sound of a car pulling into the drive and Ash turns me until his body is covering me entirely as though we're about to be shot at, ignoring me when I huff at him in annoyance.

"What the hell is O'Cronin doing here? Did you know he was coming?"

I ignore the snarl in his voice and carefully step around him to find Aodhan and Jack in the driveway, getting out of the car and grinning at Harley.

Harley doesn't look like either of them. Where he's all fair hair, blue eyes, and gold skin, his Irish cousins are dark hair, green eyes and roguish grins. Aodhan is just as tall as Harley and just as broad but without the muscle mass Harley put on in the last few years of hitting the gym hard to cope with the terror of Lips being in constant danger.

I know for a fact that he's still ripped under the charcoal tee he's wearing though.

My stomach fills with nervous flutters at their arrival

but it's not exactly a bad feeling.

They both give Lips respectful nods but Harley has relaxed a little around his cousins, enough that he can greet them with a grin.

"We're just here to see you off, I thought we might've missed you." Aodhan says with the same rogue grin on his face that Harley has when he's flirting with Lips. I hits me in my gut that they share just as much blood as Harley and I do, that he might not look like either of us but there are little signs of the O'Cronin's there.

That would have annoyed me before but after spending time with Aodhan and Jack, now… it's not such a bad thing. Liam and Domnhall were evil but so was Senior. We're not our parents.

Lips certainly isn't.

Ash glares at Aodhan but Harley and Blaise manhandle him onto the bus, laughing and joking like children.

My heart hurts just a little at being left behind but I know I need this. There's something about this next six months that feels so pivotal to me and I know if I keep hiding behind my brother that I'll never be who I want to be.

Senior is dead.

I can be whoever the hell I want to be without my father looming over me like an executioner about to swing a sword.

I just don't exactly know who it is I want to be. I thought the answer to that was free but now I am free and I'm still not happy. I'm alive, I'm a billionaire, my brother is safe and loved.

What else could I ask for?

"I think if we're quick about packing, I can get you on that bus before it leaves the state."

I give Aodhan a glare but he only laughs at me. "What? You look like you're about to cry, Beaumont."

I huff at him and turn on my heel to walk back into my house. They both chuckle and follow after me, proving Ash right in his assumptions about what they were really here for.

I wait until I'm inside the foyer before I confront them. "If Harley put you both up to following me around while he's gone then you can leave, I want some peace and quiet."

Aodhan shrugs and closes the door behind them. "He asked me to check in on you. I told him that was already the plan, I'm keeping an eye out for any of the Jackal's men that were left over from his destruction. You know I'm not going to leave anything to chance when it comes to you."

I ignore the butterflies in my stomach as I nod. That's been my only real concern about being by myself. Lips has taught me enough to know what I'm doing but the way that Diarmuid had so easily captured me still lies heavy on my shoulders.

I train with a lot more purpose now.

"Do you have any plans for tonight?"

I startle out of my thoughts and look back over to him. I finally understand just where Lips got her jumpiness from. Trauma will do that to a person and the Jackal is still alive and taunting me inside my head.

It hurts me to think about how he must be inside hers too.

"No plans. I'm going to cook for myself, probably do some yoga and then head off to bed. I have a meeting to attend tomorrow night, as do you, so an early night would do me some good."

Jack huffs and scratches at the scruff on his cheeks a little. He still looks rough around the edges, in need of a long shower and a shave at the very least, but I don't hold it against him. The loss of his love and their unborn child isn't something you just bounce back from.

"The night is early, Beaumont. How about you come to a party with us? Let your hair down a little. Why should your family have all of the fun while you stay home and do all of the work?" Aodhan grins at me and all I see in the O'Cronin charm that must have melted my aunt Iris's heart.

I'm immune to it thanks to Harley.

"I can't. I hope you both have fun though, drinking and dancing in the Bay does look like a good time."

Aodhan steps up towards me and shoves his hands in his pockets. "Why not? You say you can't, but why exactly can you not have a fun night out? The Jackal is dead, you'll be with me and Jack the whole time, no one is going to so much as side-eye you. Fuck, half the Bay knows who you belong to anyway… no one touches the Wolf or her pack."

I swallow.

There really isn't a real reason why I can't go, I just… I haven't done anything this reckless since Rory and without Lips to come save me this feels dangerous.

"Okay, but I warn you, it'll take me at least two hours to get ready. I'm not some Mounty girl who can just throw some rags on and call it good."

Aodhan grins and shrugs. "I'll raid your fridge for beers, we know where the *theatre* room is."

He says theatre like it's an insult but I'm used to the way he speaks now so it doesn't upset me at all.

It takes me almost three hours to get ready, mostly because I have no idea what I should wear to something like this. White is the obvious choice but this isn't an official outing so I don't necessarily have to. Nothing red, that much is for certain and nothing in any of the colors that are already taken from members outside of our allies.

It's stupid and it's foolish, but I stick with something safe and I wear black.

Lots of people wear black so it's not as though I'm

doing anything wrong but I'm also trying very hard not to provoke anything from Atticus at the moment and showing up to the docks of the Bay at a party in his colors seems reckless.

I do it anyway.

"Holy shit. That's a fucking dress."

I roll my eyes at Aodhan as I come down the stairs, my legs as steady as ever even in ten inch stilettos and such a short hemline. "Well done on your keen observation skills. Honestly, sometimes I wonder about you, O'Cronin."

Jack scoffs and mumbles, "I think he meant that you look like sex on heels and he's a little fucking worried about taking you into the party like that. We're going to be working overtime keeping hands the fuck off of you."

I glance down and smile at the long lines of my exposed legs. "Good. There's no point going out if you're not ruining someone's life."

Aodhan tips back his head and laughs. "There she is! There's the Ice Queen. I thought we lost her for a second, my cousin would've been pissed."

I roll my eyes at him again and then I take his arm. He looks a little shocked that I'm touching him but I've always been a tactile person. There's never been a shortage in family that would hold me or take my hand when I needed it.

It never occurred to me that maybe he'd object to it.

Jack gets the door and then we walk out to the car. It's a classic, an Impala that I know Harley drools over every chance he gets. It isn't pristine, the seats all need some work, but it's still a very nice car.

Aodhan helps me into the front seat, a little clumsy like he's never shown this sort of chivalry to a woman before and he's winging it. Jack climbs into the back, folding his legs up with a grunt. I take a second to check them both out and I feel just a little over dressed. Both of them are in jeans, distressed from wear and certainly not a fashion choice, and while they're both clean they're not at all dressed for the occasion.

"Where did you get the Impala? It's a new purchase, right?"

Aodhan starts the engine and the roar is like nothing else. I'm not exactly a car person but I spend enough time with Harley and Ash to know the ins and outs. Ash prefers his European sports cars over the grunt of the muscle cars but it's all variations of the same equation.

"It was Domnhall's. I wanted to sell it, fuck him, but… it's too fucking pretty for that shit. So instead I drive it around doing shit for people he hates and enjoy every second without him."

Jack changes the subject, steering it away from their dead scumbag relatives and onto safer topics.

I check my phone as he talks and try not to laugh at

the stupid messages I'm already getting from Lips and the guys. I should not miss them yet. I definitely shouldn't miss them the day they've left, I woke up with Lips and Ash arguing in my bedroom about waking me up. Ash wanted to force me onto the bus because he couldn't bear to leave me behind.

He messages tell me he's still feeling that way.

I hesitate for a second and then I snap a photo of myself in the car with the O'Cronins, my outfit and red lipstick clearly in view and then I send it to her with a single line of text.

*Wish me luck, the Bay isn't going to know what hit it.*

Aodhan chuckles at me and says, "You know they'll turn around and come back for you, right? There's no way they'll let you go."

My phone buzzes and I hold my breath a little as I check it.

*Down at the docks? Illi is around, text him if you need anything. Have fun and remember to stab first. I love you.*

I refuse to get weepy over Lips trusting me. I refuse to cry over her finally feeling comfortable telling me she loves me, that we're as close as blood these days and the universe brought us together to start this rag-tag family together.

Great, maybe I will cry.

"We have, what, four hours maybe until they get here?

Let's head straight for the bar when we get there." Jack snarks from the backseat and I huff at them both.

"They're not coming back. I can go out if I want to, I'm not their prisoner."

Aodhan grins and I'm tempted to ruin his life. They're both baiting me to convince me that this is a good idea. They want me angry and fighting back about going out so I enjoy my night but… I'm still on the fence about it.

I wish I wanted to go out and drink and find some stupid man to spend the night with. I wish I wanted to act my age for a minute but really I just want to stay home and plan out how to take control of the Bay completely.

How could drinking and sex compare to total world domination?

"There's still time to plan tomorrow. I'll even help out with it, I've met half the fucking Bay already. I'll know whoever you need me to know."

I slide me phone into the pocket of my blazer as the lights of the Bay slower start to get less reliable the closer we get to the docks. There's a reason this area is called the slums, the city doesn't exactly care about this place.

"Have you met Colt or Chance Graves? Or Grimm? They've all spent time here before and Illi has met Colt a few times. They're all on my list."

Jack groans. "We've met them and I hope that list of yours is a hit list."

Aodhan gives him a look in the rearview mirror. "They're the Wolf's blood, you might wanna shut the fuck up."

Jack shrugs and it's a little suicidal, like he's kind of hoping that speaking like this will end it all for him.

"Colt is… fuck, he's not so bad. He's a biker and the whole lot of them are fucking assholes but he's got a line. He's not like Grimm, he's good enough I guess. Chance is another story."

Illi has said as much.

Chance sent his brother down here instead of himself to die at the Butcher's hands. It sounds exactly like something Joey would do and we've been careful about making sure the guys don't hear too much about him until we decide what we're doing about these siblings of Lips'.

Ash for one will gut him without second thought if he is a threat to Lips.

Harley and Blaise too but after living with Joey for so long and having his hands tied by Senior, there's no way Ash would ever let it come to that again.

The problem is we need to be sure about him before we do anything.

"Grimm's a piece of shit. I wouldn't go after him unless you've got the fire power and his death is a sure thing." Aodhan says, a frown on his face as he pulls into the parking lot.

He cuts the engine but none of us move.

He stares out of the windshield for a minute before finally he sighs and says, "Look, there's something else you need to know about Grimm if you're digging around in his shit. He's trying everything he can to infiltrate the Unseen and take them out. He's sure they put a hit out on him and he's fucking insane about it."

I tilt my head at him. This is news. "How do you know that? What hit?"

He unbuckles his seatbelt and runs a hand over his face. "I've spent a lot of time at the fishing dock, further up the coast. I've heard a lot over the years and the Demon's like to hang out up there, it's far enough away from the Unseen that they can party up there after they blow shit up. Well, one of the things I heard is that the Devil is stalking Grimm. He's killed dozens of Demons, probably fucking hundreds over the years, and Grimm thinks the Unseen have paid him to do it."

I swallow and keep my face carefully blank.

There's only a handful of people who know about Nate and Poe, we voted and decided to keep it that way for now. Poe is fifteen and she lives too far away for us to just get it out there about the blood ties.

What if someone came after her thanks to Lips?

None of us could live with that and, worse, what would happen if Nate lost his most beloved little sister, the anchor

that has kept him in some sort of sanity for his entire adult life?

Absolutely not.

"Right. So do you think the Unseen put the hit out? Why does Grimm think so?"

Aodhan unbuckles my seatbelt for me and Jack climbs out from the back. "The Unseen didn't put the hit out. No one but God and the Beaumont's could afford his prices."

The warehouse looks the same as the last time we were here for the meeting.

Still too many people packed in and even without the strict dress code the girls are barely covering themselves. There's more than a few of the Viper's guys walking around shirtless, their tattoos on show like some kind of badge of honor. I slipped my blazer on as I got out of the Impala so my own tattoo is covered so even when the blacklight hits me there aren't any signs of my allegiance showing.

It doesn't matter.

Everyone knows who I am and they all for sure know who Aodhan is.

I startle when he takes my hand, threading our fingers together in a way that makes my heart squeeze in my chest. We haven't spoken about what happened in the Jackal's lair, not once, but I also don't want to think about him

treating me like I'm made of glass. He hasn't so far but something has shifted between us now that my family has left town.

The crowd parts for us but it feels different from the last time I came to a party down here. The Stag has the respect of the Mounties because he's a member of the Twelve but has none of the renown of the Wolf. He doesn't have the Butcher on his side.

He's not hiding in the shadows waiting to slit your throat.

He has the name but not the reputation yet and infamy takes time to establish. I've been thinking about it a lot over the last few weeks, about what would be most useful to us and what gaps there are now amongst the Twelve that we could capitalize on.

Money isn't an issue but we have to run the Game again and I don't want some newcomer to mess with the peace we've found for ourselves.

"A cocktail or a wine? They're probably all shit, any chance you drink straight spirits?" Jack says, leading the way over to the bar.

Aodhan grins at someone we pass tipping his head and I glance over to find some guy waving at him from across the bar. We're surrounded by Mounties and I think if it were a little less deafening in here I'd hear the panties hit the ground around us at the cheeky grin on his handsome

face. There are more than a few glares from girls around us when they see our linked hands and I fight the urge to roll my eyes.

I was hoping to be done with the catty bullshit when high school ended.

"A margarita please and in a clean glass, Jack, make sure it's clean *before* you watch them pour."

He salutes me and Aodhan helps me into one of the bar stools, his body covering me like he thinks I'm about to be shot at. It's ridiculous and I try to relax a little so he'll relax around me as well.

When I made the decision to come out for the night I also decided to have a good time with people I think just might be my friends. The hand holding has changed things slightly but still, I want to have a fun night.

Aodhan slides into the bar stool besides me, grinning and tipping his head at someone else behind us.

I side-eye him, channelling Lips because no one side-eyes boys bullshit better than her thanks to all of her practice. "Is there anyone down here you don't know?"

Jack slides drinks towards us both and then stalks off, sharing a look with Aodhan before he goes.

What's that about?

"I'm not sure you can talk, Queenie, your blackbook is overflowing."

I inspect my glass before I take a sip. The margarita

is strong, all drinks in the Bay are, and I hold my wince in. "It's not though. Not with the people we need at the moment and that's on my to-do list as well."

He smirks at me and downs his glass, whiskey neat just like Lips, and then nods his head at the bartender for another one. The guy doesn't blink at the fact he has a member of the Twelve here drinking which says either Aodhan is here often or the bartender has been around for a lot of meetings.

"We're supposed to be enjoying the night without thinking about work. Come dance with me."

I look at him over the rim of my glass. "Why?"

He huffs and leans in close to my ear. "Because I'm sick of seeing you hide away. You're more powerful than anyone except the Wolf herself. Why are you hiding behind your brother when you could take the power for yourself? Come dance and forget about it all."

I huff at him but out comes that grin of his again and I tip my head back to down the last of the glass with nothing but practiced ease. I might not drink like the guys did during high school but I'm no stranger to a good cocktail.

Not that I'd call this one good.

It's passable and the glass was clean so it'll do.

"Atta girl. Do you want some shots before we head out there? Have you ever danced in the Bay? Fuck, those heels might not work out."

I shrug and take the new margarita, downing the entire glass in one go. I watch as the grin on Aodhan's lips turns into a cackle. "Good to see the Wolf taught you how to survive down here, Queenie."

I set the glass back down on the bar and lean into him, his eyes dropping down to the slash of deep red across my lips. "Well? Show me how Mounties dance, O'Cronin."

He grunts a little under his breath and slides off of his seat, his hands wrapping around my hips and pulling me into his body. I tip my head back to look up at him and I don't care that we're in public. I don't care that we're both infamous here, that there isn't a person in the crowded bar area who doesn't know exactly who we both are and how we met.

They might think they know but they don't.

Even Lips doesn't know and there's something intimate about that, something about our relationship that's just for us. I'll tell her everything eventually… she's my family and my closest confidant, but for now I just want to figure out what this all means to the two of us.

I try not to think about Atticus and what he'd think of this. He was willing to give me up so why would I think about his opinions?

Aodhan takes my hand and leads me into the crowd without kissing me but I can feel the tension build between us, like it's hanging there and waiting for one of us to cross

the line.

I can't dance Mounty style, my hips definitely don't move like Lips's do no matter how hard she's tried to teach me, and the heels don't make things easy but I've done enough years of dance and with two margarita's warming my blood I can make it work. Aodhan doesn't seem to care that my style isn't the usual dirty grind he's probably used to, his hands stay on my hips and he keeps dragging me back against him until I think that maybe this entire night has been planned, that he showed up to my house to drag me out here to have some fun and wreak havoc on my body and soul.

I think I'm going to fuck Aodhan.

A hand clamps down over my arm and jerks me away from his body. Aodhan snarls but when he looks up he pauses a little.

# Three

I don't have to look up to know who it is, the smell of his cologne and the feel of his hand on my skin like a brand is enough for me.

"What the hell are you doing bringing her here? Are you fucking insane?"

The alcohol is still thrumming through my system, warming my blood up and loosening me up, so I laugh at him.

Once again, Atticus Crawford is here to wrap me up in cotton wool and protect me from living my life.

I might be just a little tipsy but I remember not to use his name. "Stag, I'm getting another drink. Is Jack there? I need another margarita."

I step away from them both only to find Luca waiting behind Atticus. He grins at me and holds out an arm to me.

I don't want to but I don't want to listen to Atticus scold me like a child either so I huff and take it.

"What a lovely surprise, Miss Beaumont. Let me help

you out to the car."

I shake my head but he pulls me along with him anyway. "I'm staying here with my friends. I'm having a good night."

Luca doesn't stop, he just nods and coos at me under his breath as though I'm drunk enough not to realize he's walking me out of the warehouse.

I've had two fucking drink's and I don't want to leave.

"I should warn you that I'm armed and not in the mood to ask again." I say, and he stops with the cooing but doesn't slow his steps down at all.

"I get that but the Crow also isn't in the mood and finding you down here tonight might have just sent him off the rails. He's already stretched pretty thin."

There's men dressed in black suits everywhere now and pulling a knife on Luca now would only risk getting me hurt.

I don't want to think about what Aodhan would do if that happened, or if Lips caught wind of it, so I walk out with him. I still have my phone and I'll just call my Mounty if I need to. I don't *want* to but I can.

I get marched out of the building and into the parking lot. The night air is warm, too warm for the blazer I'm wearing thanks to the dancing, and I'm sure I look like a mess. I don't really care all that much about what people think of me but this is not how I wanted my night to end.

I'm reconsidering stabbing Luca when a voice calls out to us both, "Get your hand off of her before you fucking lose it. Fuck, you might lose it anyway, I'm not in the mood for dealing with political bullshit."

Oh thank God.

I turn to find Illi leaning against Atticus's car, a cleaver already in his hand and a savage smirk across his face.

Luca stops but his arm stays around my waist. "It's none of your business, Butcher, why don't you head out to find some chump to bleed out?"

Illi straightens up. "I have, dickhead. Any last words before I ruin your fucking suit?"

I hate this.

I hate that I'm still just the fucking pawn to be fought over.

I get out my phone.

"What's happened? Illi hasn't called, I'll get him on the line."

I huff. "He's here. I was drinking and dancing with A—I mean, the Stag and then the Crow showed up and beat his chest because I'm too fucking delicate to dance at a party. I think Illi might cut Luca's head off. Has he done that before? I assume he knows what he's doing but probably not good for our alliances if he does."

There's a pause and then Lips swears under her breath. "The first fucking night we're away. Let me call Atticus

and ream him. You're allowed to fucking live."

There's a crunching sound and then Atticus says from behind us, "Get in the car, Avery."

I refuse to turn back and look at him so I miss Aodhan arriving and taking him to the ground in a single move, Luca cursing under his breath and finally letting me go so he can help out his boss. I can hear the struggle and the sounds of fighting but I don't so much as glance behind me.

I ignore them all and look up at Illi.

"Take me home. I'm done with this bullshit."

I wake up before my alarm clock and just lay there in bed staring at the perfect white of my ceiling.

There are at least a dozen things I could be doing right now that aren't lying here moping. It goes beyond just looking into the Graves siblings for Lips, I've been thinking about filling up my manipulation roster with senators and FBI agents now that I'm out of high school and our family might need bigger hitters in times of need.

I also don't want to have to call Atticus for everything.

I can't keep relying on him for everything and if he really is intent on giving me up then I'd like to cut all ties with him. The fact that he's another member on the Twelve and someone who may be a danger to Lips in the future

means that unless he's voted into the family then he's a risk.

I can't let my heart get one of us killed.

I'm not saying I'll be able to let my love for him go… I'm not sure I'll ever be able to do that. Loving Atticus Crawford is so ingrained in me that it's now instinctual. I think I could give up breathing easier than giving him up and, though he refuses to do anything about it, I know he feels the same way. There's something inside of me that recognizes that in him.

But loving Atticus doesn't mean that I can't live a fulfilling and great life without him. Watching Lips and the guys navigate their poly life has taught me just how much you can love multiple people and all I have to do is look at Aodhan to know that maybe that's possible for me. The things that happened in the Jackal's lair…

I can't think about that.

Not without ruining my day and spiraling into a pit of despair and self loathing. I've never hated myself before that moment and it doesn't matter how many times Aodhan has reassured me since we were rescued, I can't shake the feeling that now I'm a monster.

I've lost my moral high ground and for someone who has based all of my actions on being better than others, this is *fucking* hard.

I'm better than Senior because I use my manipulation

to protect not kill.

I'm better than Joey because I would never let my father use me to hurt my brother.

I'm better than the girls at Hannaford because they only care about their social standing so it will give them all the riches in the world. I care about using it to stay alive and protect what's mine.

I'm better than the Jackal because I'm alive. I won.

I check my phone and find a stream of messages both in and out of the group text. Lips is worried, Ash is furious, Blaise is making jokes, and Harley is sending me photos of Aodhan's black eye thanks to Jack's photography skills.

I wonder how Atticus is looking this morning.

I get up and take a long shower. I scrub myself raw, washing out my hair and brushing my teeth twice like that will somehow help the situation I've found myself in. Then after I'm dry I moisturize everything, blow dry my hair, curl it, pin it up to perfection, and dress in something that makes me feel as though I can eviscerate my enemies without second thought.

Alexander McQueen is excellent for that.

I'm downstairs fixing myself a coffee when the security sensors Jackson set up before we moved in are tripped and I move over to the security monitor that's tucked away in my butlers pantry.

I sigh at the sight of the Rolls Royce but it turns into a

giggle at the sight of the black eye Atticus is now sporting. Serves him right for ruining my night.

My phone buzzes.

*I'm on my way.*

I send Illi a quick stand down message and then I turn my phone on silent before tucking it into my pocket, running a hand down the sharp lines of my jacket. If there's anyone I would want to see today wearing these clothes then Atticus would be it.

I needed the redemption of making out drunkenly with Aodhan last night. I needed the high of finally crossing that line with him now that I don't have my brother breathing down my neck. What right does he have to ruin my night?

I take a deep breath before I open my front door to him. He's wearing a Tom Ford suit and a pair of Prada loafers, charcoal socks and a Rolex. It's the one I gave him years ago which almost takes my breath away but there's a file tucked under his arm so clearly this isn't a social call. Luca is with him of course but in the light of day I really don't want to see him.

He was the one to find Aodhan and I in the Jackal's rooms.

Don't think about it, Avery. Harley's words echo in my head, *don't drown.*

"We need to talk."

I frown at Atticus but he looks at me, unrepentant for

his lack of niceties. "You have my number, a phone call would have done the job."

His hands slide into his trouser pockets. "Can I come in or are you going to insist on doing this out here? I'm not going to hurt you now you're alone here."

I roll my eyes at him and step aside. "Just you, I'm not having your men walk their dirt through my house."

It's only Luca outside but I can't look at him, let alone say his name. Atticus frowns slightly but when he glances back at Luca he's already leaning back on the car with his sunglasses back on, looking up at the clouds like that's a useful pastime.

I understand he's being kind and giving me space but Atticus doesn't. He's keeping his word to me and lying to his boss.

I'll need to remember to tell Ash and Harley to ease up on him a bit.

I walk Atticus through the foyer and into the kitchen. He looks around politely but I have no doubt he's already got the layout of this place on file. I once invited him here to see it when the renovations were still underway but he'd told me he was too busy. It hurt back then… still stings to think about but at least now I know why.

He was trying to keep his distance as much as possible so no one would ever find out about me.

I sigh just thinking about it and he casts me a look as

I gesture at the table for him to take a seat as I fix us a cup of coffee each. He doesn't make a move towards it, just stands there within arms reach of me like this isn't my home, like it isn't wired to the hilt with security that a member of the Twelve himself monitors for the Wolf.

"I can go out if I want to. It's none of your business who I spend my time with, Crow." I speak firmly but quietly, keeping my eyes on the task at hand.

I can hear his irritation at me using his Twelve name and mentally I give myself a point for it. "It's not as simple as just going out, Avery. I'm not trying to control you but there are bigger things at play here."

I tilt my head at him. "Fine. Tell me what these bigger things are and I'll promise to take them into consideration."

His eyes narrow just a little bit and he stops to look me over properly. I've taken too much care in my appearance to be worried about him noticing a goddamn thing wrong with me. If there's anything I can do perfectly in this world, it's dress to impress no matter the state of my world.

"I came here to do just that. I wasn't  expecting you to be on your way out though. Spending the day with the Stag again? Or is the Butcher taking you out to some hovel in the Bay?"

I turn to face him as I turn the coffee machine off, wiping my hands on a clean towel even though my skin itches to wash them properly. "Neither. I'm preparing

myself for the night ahead of us. Why shouldn't I look my best to represent the Wolf at the Twelve meeting?"

He grimaces and I give myself another point. Of course I'd be wearing this stunning white suit, full of lace and skin bared in the most unlikely places for the Twelve meeting.

I'm not exactly subtle when it comes to my loyalties.

He finally takes a seat, sliding the file across the table to where I take my seat after I place our coffees down. He picks up his cup like it's been years since he last touched one. I'm sure it has been but I don't start my mornings without caffeine. Not ever. My eyes drift down slowly to the words written in his perfect lettering in black ink across the front of the file.

The Lily Heart Killer.

I shuffle through the pages but all of them show the same thing over and over again. A serial killer who kills indiscriminately, men and women of every race and age. No pattern in victimology to be found, none of them linked except for the signatures in the way their bodies are left behind. The chests carved open and their hearts removed with precision. The women have a lily planted in the open cavity and the men have dirt sewn into the chests. All of the victims are left with a scripture from the Bible, referencing men of God.

And the Devil.

"This doesn't mean it's him." My voice gives away

nothing, not the fear pooling in my stomach or the way my heart is pounding in my chest.

Nathaniel Morningstar Graves may be Lips' brother but he's also a threat to everyone who wishes to continue breathing. I have no doubt that he would kill me and my family without a  second thought if he so much as suspects we have become a threat to his blood.

He's not on my list to look into for a reason and Atticus is risking us both by digging into these murders.

He doesn't show any fear about the repercussions of his actions. "He's a player on the board, if we overlook his actions purely because of fear then he has an advantage over us."

I straighten the pages back up and place the pile back onto the table. "He already has the advantage. He's the Devil. There is no stopping him."

Atticus shrugs. "The Devil is only the name he has chosen for himself. He's still a man and can be taken out if handled correctly."

I sigh.

I can't help it, I can't help but feel as though he's trying to force me to choose and there are a lot of things I would choose Atticus over but my family isn't one of those things. He should know this already and the fact that he'd even try this pisses me off.

Unless there's more at play here. "Why would you

want to take him out? What exactly has he done to you?"

Atticus stares at me, assessing my every breath. I think half of the reason I've become so good at reading people is because I've tried to see what he sees when he looks at me this way.

The other half would be surviving Joey and Senior.

"He's a serial killer. Have you suddenly become tolerant of criminals who kill dozens, if not hundreds, of people?"

I try not to show my irritation at him. Of course he'd bring up my father, bring up the hell that was my childhood dealing with a man who enjoyed collecting girls and women to rape and torture to death.

Am I so sure Nate is different?

No. I'm really not, but it isn't my decision. Lips gave me all the time I ever needed to decide on my blood, how could I possibly offer her less than that?

"Ash has killed for me, and I know that there isn't some magical number that he would stop at just for the fear of killing *too many* people. The Wolf has killed dozens at least. The Butcher hundreds for sure. How many men have you killed, *Crow*? How many deaths have you ordered? I'm not sure you should throw stones."

The corners of his mouth turn down at me calling him Crow again but that's exactly what I wanted to happen. I want it to be a direct hit because he needs to remember that

he's not innocent here. Just because he's righteous in his own mind that doesn't make it any better.

Lips has always killed for a reason.

Illi has too, for money or for love. Why is that any different than Atticus?

I slowly push the file back over to him. I've read the contents and there's nothing in there that I couldn't find for myself if I needed to. He stares at me for a second but even though I just woke up, I'm too tired to deal with this anymore.

"I'll see you out."

He sighs and stands up. "We can't be friends anymore?"

I scoff at him, the derision dripping from my tone. "I don't want to be your friend. I have never wanted that and, frankly, I don't think the Crow of Mounts Bay has friends. He has people that he cultivates alliances with, people that are useful to him. I am no one's pawn, not even yours."

I start towards the door but I can't help but see the smirk on his face that chips away at the ice casing on my heart. "Floss, you don't have friends either. You have family and pawns. You think I don't know that you vetted the Wolf before you let her in? We're the same that way."

I squeeze my eyes shut.

It's always been easier for me to shut out that he's the reason I was given that name, that he's the reason I don't want to be called that nickname by anyone who isn't my

family and only because they've called me that for so long that I'd have to explain why I wanted them to stop.

Ash would not take it well.

I wait until we're back at the front door before I reply to him. "Maybe you're right, maybe I don't have friends but you're the one who chose to not be a part of my family. You wanted to give me up for the greater good so now you get to live with that choice. You don't need to protect me and you definitely don't get to tell me where I'm allowed to go. Goodbye Atticus."

# Four

I'm not proud but I definitely go back to bed after Atticus leaves.

It's that or I'd have to redo my kitchen and I'm very conscious of the fact that I have to go to the meeting and I don't have time to have a full-blown cleaning meltdown.

I can save it for later.

When I finally have to get up I pick out my outfit with the utmost care.

A de la Renta dress that falls just below my knees, a Balmain couture tailored jacket, and a pair of Choo's on my feet, I'm dressed entirely in white and with the same understated wealth that anyone born in my social circles is. Nothing with garish logos but still dripping in money.

None of that matters to me anymore.

I'm dressed in white because I'm attending the meeting as the Wolf's proxy, the delegate she's sending in her stead to sit in the meeting and make decisions about how the next Game will run. She trusts me with this and I'll do

everything in my power to not only make the right decisions but also to learn what I can about the other members here.

I need to watch them all carefully, pick up on what their plans are, and make our own moves on the board accordingly.

Illi arrives on time to pick me up, the BMW he drives immaculate and a lingering scent of Odie's favorite perfume in the air.

He gets out and opens the car door for me, cracking a joke about not dressing to the occasion.

I slide into the seat and wait until he's back behind the wheel and pulling the car back down the driveway before I answer him. "I'm proving a point… and I'm gathering data. We need to know who here is going to question Lips and our family."

He drives a lot like Harley, like the car is an extension of his soul and I'm sure that he'd love to be racing his way over to the warehouse that has been chosen for the meeting but with me in the car he's showing restraint.

It's sweet in a *very* Butcher way.

"The kid is lucky you're into this shit, neither of us enjoy political bullshit. Stab first and all that." He mutters, and I shrug at him with a smirk.

"Both of you have played the game for years without me. I can't pick up a gun and help defend our people the way everyone else can, but meetings? This I can do in my sleep."

Illi shrugs as he weaves through the traffic. "I'm sure you could pick up a gun if you needed to, Queenie. I think the kid and I have done everything we can to make sure that you can defend yourself if you need to."

There's a little photo hanging on the visor of Odie in a vibrant blue dress, the color of Lips' diamonds, as she sits in a cafe in France. There's this grin on her face that she only wears when she's staring at Illi and it makes my chest ache a little.

Why is everyone I'm surrounded by in love and happy and complete while I'm desperately trying to scrap together the pieces of myself so I can just exist in peace?

Great.

The signature Blaise Morrison Pity Party has somehow infected me.

Illi notices me looking and shoots me a lopsided grin. "Our honeymoon. That was the day after I cut her cunt father's heart out. He was a piece of shit, a different kind of bad than yours but still fucking shitty."

That clears my head a little. "At least you'll know exactly what not to do."

I've already congratulated him on the drive back from the party when the margaritas were still strong in my blood. He'd looked so happy.

The warehouse the meeting is being held at is one of the Bear's now ruined businesses. Illi drives up to the

warehouse and waits for a second before the roller doors slide up and then he drives through. There's enough tools and scrap metal lying around that it's obvious this was once a chop shop for cars but it's been gutted by the raids.

Illi catches me taking everything in and chuckles under his breath. "It used to be a big money maker… lots of big rigs went through here but this is the shit that happens when you side with a dickhead like the Jackal. He's lucky he only lost his business and not something irreplaceable."

I nod slowly. Lips has never told me the full story of what happened between the Butcher and the Jackal but I know enough. I know enough that I'm once again glad that the psychotic asshole is dead.

"What ended up happening to his body? I'm usually more… careful about knowing the details but after everything that happened I just left it to Ash and Lips that he was definitely taken care of."

Illi pulls the car beside Aodhan's Impala and I keep my face carefully blank at the sight of it. Illi doesn't pry into my life but you don't get to be a man of his statue in the Bay without keen observation skills.

He doesn't move to get out for a second and he grunts a little under his breath before he finally answers me. "I know you're not cool with gory shit but I took D'Ardo's head off just to be sure the little fuck couldn't have some sort of Jesus-resurrection moment and fuck our lives up. If

anyone could pull that shit off I'd be him. The body was cleaned up by the Crow, you'll probably find him stuffed somewhere in his basement like a fucking trophy."

Thinking about the Jackal's head being cut off doesn't make me feel sick at all.

If anything, it makes me feel sick to know that I wasn't there to see it for myself, to know for sure that he's definitely gone because sometimes when I shut my eyes I can still see him standing over me with a knife.

I can still feel his lips pressing against mine.

I shake my head to clear those thoughts away, it'll never be the right time or place to think through that stuff but now definitely isn't it, and then I open my car door only to find Aodhan there waiting for me.

I smile at him and take the hand he's holding out to me to help me up. "You're early."

He grins at me and keeps a hold of my hand as he shuts the car door for me. "I didn't want you facing the Crow's bullshit by yourself."

Illi stalks around the car and even when his eyes dip down to our hands he doesn't comment about it. "He showed up to her place today to get that shit out of the way so there weren't witnesses. Queenie can hold her own."

I blow out a breath and roll my shoulders back a little, shifting them in the blazer. It's stunning and fits me perfectly but that doesn't mean it's the most comfortable

thing I own .

Beauty is pain.

"I can deal with him better than you can, your face looks terrible."

His grin doesn't falter, if anything it gets wider. His jaw is bruised and his knuckles are scuffed up on both of his hands. His dark hair is tied back and instead of the roguish look he usually has he looks like some kind of tortured artist.

It's not a bad look.

The butterflies in my stomach are ridiculous, I should not be getting weak in the knees over him, but the moment Illi turns his back on us to lead the way Aodhan lifts my hand up to kiss my palm and I just about melt into the disgustingly dirty warehouse floor.

"I'm sorry the Crow ruined our night, Queenie. You were supposed to be getting a night to let loose and instead you got more fucking politics."

I shrug as we walk, leaning in close to him to murmur back, "Politics is all I know. Don't worry about it, Stag, maybe we can go out again sometime?"

We step into a large room covered in posters with naked women on them and dirty rags left everywhere that you couldn't ever force me to touch. My skin crawls and I want to run away screaming. My fingers tense around Aodhan's and he pulls away from me slowly, and when

I glance back up I see we're the last ones to arrive and there's a few eyes already on us.

Aodhan must have thought I was uncomfortable about being seen too close to him when really I couldn't give less of a fuck about what these pathetic criminal lords think.

I can't voice that now though.

Illi holds out an arm for me to take, ever the gentleman, and I slip my hand into the crook of his elbow. Atticus refuses to look at me, even with the Jackal gone and every line of my body straightens until I'm holding myself up like the ice queen Illi always teases me about being.

Let the Games begin.

"There's no point in running the Game again until the Wolf returns."

Now that the Jackal is dealt with and the Lynx isn't here throwing sultry looks at all of the men she'd like to manipulate into her bed, the meeting is much faster and more bearable than they were before.

I'd only been to one meeting before the Jackal turned on the entire institution of the Twelve but Lips had told me they were always like that. Ego stroking men and petty fighting over things that don't really matter... it's all sort of pathetic.

Everyone is looking at Atticus like he's some sort of

messiah now, the man who survived the Jackal's many attempts on his life. I wonder how they'd look at Lips if she was here? She always had their respect but something has shifted in the group, like a veil has lifted and they all see the real danger that they've been living and working with for all this time.

My words have the exact effect that I intend on them having. The Bear looks at me with that desperate loathing he now cloaks himself in. He lost everything under the Jackal's reign of mayhem; his business, his money, and his infamy. No one wants to pledge themselves to the crime lord who put everything into the losing side, only saving themselves by crawling back to the Twelve on his belly.

He's next on my list of members who need to be replaced.

"You can't just decide not to run the Game! We can't be the Twelve without twelve fucking members, that's not how this city fucking runs! And who the fuck are you to speak at this table?"

Illi's arms uncross and his palm rests over his cleaver, strapped to his thigh in a holster where everyone can see it. There isn't a man in the room who hasn't seen him in action and tension thickens in the air.

I let a smirk take over my lips, one I've worn my whole life against pathetic men who question me. "I speak for the Wolf, she was very clear about her intentions to have me

as a proxy while she was away on business. If you'd like to question this, I should warn you I have full control of her empire in her stead and I'm sure the Butcher would be very happy to deal with a washed up, useless waste of space who shouldn't be taking up a seat at this table any longer."

The air leaves the room.

Atticus purposefully doesn't look at either of us but Aodhan leans forward in his seat until his chest is blocking the Bear from my view. It's sweet of him but entirely unnecessary. Illi is the fastest man in the room and I'm wearing Kevlar, there's no need for him to be attempting to protect me.

The Bear is also a pathetic excuse of a man. He'd never go against the Wolf to try to harm me.

The Ox, who has been watching us keenly, says, "He might be all of those things, Beaumont, but he's also not wrong. This city has been running under the institution of the Twelve for decades, you can't just change the rules because there's been a shift in power. Even one as big as the Jackal's death."

His eyes glance down to Jackson's wolf insignia tattoo, right there on his hand in black ink because he's kind of an idiot who doesn't think things through.

It was a statement, one that got him kudos with the guys, but one we don't need the rest of the Twelve knowing… not unless we're going public with our alliances. With the

family we've been slowly building.

There's pros and cons to keeping things quiet, but of course he didn't consider that.

Men.

Atticus looks around the table slowly and then says, "The Jackal's actions have put a lot of extra eyes on the Bay and that isn't good for anyone sitting at this table. There's been Feds here looking into the sudden surge in missing persons and body parts being left on the streets. Now isn't the time to be running the Game, we should focus on dividing the Jackal's businesses until the Bay quietens down."

The Tiger nods along but there's still a lot of frowning happening in the room.

Aodhan looks around like he's waiting for someone else to speak up and when no one does he says, "What about the new dealer on the streets? Is no one going to mention the fact that the Jackal's little plastic baggies have been rebranded and someone is making bank on his product? A lot of money is going in someone's pocket right now that isn't a member and with that kind of capital there's bound to be a new king pin in town."

I turn to look at him.

I hadn't heard of this.

Illi squints at him a little and Aodhan hands him one of the bags. Illi stares down at it for a second, then huffs and

turns his hand so I can see it. The cocaine is still there but so is the insignia, only now the eyes have been crossed out with black ink.

Atticus stares across the table at me for the first time tonight and I meet his eyes. It could be nothing. It could be some Mounty kid just making some cash and spending it on nothing but what are the chances of that?

What are the chances that it won't be the next thing to threaten us all?

Atticus finishes up the rest of the meeting but I choose to keep my thoughts to myself. I need more information. Illi gives me a side-eye and the barest of nods so I know he's thinking the same thing but when the meeting finally ends I stay seated.

I'd called ahead and warned the Boar that I needed to speak to him.

The biker president leans back in his chair as we wait for the room to empty around us. Atticus is the last to leave, sharing a look with Illi before he does. Well, sharing a look doesn't describe it adequately.

He glares and Illi stares him down until finally he leaves.

I'm sure he's waiting just outside the door but that's none of my concern right now. I have far more important things to worry about than the man who claims to love me.

"The file you gave me is incomplete. You told the Wolf

she has seven siblings. A sister and six brothers. There's only four siblings listed here and if you add Nate and Poe then that's six. Who is the seventh?"

The Boar huffs under his breath and makes like he's going to get up and walk out. "That's it? That's what you needed? I'm not telling you shit about the last one. He's fine, lives a good life, so forget about him."

I glance at Illi and that's all he needs to shift and cover the door completely. The Boar looks at him too, his eyes narrowing as he settles back in his seat.

I cross my ankles and link my hands together in my lap. At some point they're all going to have to change their view of me from the spoiled little rich girl to the woman I really am.

The one who will stop at nothing to get what I want.

I will never be caught off-guard again. I will never ever let some little forgotten piece of our pasts come back to kill us. If Lips has siblings out there I will know each and every one of them. I'll study them until I know exactly who they are and what threats they pose to her.

I will never sit at her side in a hospital again.

I take a deep breath and stare down my nose at him. "If you don't tell me who the last Graves sibling is I will assume you are being non-compliant. I will be reporting back to the Wolf about it. She'll talk to the Devil, they're very close these days. Are you sure you want to deal with

the repercussions of keeping this information from me?"

The Boar smirks at me, shrugging and glancing back at Illi with that arrogant biker look he's perfected. "My nephew needs me keeping an eye on Posey, he isn't going to do shit about me not telling you all my secrets. You're not gonna find the last sibling and that's a good thing. He needs to stay the fuck outta this life."

I want to scream at him but that's not something I do, so instead I share another look with Illi and motion at the door. "We'll see. There are a lot of eyes on Poe now, you might find that you've become obsolete."

The Boar smirks at me as he stands. "I've been watching out for my nephew for more than twenty years… finding the Wolf ain't gonna change shit. The sooner you learn that the better. Forget about the other kids, they don't need a little girl who kills in the shadows in their lives."

He walks out, glaring at Illi as he passes him by but I stay seated, tapping my nails on the screen of my phone as I think.

I don't want to think about what will happen if Lips is wrong about Nate. I don't want to think about what will happen to us all if the Devil changes his tune. We've lived under the oppression of being hunted by serial killers before.

I'll do anything to make sure that doesn't happen again.

BREE

# Five

We leave the warehouse in silence.

I'm busy thinking about everything and I mean, everything. The Graves kids, the new drug dealer, whether the Ox will side with the Bear if things go south, how this will affect Lips, whether I should call her and tell her this now.

Illi drives the car slow enough that I barely notice the city moving past my window, my mind engrossed on what this all means.

I can't imagine a worse option for a sibling than the Devil himself… so why is the Boar keeping secrets? Why mention the other sibling to Lips in the first place?

Does Nate know who the other brother is?

Too many questions. Speaking to the Boar was supposed to get me answers, not a whole new set of problems and I can feel my skin itching with the frustration of it all. It's a bit of a squeeze, but I take my blazer off just so I can breathe a little.

Illi chuckles under his breath.

I raise an eyebrow at him. "If you've found something funny about this cluster-fuck of a night then please share, I need something to cheer me up."

We stop at the red light as he chuckles at me again as he side-eyes me. "I've never seen you do something as human as struggling to get a blazer off without taking your seatbelt off. Honestly I'm a little hurt you don't trust my driving enough to just go without."

I huff at him and fight the urge to fuss with the hem of my skirt. It's harder to contain my obsessive tendencies when I'm frustrated but joking with Illi makes it a little easier. "I don't trust anyone in our family when they're behind the wheel of a car like this one."

He looks at me with fake outrage. "This is an M5. It's fucking beautiful, there's no way you can say shit about it. What, lemme guess, you like those fucking flashy sports cars your brother drives? That's rich kids for ya, too much money and zero fucking clue about what's important in a car."

A giggle bursts out of me. It's something I've heard Ash and Harley argue about a million times, even Blaise chips in when he feels like stirring shit up, and it makes me feel both desolately lonely and completely at home.

I sort of want to cry.

"I've gotta say, it's been a fucking minute since I've

seen you laugh, Queenie." He mumbles, and I shrug.

"Not a whole lot to laugh about when I'm being treated like a child by a bunch entitled men, sitting at a table without a functioning brain cell between them."

Illi cackles before the grin on his face dims a little. "I'm fucking pissed I didn't know about the new dealer. I can't afford to get sloppy. Just because D'Ardo is gone doesn't mean shit is going to change around here. The Bay is always a melting pot of every type of bad the world has to offer. Remember that, Queenie."

I nod and frown out of the window. "Did you ever think about leaving? I know your rates, you could have left a long time ago."

He shrugs. "I couldn't leave until D'Ardo was dead… and I won't leave Lips. If she moves somewhere safer than maybe I'll take Odie back to France but she likes it here too much. She wouldn't want to leave the kid either."

I wouldn't ever leave Lips here either… or Atticus. Being the Crow means that he will always be tied to the Bay in some way and there's no way I could see him leaving the empire he built from the ground up with nothing but blood and pain and secrets.

If only he trusted me to stand by his side.

My phone buzzes in my hand. I'm expecting a text from Lips about the meeting, or maybe a goodnight message from Ash.

I'm not expecting it to be Aodhan.

*I followed the Crow back to your place. Just a heads up that he's pissed about the meeting and he brought his bodyguard with him.*

Luca.

Why do I feel like he's now stalking me? I don't want to think about the Jackal anymore than I have to and every time he shows up my mind gets dragged back to my kidnapping.

"What's happened? You look sick, what the fuck has happened?"

I clear my throat. "Atticus and Luca are at my house and Aodhan followed them there. I'm just— I don't really want to see Luca after he found me at the Jackal's place. I don't want to see him so naturally he's everywhere at the moment."

Illi's eyes narrow. "If you need me to kill him just say the word."

I huff out a laugh at him. "Why does everyone keep offering to kill people for me?"

"Something bad happened to you. I might not know what it was but I can see that maybe you need some blood spilled in your name and if that isn't what you're up to doing right now then it would be my fucking pleasure to do it for you. That's what family is for, right Queenie?"

We pull into my driveway to find Atticus out of his

car and snarling at Aodhan like he's the real problem here. Luca is leaning against the car and watching them both carefully and there's something in his eye as he stares at Aodhan that pisses me off.

Nothing that happened in the Jackal's torture chamber was Aodhan's fault.

Illi parks up and takes a deep breath before turning to me. "You're not yourself lately. I know it, O'Cronin knows it, your family all know it because they're on the fucking phone to me hourly for updates, and the Crow knows it to. He's being a fucking asshole about it because he's a control freak in a fucking suit who can't ease up his bullshit because the stick is too far up his ass."

I scoff at him and shake my head. "He's not like that with me. He's never acted like this before, he always treated me like I was important and my opinions mattered. The reason I'm furious with him is exactly that! I trusted him and all along he was lying to me. I thought I could tell him anything… and now I don't know that. So, you add that along to my kidnapping and I'm just— I'm finding my feet again."

Illi nods and hesitates with his hand on the door handle. "You got 'em right there. You just need to remember to trust them again, kid."

The slip-up with the nickname makes my heart clench a little on my chest because I know how protective he is of

Lips. I mean, he just admitted not wanting to risk leaving her anytime soon so to know that some part of him feels that protective of me too… that gives me the strength to get out of the car and face whatever it is that Atticus is angry about now.

By the time I get the car door shut, my blazer folded over one arm and my phone clutched in my hand just in case, Atticus is snarling in Aodhan's face. I only catch the end part of what he's saying.

"—if you knew there was shit going on. I will have you dead and buried before anyone knows you're gone, Stag. There wouldn't be repercussions because they'd never find you. Stay the hell away from her. Avery Beaumont doesn't belong in Mounts *fucking* Bay."

I avoid Luca's eyes as I stalk forward, ignoring the little grumble that Illi lets out at me getting too close to the snarling men. "Atticus, I am a grown woman who can make my own decisions. If I want to go out for the night I can, with whoever I want to."

His lip curls but he doesn't move an inch away from Aodhan. "And what if the drugs are being peddled by the cartel? There are three prominent families in the Bay, each more dangerous than the last. How about you ask the Butcher about what they do to girls they like the look of?"

Bad move.

I cringe before he even takes the first step but Aodhan

is faster than them both, moving until he's standing in front of me like a shield while Illi stalks forward to punch Atticus square in the jaw.

Luca finally reacts, darting forward to stand between them both as Atticus reels back, blood pouring out of his mouth at an alarming rate.

Illi doesn't move from where he's now planted in front of them both, the scowl on his face reminds me of the one he wore when we were forced to go down to the skin auctions by the Jackal for a Twelve meeting.

"That's your one and only warning, Crawford. Mention that shit again and nothing will fucking save you."

Atticus wipes the blood away from his mouth with the back of his hand, in a very non-Atticus way, and then he turns to me, his voice low enough that I can barely hear it. "I've seen your dead body before. That's not something I can so easily forget."

I freeze and my eyes dart away from the blood on the back of his hand to meet his. Cold steely gray, his gaze cuts through me until I find the last bit of my courage is sliced away and my tether to this moment is *gone*.

"Never again, Avery."

I swallow roughly and look away, finding Aodhan staring down at me but he glances away as soon as our eyes meet like he's trying to hide something from me.

Nerves start up in my stomach and I loathe the feeling.

"Nothing would have happened to her. Jack and I were watching her every fucking move, the Butcher was in the area, there was no fucking danger to her. You don't own her, Crow. She wears the Wolf's insignia, not yours, and if she wants to come out with me then there's nothing you can fucking do about it. She's as safe with me as she is with you."

Atticus's lip curls all over again, blood coating his teeth, but he doesn't get the chance to say a word.

"How did that work out for you last time? Maybe Avery should choose a little more wisely who she spends time with." Luca drawls, and the air evaporates from my lungs. It's as though Luca's words have thrown me into a vacuum and now I can't *fucking* breathe.

I need to get out of here before they all see me break.

I walk with a straight back up the steps and into my house without looking back. I shut my mind down completely, walking on autopilot until I make it all the way up the stairs to my bedroom. I know this place so well I don't have to hit the lights to make it there without breaking anything, I can arm the security alarms from my phone and the moment I do I switch my phone on silent.

I strip out of my clothes and step into my shower with the water cranked up high and just lose myself there.

There's no hiding myself from the Jackal's damage now.

87

# Six

## THE JACKAL'S LAIR

"You can kill him or fuck him, the choice is yours."

My eyes snap to Aodhan's and his chest is heaving. He didn't scream once, matter how deep I pushed the knife in. Even with the sweat on his brow he's still staring at me with clear eyes, like he wants me to do whatever I have to do to survive.

I can't kill him.

He blows out a breath and tips his head back to look up at the ceiling. I think he's seen the resolve in my face and assumed I've prepared myself to stab him through the heart. He obviously doesn't know me because there's no way I'd kill my family and he got our votes.

Killing him would be a betrayal of what we've built and I won't do it just to get out of being forced to have sex with him.

There's still a choice here and I'm making it.

We're obviously taking too long to make a move because the Jackal pushes off from the far wall and stalks over to where I'm tied to the chair, lifting a knife and slicing the straps of my camisole cleanly until the fabric falls away from my chest.

I'm wearing a bralette underneath so there's barely anything covering me, my nipples peeking through the black lace. Aodhan's eyes stay firmly away from me and instead he glares at the Jackal like he can kill him with the pure loathing he's throwing at him instead.

I've been tormented by monsters my entire life, so I know exactly what to do.

I know how to slow down my heartbeat, to keep my breaths long and even and slow, and I know exactly how to keep my face blank.

There's a reason I became the ice queen that Illi always calls me, Senior and Joey both forced me to learn to give away nothing for them to use against Ash. Everything I do is to protect him, it's always been that way, and for once I'm thankful for that.

But that doesn't mean I don't want Senior dead still.

He deserves to die screaming, not me and definitely not Aodhan.

"How boring, you're going to just kill him then? I should have known the little Beaumont cunt would happily slit his throat to save her own. You'd do the same to the

Wolf, wouldn't you? You told my little Starbright that you love her and want to protect her but you're lying. Rich cunts like you don't care about Mounty sluts like her."

Ah.

So now she's a slut because she's fucked someone who isn't him? Typical male bullshit. It's pathetic really, totally pathetic that he thinks and acts so predictably while thinking he's some sort of criminal genius.

He leans down so we're face-to-face, his breath fanning out over my cheek until I want to gag but my poker face is unmatched.

He lifts the necklace away from my chest, the little blue diamond in the cage that Lips had given me for Christmas and his lip curls at the sight of it. His fists tightens around it before he yanks it hard, snapping the chain, and of everything that has happened so far, this might be the thing that breaks me.

He slips the broken necklace into his pocket and then he slices the straps of my bralette until my entire chest is bared. I stare at Aodhan's face, unblinking and unfeeling, and he keeps his eyes unwaveringly on the Jackal. It's like we've come to some agreement to get through this, that I'll ignore it all and he'll seethe at the Jackal until he can kill him for doing this to us both.

I just need to hold out until Ash and Lips find me.

I won't think about Atticus because my heart is still too

raw over him and if I let his face enter my mind, I'll break open. I never think about him when I need to stay blank.

The Jackal chuckles but I keep my eyes steady on Aodhan. "O'Cronin doesn't seem to like you all that much, does he? Fuck, he doesn't even want to look at all of this skin you're showing. How does that feel? To know that you might be the richest little cunt in all of the country but some gutter trash Mounty doesn't want to fuck you. How about this, little Beaumont? How about you fuck him, or I fuck you? Either way, someone is being fucked tonight."

Aodhan's eyes finally snap to mine but I look away almost immediately, finally looking up at the Jackal. "I guess you'll have to untie me then, won't you, because I can't fuck anyone while I'm strapped to a chair."

A smirk stretches across his lips and from the corner of my eyes I see Aodhan trying to fight against the restraints again. We both ignore him.

"And here I was thinking you were too prim and proper to get the job done. I was hoping that either way you'd be sobbing on someone's cock. It's not fun if you're enjoying it too."

I tip my head back so I'm not looking up to him, smirking back at him because I've been trained by Lips and I know exactly how to manipulate this man. "If you want a show, then untie me."

He thinks he's calling my bluff, it's clear when he

smiles at me and leans down until our lips are nearly touching. "Are you sure you don't want me to fuck you? Because if I take these ropes off and you try to attack me I'll slit your throat and then fuck the wound. Either way I'll enjoy it, I guess you just need to pick your poison."

I stare him down. I choose my words just as carefully as I always do but I'm also very aware that he's an unstable psychopath and this all could be for nothing.

Just hold out for my family to come for me.

"I'll fuck Aodhan. If you need someone to be unwilling here then it's not going to be me."

He leans forward and his lips touch mine as he slices the ropes binding my hands together. I stop breathing altogether while I run through every option I have to fight him off if he's the one who's actually bluffing here.

Aodhan grunts as he struggles but I keep my eyes on the Jackal, not once wavering away from the challenge there.

A slow smirk stretches across his lips and his hand snaps out to grab my jaw in a bruising grip. "Maybe you're more my type than I thought, Beaumont. Maybe I'll fuck you raw after you're done with O'Cronin."

My heart clenches in my chest.

There's a loud bang and then the ground rumbles underneath us, rubble and sand falling from the ceiling like it's about to cave in on us. I stumble a little and fight

to hold back the wince at the pain shooting up my legs from my feet but it's a relief to get some distance from my captor.

The Jackal curses viciously under his breath and then stalks over to open the door. There's guards waiting there and both of them smirk at the sight of me but I shift my eyes over to look back at Aodhan. I'd almost forgotten that I'm naked from the waist up but I don't move to cover myself, no matter how badly I want to.

I can't show weakness right now.

"Get me the collar."

My eyes snap back over to the Jackal.

There is absolutely *no fucking way* I'm letting that man put a collar on me.

Relief floods through my veins when the Jackal's man walks over to Aodhan, a thick black strap of leather dangling from his hands, and I take a deep breath. I feel just a little guilty for being glad it's not me being collared but I'm sure I'm the only one with a history that makes it abhorrent.

My father collars women.

Aodhan sneers at the guy and the Jackal chuckles at him. "Wanna know what it does, *Stag*?"

His words drip with sarcasm and I swear I could choke on the male bullshit in the room. Then there's the crackling sound of an electric current and the man holding the collar

lets out a yell, his body jerking and falling to the ground. He jerks there for a few seconds and then stops.

He doesn't move again.

Aodhan meets my eye from across the room, my heart in my throat. There's no way out of this.

The Jackal smirks as he stoops down to grab the strap, buckling it around Aodhan's throat and pulling it tight so that it's pressing into his skin firmly. We'll be lucky if he doesn't pass out before our little show is over.

The Jackal flicks open his cupboard of horrors and pulls out a camera, setting it up and I try to discreetly shake out my hands where he can't see to stop them from trembling.

"I'll be watching. If you don't fuck him, I'll kill him. If you try to escape or take the collar off , I'll kill him. And Beaumont if you enjoy it too much, I'll fucking kill him."

I refuse to acknowledge him or the snickering men still standing with him. I can't look at the dead guy either because my mind will just *break* and I need to be strong right now to get through this. The door swings shut behind him and I take a deep breath.

I can do this, right?

Of course I can.

If Lips can run through a forrest with a bullet wound in her shoulder and a crazed Irish shooter chasing her, I can fuck Aodhan to save his life.

I'll just repeat that mantra in my head until I get

through this because when I finally glance over at Aodhan the Jackal is right, he doesn't look at all willing and that means that technically I'll be the predator here.

"Don't even think about it, Beaumont. The explosion means the cavalry's here so just sit down and wait it out."

I might not be able to look at it but I can gesture down to the dead body. "I know you're not blind but are you suicidal? I think we both know that the Jackal won't hesitate in killing you here and I don't like to lose."

My voice sounds far more confident than I feel but I'm an expert at faking it. There's a clear path from where I'm standing to where Aodhan is strapped to the chair so I can close my eyes and take four long steps to him. Right as I start to walk there's another explosion somewhere above us and I stumble a little, catching myself on his legs before I climb up to sit on his lap.

Atticus was the last man I kissed but I haven't been on top of anyone like this since Rory and I do *not* want to think about him right now.

"Avery, he's gone. You don't have to do this."

I stare down at him. "You have a shock collar around your neck and a camera pointed at us both. I'm not going to kill you. It's not such a big deal now he's not in here narrating just hurry up and kiss me, O'Cronin."

He huffs and strains against the leather straps around his arms again. They have more give now, he's getting

closer to breaking them but for now they're holding firm.

I lean forward and kiss him, closing my eyes because I don't want to see just how much he doesn't want to do this. I'm trying to save his life but I still have limits to what I can take.

He stays completely still for a second but when I press up closer into his chest he finally kisses me back, hesitant until my tongue sweeps over his and then he's giving as good as he's taking. I hook my arms around his neck and I try to lose myself in the kiss, to forget about the fact that we're being forced into this by my best friends psychotic stalker and the fact that there's *a dead fucking body* two feet away from us.

I don't know a lot about Aodhan except that he loves Harley enough to come for me when I was taken. He killed every man in his family that had ever laid hands on the women so I guess that's something else I know… something else that either makes this situation better or worse.

I'm fucking a man who won't hurt me.

Or, I could be raping a decent man if he really doesn't want to play along here.

Stop thinking the word *rape*, Beaumont, for fuck's sake. Consequences are for later, right now you need him alive.

I very purposely roll my hips down onto him because

while I'm a virgin I'm not completely clueless and I know that I can't do this without his dick being onboard for the sex even if his mind isn't into it.

He grunts into the kiss and then groans when I let myself get really into the kiss, moving my hips to ride the beginnings of the erection until his dick is pushing up into my pussy through the layers of clothing between us. That was easier than I thought it would be, thank God, and even when I shift off of his lap to strip off my yoga pants I keep kissing him. It's a little awkward but there's something about his lips on mine that makes this all so much less scary.

I unzip his jeans and of course, of fucking course his dick is the biggest one I've ever seen in person. It's thicker than my wrist and if I wasn't already worried about how the hell I'm going to do this without crying I am now.

Instead of letting myself panic, I just turn my brain off and move on autopilot for a minute until I can lower my heart rate. I wrap my hand around the girth of him and stroke him for a few pumps until I'm sure he's hard enough for me to do this. If anything his dick gets even bigger and I try not to wince. Deep breath, I keep one hand on his dick and hold his shoulder with the other to keep myself steady. Then I raise my hips and lower myself slowly down until the head of his cock is parting my lips, pushing inside me just enough to feel the resistance there.

His eyes widen and he opens his mouth but there's no freaking way I want the Jackal knowing I was a virgin, not with the obsession he had with Lips's untouched state so I kiss him again, biting his lip as though he'd be able to understand what the hell I'm doing here but there's no way he could.

He doesn't know me well enough, he doesn't really know me at all, except that we both would do anything to keep Harley safe and that's why we're stuck here in this little room together.

It hurts.

I can feel the second he tears through the barrier and sinks deep inside me, my breath squeezing out of my chest and choking me. I just sit there for a second, focusing on my breathing and trying not to panic, but Aodhan's chest is heaving.

I don't know if he's trying not to move and jostle me or if he's worried about hurting me, but he raises his hips just a little until I'm more secure in his lap and then he wrenches his arms until the restraints finally break.

I tense, sure that he's going to throw me from his lap and rage the hell out, but he doesn't. It's almost worse than that. He lifts a large, scarred hand up to my face and cups my cheek, pulling my face into his lips.

"I'll fucking gut him for this, Queenie." He murmurs against my lips before he kisses me, cradling me close

like I really am some precious girl to him. I refuse to get weepy about this situation, I've fought too hard for this to be about me making the smartest decisions here without emotions or worthless dreams.

"I told you, I decided what I wanted. I'm not going to cry about this." My voice is a little rough but I tell myself it's because of all of the screaming I did while the Jackal was cutting my feet up. It has nothing to do with his hands cradling my face and whispering to me like I'm something more than what I really am to him.

It feels weird to be talking like this, his dick is inside me and my blood is dripping down his legs, but his dick is still throbbing inside me and when I shift he groans.

I huff and force a laugh. "Well? Are you going to make me do all of the work here?"

The challenge lights him up but he's still fucking careful as he hooks his arms around my legs and lifts me, my arms winding around his neck to hold on as he slowly thrusts his hips.

"Fuck, fuck, tell me this is okay." He grunts and I huff at him again.

I don't want to admit how okay this really is.

I should not be enjoying this but now that the pain has subsided the thick length of his dick inside me feels good in all of the most unexpected ways and now that he's onboard there not much that I have to do except take it and

with the way he's holding me all I *can* do is take it.

He grunts like he's frustrated and my heart drops a little at the sound and then he lowers my legs back down until I'm straddling him again, one hand on my ass moving me how he wants and the other slipping between our bodies to my clit.

I thought guys were supposed to have more trouble finding it than that?

My breath catches in my throat as my pussy clenches around him at the feeling and I choke out, "I'm not supposed to enjoy it."

He grunts and pulls me in closer with the hand on my ass. "Fuck what he wants. I'm not coming until you do."

His mouth is hot and demanding on mine, nothing like the gentle and careful actions of his hands. He treats me like glass until a groan rips out of my throat.

He loses his head at the sound.

His hips surge up until my breath is knocked out of me, his fingers pressing and circling over my clit until I break apart, his mouth pressed against mine muffing the scream that tears out of me as I come apart in his arms.

His hands move to my hips and he pushes me down until he's grinding up into me, desperate for me to take in every inch of him. I can't catch my breath, my heart is racing and when hips jerk up into me one last time as he comes with a grunt, his hands grip my ass until I'm sure

there'll be bruises imprinted into my skin forever.

There was no condom so everything just feels… wet.

Somewhere, far off in my brain, I start to panic about that but mostly my brain is fixating on the hollow of Aodhan's throat where I can see the vein there pulsing with his blood and I can measure his heartbeat. With his head tipped back like it is I almost want to kiss him there but now that we've both come I feel… I feel like I can't touch him at all.

I think the panic might be setting in.

The door swings open and I tense but Aodhan's arms tighten around me. His legs are still tied to the chair so he can't just jump up and kill whoever the hell has just walked in here.

Fuck.

Don't let it be Ash.

"Holy shit. No, fuck, holy fuck."

I glance up and it's not Ash but it's not much better than Ash.

Luca stalks into the room and then turns back around to snap the door shut. "Avery, fuck, are you hurt?"

I take a gulping breath and then say, as evenly as I can, "No but I need help. The Stag has one of the Jackal's shock collars on and I don't know how to take it off without killing him, do you know how?"

He starts cursing up a storm, muttering as he strips out

of his jacket. Aodhan pushes me carefully until I'm sitting up in his lap and I cross my arms over my chest. I feel weirdly self conscious about Luca seeing me like this.

Aodhan pulls his shirt off and tugs it over my head until I'm covered. When Luca moves to stand behind him I finally look down to find Aodhan's dick still out and my blood is all over him.

I swallow and he shifts again to zip up without moving me from his lap. There's nothing stopping me from getting up. Nothing at all except I can't move away from him. I can't, no matter how much I want to.

Aodhan knows.

He wraps his arms around me and holds me against his chest. It's embarrassing now that Luca is here and the little bubble we had around us has burst but I close my eyes tightly like that will help.

"The Crow is going to bleed you out for this, Stag."

I swallow against the lump in my throat but Aodhan doesn't react at all, just runs his hand up and down my back like he can't hear the threats. I should say something. I should speak up and stop the war that could break out here but—

I'm tired.

"Where is Lips and Ash? I'm surprised you found me first." I mumble, and Luca huffs at me.

"They went to the Jackal's private rooms, where I'm

sure he wants to be found. I knew better. He wants the Wolf in his lair but you? He'd want to play with you here. Avery, if you need me to kill Aodhan, tell me now and I'll get you out of here without any fallout. I won't breathe a word to anyone about what I saw and we can say the Jackal took him out before I got here. Say the word."

There's a click and the collar finally comes off but Aodhan doesn't move and I can't pry myself away from him.

"If anyone needs to die for what happened in this room, it's me. I was the one who forced him."

My voice cracks and Aodhan's arms tighten around me. "Take out the camera. She doesn't fucking need that looming over her. Throw me your jacket, I need to get her cleaned up. Avery, just breathe."

I didn't realize I'd stopped but I tuck into him tighter and take a deep, gulping lungful of air. Luca grunts and frees Aodhan's legs before he goes to do as he says, compliant now he has a little more information.

I'm sure he's seen enough of what the Jackal enjoys to make his own assumptions about what happened.

Aodhan uses the shredded remains of my camisole to clean me up and then he helps me back into my scuffed up yoga pants, his hands gentle and always conscious of the bloodied mess my feet are in. There's a steady stream of blood trickling out of the stab wound in his stomach but he

doesn't pay it any notice at all.

Makes me wonder if it's not the first time he's been stabbed.

Once Aodhan has me tucked into Luca's jacket he helps me to my feet, holding my hips until he's sure I can stand without my legs giving way. All of these little things he's doing, all of the little things I have no idea how desperately I need until he's giving them to me, I feel so unworthy of them all.

I didn't give him a choice. Even before the Jackal forced our hand with the collar, I'd decided what was going to happen, not him.

I can't look at him.

Aodhan steps in close to me so that he's blocking Luca from my view, his back to the other man like his presence means nothing to him. I find it oddly comforting… like this moment between us was real and we did survive this together.

I'm so confused.

"What was the necklace he took from you?" Aodhan murmurs and I startle. I didn't think he'd notice something like that.

"It's… it was a gift from the Wolf. Something that means a lot to us both, it's something very personal to our family."

He swallows and nods before glancing up at Luca.

"You trust him? Can I leave you with him and know you're going to make it out to the Wolf? He offered to kill me for you so my guess is yes but I need to hear it from you."

I glance over to Luca but he's watching us both carefully. Shit. "Yes. I trust him."

Aodhan nods and hands me the gun Luca just handed him. "Shoot first."

And then he disappears, stalking out and into the lair like he's going to find the Jackal and slit his throat for what he's done and… God, I hope he does. I hope he gets that kill for us both.

I think I'm in shock.

Luca waits for a second and then motions towards the door until I follow him out. There's men waiting at the end of the hall dressed in suits so I'm certain they're Atticus' men.

I have to speak up before there's a chance they can overhear it.

"Luca… I don't want Atticus to know." I whisper, and he nods.

"I'll take it to the grave, Avery. Chin up, if they ask why you're crying remember how badly your feet hurt."

J BREE

# $\mathcal{S}$even

## AODHAN

Watching Avery's stiff back as she walks into her giant, empty fucking mausoleum of a house on heels that could kill a man is a special form of torture.

Not just because she's the most fucking heartbreaking woman to look at that I've ever met but because I know just how broken she is inside right now and there's nothing I can do to fix it.

Nothing except to break Luca's jaw.

So I get right onto that.

The Butcher chuckles under his breath when my fist connects with the asshole's jaw, his attention still on the door Avery just walked through so the blow lands fucking *perfectly* and sends him to him knees.

The Crow snaps at me, "Maybe you should wait until you've built a name for yourself before you start burning bridges, Stag."

The Butcher scoffs from behind me but I keep my eyes on the asshole spitting blood out onto the driveway. "You speak to her like that again and I'll fucking kill you. I don't care who you belong to, I'll take you the fuck out."

The Crow snarls at me again, "You might have taken your seat on the Twelve during a war but that isn't how this works."

The Butcher steps right up until he's chest-to-chest with the Crow again. "Nah, that's exactly how this works. The Wolf has made it clear that anyone who fucks with Avery is dead. Keep your *inductees* in line before I do."

Luca straightens up and rolls his shoulders back like he's ready to fight back but his eyes are wary of the Butcher.

I get it.

The man is a fucking machine, bigger and more deadly than the three of us put together, but Luca still looks ready enough to jump in for his boss so I guess that's something.

"I will deal with the new dealer in town. Keep your noses out of it and stick to what you're good at. Contract killing and drinking yourself to death with errant bikers." The Crow sneers and then he steps away from the Butcher, jerking his head at Luca until they both climb into the Rolls Royce and finally leave.

The Butcher watches as the taillights disappear down the private road, his arms crossed and a scowl on his face that I'm not sure a lot of men see and live to talk about it.

"You told Arbour you were with her the whole time."

I nod slowly and he pegs me with a look. "So why the fuck is she shaking over seeing that asshole? What the fuck did he do to her because I don't give a fuck who his boss is, that girl is family. She risked everything for the Wolf and that loyalty means a helluva lot more to me than some bullshit gangster club you're in."

It takes me a second to realize he's talking about the Twelve. I guess it still feels a little fucking foreign that I won the Game and now I sit at that table.

I did it to get rid of the abusive men in my family, to keep food on the table, and to stop the women from being murdered.

I never gave a shit about power.

Not until I saw the girl who wields it like a weapon.

Now it's all I can think about. All of the little power plays in the Bay, all of the players on the board, the business men and the senators… every last one of them is on my radar now because I need to be sure that she's safe.

I glance at him and, though it might be signing my own death warrant, I shrug at him. "I was with her and he didn't hurt her. Something happened in that room and he knows about it… she doesn't want to be reminded."

He frowns at me. "Why is she okay with you then? If you were with her then why aren't you a reminder too?"

I'm not going to talk about it with fucking anyone so

I deflect. I lift my shirt until he can see the scar there, still red even though it's healed up perfectly. "I guess the knife she pushed into my guts was enough to make me a safe place. Besides, she knows I'm not gonna say a fucking word about it. I'd rather fucking die and I've proved that to her. Luca though? He's loyal to the Crow. He could start running his mouth and bringing up shit that might just break her."

He stares at it for a second and nods, the corners of his mouth twitching up. "You're lucky the Wolf taught her where to aim. She wouldn't have hit anything important by accident."

I smirk back. "I'll remember to thank her when they all get home."

He nods and the smile drops away from his face. "There are a lot of people on our list to die for what's gone down, anyone who gets away is a risk."

Is he… are we about to be working together? What the hell has my life become that the most infamous killer in the Bay is making plans with me about taking people out?

"I'm finding Diarmuid. I'm finding that fucking cunt and I'm killing him for what he did."

He nods and looks back over to the door, but there are lights on upstairs so Avery has clearly gone up to bed.

"I have some people already looking into where he disappeared to, I put some feelers out."

I nod. I have no doubt that the Butcher's information network is much bigger than mine is but Diarmuid is still my problem to deal with. "I want the kill. I'm grateful that you're helping track him down but his death should be mine."

He shrugs at me. "As long as he's gone, I don't really give a fuck who does it. I was gonna offer to bring him to Queenie but she's not into blood-soaked scenes. The kid might want it though."

I'll call the Wolf myself to put in a claim.

Diarmuid didn't just betray the family, he was just another black mark against the O'Cronin name and I'm fucking over that shit happening. He's the last male of that generation left breathing and I'll be happy when he's in the ground.

The Butcher claps me on the shoulder and I turn away from him to stalk back over to the Impala. It's late enough out that I should really head home and try to get some sleep but I know the second I shut my eyes, all I'm gonna see is Queenie's face.

Her face at Luca's words, her face when she watched her family drive away, her face when she sank down on my dick at the Jackal's orders and bled down my fucking thighs.

"O'Cronin."

I glance back over my shoulder at him and he's standing

there, a cigarette hanging out of his lips and his keys in his hands.

"You're a part of the family, call me Illi."

# Eight

## AVERY

I barely sleep for the next few nights.

I spend my days working through the information the Boar gave me about the other Graves siblings and start putting together some profiles for each of them. Colt is exactly what Illi said, a decent biker who is very clearly forced to play by his psychotic father's rules. Chance is a wild card, nothing he does ever follows a pattern or reasonable thought process. He's definitely going to be the one to watch out for because everything I see is a warning sign.

It's all a little too Joey-like for my comfort.

There's Wyatt James who lives in Colorado. Single, works as a cop which is kind of hilarious, and other than a photo of him in uniform, his file is almost entirely empty. A blue-collar, upstanding citizen with eyes that I'm now finding all of the Graves siblings share.

It's a little creepy.

The Boar failed to mention to Lips that her brother Noah Ramsden, six months younger than her and born in Utah, is dead. A drug overdose at the grand old age of seventeen, his mother was a junkie and he spent his entire life in and out of juvie for dealing and stealing offenses. The photo in the file is from grade school and he was a cute kid, far too skinny and a bruise on his cheek that mottles his skin. I make a lot of notes about him because I know for sure that Lips is going to have a lot of questions.

I won't be surprised if there's a trip to Utah in our future.

So with Nate and Poe, we know six of the seven siblings. With Atticus already looking into Morningstar it's probably not a good idea to hand him this information and ask for his help. I'm sure he already has eyes on it but other than the eyes, there's nothing on these pages linking the siblings with different surnames.

I wonder how the Boar found them in the first place?

I'm up early with a face mask on, lying on my bed texting an old informant about DNA profiling when a text comes through from the Coyote.

*Heads up. A search warrant was just issued for your house by the MBPD.*

I sit up in my bed and hit dial.

Viola Ayres, the late Senator Ayres daughter and the

tech genius girlfriend of the Coyote of Mounts Bay's girlfriend picks up. "You don't have time to ream us for waking you up, start hiding your shit."

I scoff at her as I get up, straightening the hem of my nightgown. "What exactly do you think I keep stashed in my house? There's nothing here for them to find."

I'm careful even in my anger to not say anything that could be used against me if they're also tapping me lines. Viola is a little less cautious which makes me wonder how secure the Coyote's phone line must be.

I can't imagine Jackson ever choosing his words with care.

"Well, what's the phone call for then? I didn't think we were close enough to sit around gossiping."

I tip my head back and stare at the pristine white of my ceiling while I try not to lose my cool. "What is the warrant for? I haven't done anything that would require police to come and destroy my house so who the hell is coming after me? I need to know before I start making phone calls. We're on a time crunch here, Ayres, you're spending too much time with Jackson and turning into a pain in the ass."

She huffs down the line at me and I hear the clicking of her fingers on the keyboard. "Your guess is as good as mine. There's a gag order on the warrant so only the Judge who signed it and the Police Chief know what it's for."

The Police Chief.

He was in Senior's pocket for years, cleaning up after him and getting rid of evidence trails have earned him an obscene amount of money for a man of his calibre.

Maybe this is just his anger at having his side hustle cut off.

He's on my list of people to replace anyway, maybe this will just speed things up for me.

I take a deep breath and then I get to work.

By the time there's a knock at my door, an over-the-top thumping of a fist like the man doing it enjoys the power he thinks he has a whole lot, I'm dressed entirely in white again. I'm lucky I look great in the color because with all of the power plays I'm having to make I'm wearing it a lot.

I've already called Lips, Illi, and, although I didn't want to, Atticus to let them know exactly what is happening.

Atticus is on his way.

Illi too but they're both planning very different actions for what is happening here. The Butcher will be mentally planning out every second of carving these men to pieces for daring to show up on my doorstep.

The Crow will be plotting out exactly why they would be showing up.

Either way, they won't find a thing.

"Avery Beaumont, open up! We have a warrant to search the premises and we will break the door down if required."

Oh, I wish they would.

I wish they would break down my eight thousand dollar custom door because the hellfire I would rage down onto them for daring would be so satisfying. Even without the resources I usually borrow from Atticus, there's a lot of options I have for myself.

I need to fill my black-book a little more.

Maybe instead of trying to find myself I should just get back to what I'm good at and start ruining peoples lives, manipulating them into being under my thumb, and then I'll feel a little more comfortable in my own skin again.

I walk to the door and unlock it, pulling the double doors both open wide with my head held high and my posture perfect in my eight inch heels.

Half of the men standing there in riot gear look a little dazed at the sight of me. I know exactly which ones are dirty cops, they all gulp at the sight of the Wolf's most trusted confidant standing before them dressed entirely in white, but the others are not expecting to be here to search the house of someone like me.

A nineteen year old girl, dripping with old money and good breeding.

The only person who doesn't look shocked or

concerned is the Police Chief, George Drummond, who's standing there with a sneer curling his lip up at me.

I give him my signature icy look back.

He holds up a folded piece of paper in one of his meaty fists. "We have a warrant to search the property, all of the buildings, and cars. Doesn't matter who you call about it, Beaumont, this is happening today."

I shrug and hold out my hand for the paper, not because I need it but because I'm playing along. "Is there something specific you're looking for? It may be faster if you tell me."

His lip curls even more. "I know exactly who you are and what your family does. I'll find her, no matter how fucking well you try to hide her."

Her?

The men all start moving, some searching outside and others walking past me to get into the building but not a single one of them brush against me as they pass.

Their Police Chief might not see it, but the men all seem to know who the real danger here is.

"I'm not sure who you think I'm harboring here but I assure you, I'm home alone. My brother is out of town, so he definitely hasn't snuck some girl in here without me knowing."

I don't know how much he knows about how my family is made up but it's probably for the best that I leave Lips' name and their relationship out of this for now. It might let

me get a feel of what the hell is actually going on.

Drummond finally hands me the piece of paper and steps forward, his face flushed in anger and sweat beading on his forehead so he looks like he might be in danger of a stroke. "I will find my daughter, Beaumont, and if you've harmed her in any way I will throw the fucking book at you. I know exactly where your families skeletons are buried."

Lauren.

That stupid, star-eyed, dreamer of a girl that Lips always felt sorry for is the one who's missing. I haven't seen her since I left Hannaford Prep, I haven't even thought about any of the stupid bitches we were stuck there with since then, but it doesn't matter. If she's missing and her father is the Police Chief? Probably something worth knowing about.

I raise an eyebrow at him and say in my coldest tone, "Of course you do, Drummond. You helped my father bury them."

When Illi arrives I'm sitting on the love seat in front of my house, the one Harley insisted we have for him to cuddle up with his Mounty. The pillows have been slashed open, because in true Mounts Bay PD logic I must be keeping drugs and cash in the fucking cushions… that or there's a

ransom note in there for Lauren.

"What the fuck have those fucking pigs done to the place? Where's the fucking respect for shit, I'll gut them Queenie."

I huff at him, pissed the hell off, and shrug. "Probably best to not announce our murder plots out in the open. I wouldn't want to spend the rest of the day getting you out of lock up."

He glares over at the cops with a clenched jaw, his arms crossed over his chest and a scowl that speaks of murder. "Nah, they gotta take you in for that shit and I'd be bleeding the whole lot of them out before they got the chance. What's all this about, anyway?"

I shrug and glance over my shoulder at where Drummond is standing and yelling at three of his officers because they aren't finding anything to take me in for. "The Police Chief's daughter is missing."

Illi huffs. "And what the fuck would you know about that? Do you spend a lot of time with pig's kids without me knowing about it?"

I would smirk at him but the state of my house has made any joy impossible. "We went to Hannaford together. Drummond used to pant after my father's cheque book. I think he's paranoid that we took Lauren as retaliation… but I don't give a fuck about stupid little girls who don't know when to keep their mouths shut."

Illi nods and then I watch as he squares himself up, broadening his stance until he looks like he's gotten even wider. There's footsteps as Drummond approaches us but I won't lower myself to look at the pathetic man anymore than I already have.

"I will find her and I will have every last one of you locked up, the keys thrown away, for taking her."

Illi rolls his eyes. "I don't know who the fuck you think you are, but no one give a shit about you. Police Chief who lives in billionaire serial killer pockets? You're fucking nothing to me or Beaumont. Nothing but a fucking tantrum throwing pig."

That has me smirking and I glance over my shoulder at the blustering man still standing there failing to get a word out in his anger. "I'll be billing the city for all of the damage here. Expect to see me again soon because I'll have your job for this."

Illi scoffs. "I'll have his fucking throat. Sleep tight, cunt, I know where you sleep."

Drummond has the sense to look at least a little worried about that but the officers around us who hear it practically shit themselves. I've forgotten what it's like to look at Johnny Illium and see anything other than the fiercely protective family man who will throw down for his people without hesitation.

He must be terrifying to these gutless idiots.

It takes a half hour before they all finally get in their cars and leave us to my utterly destroyed house. I try to send Illi home, if anyone can clean this place up single-handedly it's me, but he gets it in his head that they've planted something here. The idea of there being surveillance on me literally curls up in my gut and threatens to choke me with bile so I keep my mouth shut while he searches the entire place with a fine tooth comb.

I throw out most of the soft furnishings.

There are dozens of broken chairs and every last one of Blaise's guitars that he left behind are too damaged to rescue. The orgy sized bed in their room has been completely gutted with what looks like a machete and Harley's books are all over the floor. All of that pisses me off but the real thing that lights a fire in the deepest, darkest corners of my soul are the shredded remains of the clothes Lips left behind strewn across her floor.

They'd had to pack light for the bus and there were shirts she'd stolen from the guys that she didn't want to risk losing so when I find the pieces of the cashmere sweater of Ash's that she was not-so-discretely obsessed with I think I lose my mind a little.

Okay.

I definitely don't lose my mind but I go beyond the shallow anger at my house being messed up because those torn up clothes mean something to Lips. As a kid

who struggled to clothe herself, who didn't have anyone to love her or give her any sort of security, the clothes that her guys gave her mean something and Drummond has stomped all over it.

I will salt the Earth.

I will burn the entire department down to the ground and build something back up in it's ashes that belongs entirely to me.

For the first time in *months* I feel purpose again.

My job is to stop this shit from happening to us.

I move back down to the kitchen to find Illi in there with a beer out on the counter and a glass of wine already poured for me.

"Did you find anything?"

He shakes his head. "Nothing. I'll get the Coyote out here to go over it again, I doubt they would give up this opportunity to get eyes in here."

I shrug. "I guess I'll have a quiet night tonight until then. What a shame, I was planning on some naked ritualistic sacrifice."

He tips the beer bottle back and gulps it down. "Fuck, that would be something to see. Queenie sacrificing a goat."

My nose wrinkles at him and I ignore his chuckle. "Where would I even find a goat? I'm far more comfortable with human sacrifice."

I pick up the wine glass and sip it slowly, staring at the crack in my marble countertop and wondering how the hell they even managed to do that.

Illi finishes the beer and grabs another one.

I clear my throat. "I need some help."

Illi shrugs without a second thought. "Sure."

I quirk an eyebrow at him. "You don't want to know what it is first? I could ask you anything."

He chuckles under his breath and finishes off the second beer like it's nothing. "You never ask me for help. Lips does, and the guys do, but you never ask me for help so this is something big and it's going to be complicated as fuck but whatever you need, I'll do it."

I nod because it's true enough. I check my phone for a second and find missed messages from Atticus about the warrant. He'd gotten a judge to cancel it, which was why Drummond finally left, and he's looking into why they were really here in the first place.

I didn't tell him about Lauren.

I take a sip of my wine again and then choose my words carefully, aiming for vaguely detailed. "There's a Gala coming up that I need to go to. I need to update my resources and that will be the best place to scout out some options."

Illi shrugs. "And you want me to go with you? Fuck, you're going to make me wear a suit, aren't you?"

A smile tugs at the corner of my lips. "I'll have a Tom Ford delivered to your place, do you know all of your measurements? Odie knows how to take them, I'm sure you'll enjoy the process."

He grins at me, radiating smug male energy that would piss me off in anyone other than him because I'm very aware just how much he loves his wife. "I guess I can get on board with that. Anything in particular we're looking for at this fucking thing?"

I stare over at the destruction of my house. "I need a good cleaner… maybe a new lawyer so I can make the MBPD weep into their morning coffees everyday for the rest of their hopefully long lives."

Illi nods and moves to throw both of his empty bottles out but I'm not sure why he'd bother because the contents of my trash can was dumped out into a pile in the corner.

My skin starts to crawl just looking at it.

It takes me half a minute to order a skip bin to be delivered to my house and when I convince Illi head home for the day I get to work cleaning the mess up. I guess I was due for a design change anyway.

By the time I have everything cleared out that was destroyed I'm angry and frustrated and not at all in the mood to cook so I order Thai takeout and call Ash to whine.

I'd messaged him when I found out about the search warrant and I can say for sure that I'm glad he's not here

at the moment.

"Did that fuck Jackson check your house yet? I don't want you staying there if there's pigs watching you."

I huff. "He checked his security and there's no bugs. They did put trackers on all of the cars though so I won't be driving until they're gone."

"Are you fucking kidding me?! I'm coming home. Fuck this, I'm leveling the fucking city for this."

I laugh at him but I keep my tone light. "I'm glad it's your precious cars that sent you over the edge."

There's yelling and laughter in the background and I feel a little guilty about worrying him while he's supposed to be having a good time. "Don't come home. Honestly, figuring out plans for kidnapped girls and new drug dealing king pins is my idea of a good time. I'm safe. You can check in on the cams whenever you need to and I promise that I won't let anyone touch your cars. I love you. I want you to be happy."

He exhales for long enough that I'm sure he's torn but finally he says, "I love you too, Floss. If anything happens to you again… none of this is worth it if you're not safe."

I swallow roughly as the doorbell rings and I hang up to answer it.

The takeout delivery guy is young and definitely not from around here because he stares at my house in awe. It's funny and not something I used to so I try to

He hands over the bag and turns away, he feet stumbling a little.

"Oh. Did you… ah, did you know about this photo here? I think someone is pulling a prank on you."

My stomach drops as I turn around.

The guy points at the other door, the side I didn't open and when I take a step out to look at it, slowly bend down to set the bag of food on the ground so it doesn't slip through my fingers as I stare at the photo of myself that's been nailed to my front door.

My eyes are crossed out in blood.

# Nine

It's annoying to have to call Illi right back to my house but there's no way I'm sleeping here alone tonight if I have some crazed stalker sending me death threats. I think twice about messaging Atticus about it and instead I call Aodhan to tell him.

He comes right over.

I open the door for him and he grins at me, leaning down to kiss my cheek and I take in a deep lungful of his cologne. He smells like he just got out of the shower and my mind starts wondering about what it is that he's been doing while my life was getting more complicated.

The smirk he gives me is all sorts of teasing Irish charm. "Do you ever wear normal clothes? Like, shirts and sweatpants? You always look like you're about to have dinner with a diplomat when shit goes down."

My legs should not get weak at the rasp of his voice, I'm better than that, but the sound of it tugs my mind back to that little bubble we were both in… when my mind

forgot that the Jackal was the one making the decisions. I shrug. "These are normal clothes for people who aren't Mounty street urchins. You might want to raise your bar because I'm not lowering mine."

I ignore the flutters in my stomach at the low chuckle he gives me, his hand slides slowly down the bare skin of my arm until his finger thread through mine. "You raise a lot of things in me, Queenie, don't worry about that."

There's another booming knock at the door and Aodhan groans as I pull away from him to let Illi in.

"This is high school all over again." Illi snarks out, his hair wet like I got him out of the shower to be here, and Aodhan quirks an eyebrow at him.

"I can't imagine you walking the halls of a high school but I've got to tell you, it was *nothing* like this for me."

I roll my eyes at them both but I am happy to see them getting along a little better. "He's talking about my high school experience, it was full of stalkers and serial killers. All we need now are some heads to show up in cardboard boxes."

Illi tips his head to the side like he's considering it. "Look, that might be exactly what we need here. Maybe you should call Lips and set something up with the psycho."

I stiffen a little but Aodhan doesn't make a comment, thank God. Something about Atticus's reaction to Nate makes me nervous for him to know about Lips' brother.

"That is an option on the board… I knew taking care of the Jackal and Senior wouldn't be the end of things but I was hoping for a break at least."

Illi huffs and runs a hand over his face. "Please don't tell me you have an actual murder board hung up somewhere in this fucking place that the pigs just got an eyeful of? The Feds will end up on our fucking tails if I have to go kill them all."

I could keep it a secret.

I could but I won't because while my family is away these two have become my safety net and if I'm now being threatened then they should know about my panic room, custom built and completely undisturbed by the police raid.

I turn on my heel and walk over to the bottom of my huge and very ornate foyer. The grand staircase is made out of what looks to be solid marble.

It's very impressive, something I spent months designing and then almost a full year to be carved out and installed to perfection.

The opening to the basement is impossible to find but I spent my childhood in the Beaumont mansion, so it's only right that I know exactly how to hide a basement opening.

Illi and Aodhan both watch me open it and when I straighten up I've never seen Illi look so impressed before.

I try not to preen.

"I need one of these. Queenie, who the fuck did you get to do this?"

I chuckle under my breath and step over the small marble lip, startling a little when Aodhan grabs my elbow with gentle but firm fingers.

I smile up at him. "I'm okay, I spend most evenings down here."

He doesn't let me go, if anything his fingers tighten and he walks down the stairs into the darkness with me. "Do you come down in those heels? Fuck, what am I saying, of course you do. Staircases mean nothing to the Ice Queen."

I chuckle and then fight a blush away from my cheeks when Illi starts huffing and muttering under his breath about us both. I'm very glad neither of them can actually see me.

"Are there lights done here? I'm almost worried you're about to murder us both down here." Illi mutters, which is rich coming from him.

His murder room is also in the basement of his warehouse.

When I mention this to him he just laughs, that loud and booming sound that bounces around the stairwell. It does mean a lot to me that he'd even crack those jokes with me though, that there was even the possibility that I could kill the infamous Butcher.

If anyone could kill him it would be me.

I'm the least likely to even try out of our family and that means I'd be the most successful in an attempt. That's the real reason we need to be so careful of who we trust, of who we let into our family because there's always the possibility that they'll betray us.

Like Diarmuid.

We didn't even let him in, not really, we just named him as an ally and he used that to get past Atticus's men to kidnap me. Everything that happened in the Jackal's lair is his fault.

Aodhan leans in close to my ear to murmur to me, "You're shaking, Queenie."

Right.

No more thinking about that, we have a stalker to find.

That photo might not have been a planned shot but the fact that the person who left it knows where I live? I've been careful about keeping my address private so either they have access to police records or one of the Crow's men have leaked that information.

I'll have to mention it to him but I'm not chasing it up now.

I hit the lights when we get to the bottom of the stairs and Aodhan rubs his free hand over his face, squinting at the sudden brightness. Illi blinks around at everything and I think I've actually managed to shock him with my set up.

One entire wall of the basement is covered with all of

my current issues. In the middle, there's a photo of Grimm Graves. He's a mean looking asshole of a man but there's no mistaking that he's sired all of the kids in that file that Atticus gave me.

Let's hope the unmistakable eyes are the only trait of his they all share.

There's pages and pages of his crimes already pasted on that wall. Drugs, kidnapping, rape, murder, extortion, the man has no sort of moral code whatsoever. I have each of the men on the Chaos Demon council up there too, all of them with rap sheets as bad as their president.

Colt and Chance are currently grouped with the other siblings and their files are thinner than Grimm's but I'm not convinced that's only due to age.

Nate and Poe are not there.

We know for sure that they're both family, no matter what Atticus may suspect.

I expect them both to gravitate to that section of the wall, probably because it's the most interesting spot in my opinion, but Aodhan heads straight to my intensive investigation on the whereabouts of Diarmuid O'Cronin, his uncle and the man responsible for my kidnapping.

Illi heads to my list of high society figures that were owned by Senior, every last one of them the scum-of-the-Earth types who would buy at the infamous Bay skin auctions. Thank God the Vulture is dead.

"I know this guy, why isn't his name up here or any information?" Illi murmurs, pointing at one of the photos.

I arch an eyebrow at him. "Bingley Crawford? You mean Atticus's older brother? His name isn't up there because it's already seared into my brain forever thanks to being forced to spend time with him as a child."

Illi is very good at hiding his tells, one of the best, but I'm even better at spotting them.

I supposed he met Bing at the auctions… it would be just my luck that he probably bid on Odie and Illi has a score to settle with him.

"The entire Crawford family is awful. All of them except Atticus, so if Bing did something terrible please just— please don't kill Atticus for it. I won't stop you from hunting his entire family down and bleeding them out though."

Illi cocks his head and jabs a finger at the photo. "Where is *Bing* these days? You know much about what he's up to?"

I shrug and glance over at Aodhan but he's engrossed in the Diarmuid information. "He's the middle child so I know more about where Holden is than Bing but I'd assume he's still partying in the Maldives with the underage prostitutes he enjoys. Atticus has made very sure that Bing hasn't been around me since he cornered me at a party their father held and told me he wanted to feel how

tight a Beaumont cunt was. I was thirteen."

Illi nods slowly and I can practically see him running numbers in his head.

I open my mouth to question him more but Aodhan cuts me off, "Who do you have following Diarmuid? Who took this photo?"

I leave Illi to stare at Atticus's twisted family tree and walk over to Aodhan. "An old police officer who was fired for trying to investigate the auctions. I've paid him a lot over the years, I trust him as much as I can trust someone outside of my family. He's been offered money before to lie to me and not only did he refuse, he killed the man who offered it to him. I give him big bonuses."

Aodhan chuckles. "I guess being richer than God has its benefits."

I shrug. "I haven't found many downsides. I won't ever feel bad about having the resources at my disposal to take over the Bay now the Jackal is gone."

He shrugs and says, "So where is the warning photo? It's not up here."

I walk him to the small lounge chair I've fallen asleep on more times than I can count and grab the photo. I'd stashed it down here the moment I'd found it just in case the MBPD came back for some inane reason.

Illi frowns at the photo and I watch him carefully. "You know him?"

He nods slowly. "Yeah, not by name but he was known on the streets as the Collector."

I fight the urge to roll my eyes. Typical Mounties, everyone has a stupid code name. Aodhan smothers a snort at me and Illi shoots him a look until he gets a good look at my face too.

"You can't talk, Queenie, whispers are already starting on the streets about you. The Stag shouldn't have paraded you around the party down at the docks if you didn't want a name of your own. The Queen of Mounts Bay… has a ring to it."

I finally just let my eyes roll with a huff. "Could you not have picked something a little more… classy? I don't at all feel very queen-like."

Aodhan chuckles again and crosses his arms. "I'm sure you could give any royal a run for their money in the manners department… and shoes."

I refuse to preen under the assessment but I can't deny that it's nice to have someone notice the care and effort I put into my appearance. Life outside of the snake pit of Hannaford is actually pretty nice.

"Where was this photo taken, Queenie?" Illi says, his attention back on the photo and he's frowning again.

I shrug. "It's from the party. I've been digging into the political web of the Bay, preparing for the Game and everything that will come with… I assume I've pressed

someone's buttons a little too hard and now they're sending me threats."

Illi places the photo on a blank section of the wall and sighs. "This is a very specific threat though. The Collector is dead. The Crow paid Lips a black diamond to kill him. It was the very first favor he ever gave out. I remember it so fucking clearly because D'Ardo almost busted a fucking nut over it. He was convinced the Crow was trying to make friends with her, amped up the assassination attempts and sent a whole lotta chaos his way."

I frown and set forward. "Atticus paid her for his death? Who was he? What exactly did he collect?"

Illi shares a look with Aodhan that would infuriate me if it were anyone else. They're trying to gauge how much exactly I can handle of this story and though I know it comes from a good place, it's entirely misplaced.

"Girls. He collected women, or children didn't he? It's some sick story of a perverted man isn't it?"

Illi shrugs. "Sort of. He didn't ever touch them or hurt them, he just... kept them. When Lips killed him she set the girls in his penthouse free and none of them had been assaulted beyond the head wounds to get them into their cages. He fed them, gave them clothes and beds... but they were all kept in glass cages."

I slowly sink down onto the lounge and prop my chin up on my fist with a sigh. The sexual perversions of men

are disgusting but understandable to me. A childhood of growing up in the Beaumont Manor means I understand exactly what the darkest of sexual fantasies can be, but this? This isn't something I understand. The power men wield has always tied into their sexual urges.

This absolute power with no sort of bodily harm is strange.

"Yep. Lips never could fucking understand it either."

Aodhan sinks down in the seat next to mine and tips his head back to stare at the ceiling. This all feels so… normal. As if we've done this a thousand times before and I have, just not with these two men. But I trust them both, I trust them enough to be sitting here in my basement without the constant guard of my brother here with me.

Aodhan sighs and rolls his head on his shoulders to look at me. "It's a threat. Clearly it's a threat to you but it's also a threat to Lips. Whoever posted it there wants you to sweat over how much they know."

Illi grunts and pulls out his phone, tapping away at the screen. "Well, we know that they've walked their ass up to the front fucking door so this place isn't safe until we lock it the fuck down. Question is, why the fuck didn't the Coyote catch this?"

He lifts the phone to his ear and then snarls into it, "You're on my last fucking nerve, asshole, and I'm about to come call into your bunker for a little chat… yeah

well, what the fuck happened to your security at Queenies place… no, I'm sure there's been a breach, I'm staring at it… you have ten minutes, make them count."

Aodhan snickers under his breath and I cast him a look. He shrugs, "It's funny when the threats aren't being aimed your way. You wanna come stay at mine, Queenie? It's not as pretty as this place but you'll be safe there."

Illi huffs. "Like fuck. She's coming back to my place. Odie will be fucking thrilled to have you, she's been at me about putting together the nursery and I'm sure she'll appreciate your taste a helluva lot more than mine."

I roll my eyes at him. "Let me guess… you wanted a cleaver mobile for the crib? Blood spatter decals on the walls?"

He grins at me and shrugs. "Hearts in jars on every surface, just so the kid knows what Daddy does to anyone who comes after the family."

I smile at him because how could I not? It's too sweet how much he loves his wife and I know for sure that it doesn't matter how high his body count is, that child is going to be loved more than any Mounty has been before.

Aodhan grimaces a little. "Please don't say Daddy around me again until the baby is here, I think my soul just left my body."

Illi roars with laughter and Aodhan looks a little sick.

I roll my eyes at them both. "I'll pack a bag. Do me a

favor and don't tell the guys? I'll call Lips and tell her but Ash will try to come home and I don't want to cut his trip short."

Illi shrugs and agrees easily enough, I guess he only really answers to Lips and even then she has never treated him as anything other than an equal. A beloved friend who's in this fucked up life with her.

Aodhan traces a finger down the back of my hand idly, like the touch of my skin is helping him think and I'm not sure I can take all of this casual touching. I don't want it to stop, but I need to know what the hell we're doing.

Have I given up on Atticus?

Does Aodhan actually want me or is this some sort of… weird obligation thing, like he's still feeling awful about the sex we'd been forced to have?

I don't know.

I'm too scared of the answer to ask.

# Ten

I refuse to spend more than a night at the Illium household.

Not because I don't love seeing Odie, she really is a great friend to have and catching up with her now that she has the most perfect little bump is exciting, but I have no interest in being holed up and under a constant protective guard again so I arrange for even more security with the Coyote and once every inch of my property has sensors, cameras, and alarms I head home to redecorate and to plan out my outfit for the Gala.

I plan on making a statement.

The Morrison Family Charity Gala is held at the Alexandria Ballrooms in LA every year.

There's only ever a hundred people invited with plus ones that are personally vetted by the Kora board. Now that I have more than half of them under my thumb it's easier than breathing to get an invite for myself and Illi.

He could show up in his leather jacket and blood spattered jeans if he wanted to.

That's not the statement I want to make here though, I'm looking at kitting out my own black book and though I want the people in it obedient. I want them terrified of the right things.

Illi could murder them.

I'd ruin them, I'd take every last asset they owned and drag their names through the mud. I'd break them so completely and then I'd kill them.

But that's for another day, for now they've all been loyal and obedient.

It takes me half a day to get ready for the event. It's not just about throwing a dress on and a little makeup. It's all about the prep work, there's no point building a look on poor foundations.

I once tried to explain this to Lips and she stared at me like I'd lost my mind.

Someday I'll make her do the full gala experience and I know for sure that there'll be three idiot guys drooling all over my hard work. I shouldn't think about that because it just makes me upset to think about how no one will appreciate the effort I'm going into tonight... well, no one will want to rip the dress off of me but at least I'll have them all fearing for their lives.

I'm not sure which one I'd prefer.

I dress entirely in white, once again making sure that my allegiances are on display, though I'm not sure anyone

attending would even know about the intricate color systems of the Mounts Bay Twelve.

Probably more than I'd think.

I choose a Galvan dress that is more sparkle than substance, the split up the thigh meaning that it's going to be a no underwear sort of event, though the longer sleeves subdues the look to something classy enough for me to wear. I have nothing against showing a lot of skin, but half of the battle with high society is the image they all hold in their minds of you and I want them to be terrified, not gossiping about how much skin I have on show.

I choose a pair of Louboutin's, my personal favorite designer and though the shoes aren't comfortable the stiletto heel is sharp enough to slit a throat if I had to.

I straighten my hair and slick it back so it hangs around my shoulders in a dark curtain, my eyeliner is winged and my lips are my signature shade of blood red.

Illi lets himself in downstairs while I get ready but when I start down the staircase I find Aodhan standing there with him.

Neither of them notice me when I first start down the stairs, a silk YSL clutch in one hand and the other holding the marble railing, but when Aodhan glances over his shoulder at me butterflies start up in my stomach.

I guess someone is enjoying the effort I've put in.

"Holy shit." He mutters and Illi huffs at him.

"Wipe your chin, for fuck's sake. I'll call Ash to come kill you if you pop a tent in your pants right now. I'll fucking do it, just for funsies because I don't wanna see that shit."

I level a savage glare at him but he grins and shrugs at me. "You look like you're about to kill your husband for his oil fortune, Queenie."

I grin and wave a hand in his direction. "That was the exact look I was going for so my job here is done. The suit is perfect, by the way. You should wear one more often, catch your enemies unaware."

He huffs and kisses my cheek, a hand on my elbow in such a brotherly way that I feel a pang in my chest again for Ash and Harley and even Morrison with his mopey ways.

Aodhan finally finds his words. "You look fucking stunning, don't listen to Illi. He's blinded by his love for his wife, he can't see just how fucking—"

"Did I not just say I'll call the cavalry home? Keep running your mouth about her and you'll be waking up in the morning to Ash gouging your fucking eyes out with his bare hands. I've seen him kill, you know? I've seen just how *Beaumont* he really is when you fuck with one of his girls and there's a reason I trusted him with the Wolf's safety while they prance across the country."

I snort at Illi. "I thought you trusted Harley with her safety? He'll be devastated to find out you replaced him."

He shrugs. "That's a given. Arbour is a Mounty, of course he can take a swing and shed a little blood. No way you can breathe the air down there and not be a little fucked up."

I roll my eyes at him and then with a pointed look shoo him off so I can speak to Aodhan without his threats. He waits until Aodhan isn't looking and then grins at me like this is all just one big joke to him.

Asshole.

"You really do look fucking beautiful, Queenie."

The way his voice dips low makes me believe him too. "If I didn't have the lipstick on I'd let you kiss me, O'Cronin, but I need to look my best. What are you doing here, anyway?"

He huffs out a breath and scrubs a hand over his face. "Illi mentioned you guys were heading out and I thought it would be best if someone was here to keep an eye on the place while you're gone, just in case they wanna drop off another clue. Now I'm fucking glad I saw you before you left… fuck me."

He says it like a prayer but I lean up into his space and enjoy the way he stops breathing. "If you're here when I get home… maybe."

I smirk as I turn and walk away, enjoying the muttering he does under his breath and the way he clutches at his chest like I've stabbed him.

Again.

Illi helps me into the BMW and shuts the door behind me, ever the gentleman, and then he gets us onto the highway. I can wear a seatbelt without ruining my dress but when I mention this to him he shrugs.

"I already told you you're safe with me. Just sit there and enjoy the drive, we're close to two hours away so maybe get a nap in, kid."

There's no way I can sleep with all of the planning and mind games and plotting happening in my head.

No rest for the wicked.

My phone buzzes with a text from Aodhan and the butterflies start a riot in my stomach.

*I can't wait to strip that dress off of you when you get back.*

My thighs clench together and I have to remind myself that I'm not wearing underwear and the fabric is very thin. Probably not the best idea but too late to reconsider now.

My phone buzzes again and I find a message from Lips there.

*Illi sent me a photo of the dress. Try not to run away with Atticus when he sees you in it.*

I scoff at her but before I can reply she sends through a photo of her own. They've stopped into a bar in some little town on the road. Blaise has an arm around Finn and a grin on his face while Harley scowls at them both with a

beer at his lips.

Ash is staring into the camera and there's no doubt that Lips is the one behind the camera. He doesn't give anyone those soft eyes but her, the smirk on his face a loving thing rather than the one that he gives everyone else that drips with acid.

His hair has grown out a little, curling at his temples and, sitting at the bar in a pair of jeans and an old Vanth tee, he looks like a normal teenager. He looks happy and tired and in love and so at peace with everything and I've never been so fucking thankful to the little lost Mounty girl we tormented through freshman year.

The worst part about the gala is coming face-to-face with Blaine Morrison, the namesake of the Gala, standing in the center of the room talking about how fucking amazing his life is now that he's once again a single man. It doesn't matter that every last person here knows that he abandoned his oldest son, gave up custody of his infant son, and is in a bitter divorce with his wife after years of mental and financial abuse, every last person attending flock around him like he's someone worth knowing.

Illi scoffs at the sight. "He's on our kill list, right? Want me to do it tonight? Quick and easy, no more deadbeat

daddy wasting good oxygen."

I smirk at him and murmur back to him, "Lips has dibs on his death, she was very clear about what she has planned for him. We just need Blaise on board first."

He huffs and holds out his arm for me to take as we walk towards the bar area. The socialites all stare at us with varying levels of fear and disgust. A few look at Illi like they'd be open to him bending them over a table somewhere out of sight which has him rolling his eyes.

I make note of them all.

Every detail counts in the games of war.

Illi orders us both drinks and then, as he sips at his whiskey, he murmurs, "So, who's on our hit list? Please tell me I can kill someone tonight. There's not enough... fear in this room."

I sip delicately at my champagne and raise an eyebrow at him. "Dead socialites and businessmen are no help to me. I know it's hard to put up with them all but I need some very specific skill sets."

He grumbles under his breath and orders another whiskey, downing the last of his glass in one gulp. I start people watching, observing who was invited to the gala this year and who has been left from the list.

I'm approached a few times by people who aren't on my radar at all, gossip mongers who are only after the scoop on what really happened to my father. Everyone

knows he's dead and on paper it was a heart attack. The gossip rags had labelled it a 'broken heart' after losing my mother and Joey.

I broke every piece of china in my house the day I read it.

Ash had taken it a little better, he'd gone for a run until he couldn't breathe anymore, and Lips had eventually taken him to bed early. When I told her the next morning to never tell me what happened in their bed she rolled her eyes at me and told me he'd just laid there listening to her duet with Blaise on repeat.

He's a total sap for her voice and the day she sang in the chapel back at Hannaford, her raspy tones casting a spell over all three of her men like she was some sort of siren.

I cut the gossiping bitches down the moment they bring up my father and send them on their way, ignoring Illi's chuckles and huffs at all of the niceties and social cues they all follow. It's as easy for me as breathing, something that was drummed into me before I was even conscious of it, and I keep my attention on what is happening around the Kora board members.

Easiest to go through them to collect more people.

I'm sipping and glaring at Blaine when I feel a presence besides me, the scent of the Hermes perfume that comes with her screaming money.

I glance over, ready to just tell the gossiper to fuck off, but I don't recognize this woman.

Perfectly styled blond hair, a stunningly understated Missoni gown, with neutral makeup and a red lip shade that might even be the same as mine.

I meet her eyes right as we're both finished assessing each other. She smiles at me and there's a flirty edge to it, something just a little too friendly. "The Galvan was a great choice, it fits the lines of your body perfectly."

Illi smothers a cough next to me but I ignore him. "I know better than to attempt a Ferragamo nightmare at a gala like this. Missoni is a good choice, a little safe for my tastes."

Every other woman I have interacted with tonight would have been pissed at that comment but the flirty smirk just widens on her face. "You must be Avery Beaumont. I've heard so much about you. How bold of you to bring the Butcher of the Bay so far from home but I suppose you've leashed him appropriately. Who knew he could look so good in a suit?"

It's only through a lifetime of practice that neither Illi or I react. Although we haven't tried to hide who he really is, we weren't expecting someone to call Illi out like this and to call that stunning suit of his a leash?

Who the fuck is this bitch?

I let my eyes fall back on Blaise's idiot father as I sip

my drink. "What a shame, I've heard nothing about you."

The woman's head tilts like she's being coy and I suddenly feel like I have no idea what is happening here. Is she actually flirting with me? Is this an act? Has she taken a hit to the head and thinks it's funny to play with people who will murder her without second thought.

"Welcome to the bigger pond, Floss. Take care not to be eaten alive."

What the hell?

Illi and I watch as she sashays away from us, the target painted very clearly on her back from the both of us because I might not know a thing about the woman right now, but I'm going to know everything about her the moment I leave this gala.

"Is there someone you can call about her? Fuck I think she wants in you, Queenie. I'm not sure whether that was a sex thing or a blood thing but either way you're on her radar."

I shrug and lie through my teeth, mostly to comfort myself. "She's probably just some bored socialite with a Fed for a husband. Or a high profile drug lord selling cocaine in back rooms at these sorts of events."

Illi huffs and shakes his head. "Fucking rich people."

I smirk at him and we both stand there and watch as the woman works her way around the room. Every person she approaches greets her enthusiastically but every action is

laced with fear.

Who the hell is she?

Illi progressively drinks his whiskey's, one after another and I'm expecting him to actually get drunk but when I mention that to him he rolls his eyes at me. Apparently he's like Harley and has a ridiculous tolerance. I slowly sip at the champagne and just people watch, soaking in every last interaction around me until I have a running list to work with.

I don't see Atticus arrive, I don't even realize he's here until he sneaks up behind us from the other end of the ballroom.

"Are you trying to get yourself killed?" He murmurs in my ear, and I sip at the champagne in my hand as though it doesn't affect me at all.

Illi huffs and crosses his arms over his chest, still as fierce as ever in his suit. I glance over at him but he's shaking his head.

"And what exactly have I done now? Am I not allowed to speak to people anymore?"

Atticus steps forward and takes the glass out of my hand, setting it down on the table behind us. I glare at him but he ignores it.

"Amanda Donnelley is not someone you own. She's someone you court to get information from. You pay her, you owe her favors, you kill people at her request so she'll

open her books to you."

I purposefully keep my eyes away from the smiling banshee of a woman, grinning and giggling as she drapes herself over Blaine Morrison. For that alone I want to rip her throat out but the words out of Atticus's mouth just make it worse.

"Is this your way of telling me you've been whoring yourself out to her to build your empire? I'm sorry to tell you that I'm not going to play that game. I don't kneel for anyone."

Illi murmurs praises under his breath but Atticus's eyes narrow at him. "You belong to the Wolf. So does your little psychotic guard dog."

I lean down to retrieve my drink and smirk at him. "We stand with Lips. We always have, being indicted just means that you know where my loyalty lies. If I gave a fuck about the validity of the politics of Mounts Bay I'd join the Game but I'll have a seat at any table I want."

Atticus stares at me for a moment and then steps back to motion at me to follow him, the look on his face expectant and demanding. When I glance back over at that Donnelley hag again he grabs my arm and tugs me to his side.

A snarl rips out of Illi but I shake my head at him. "I'll be fine, Illi. Have a drink, I'll be back in a minute."

# Eleven

There aren't that many places to speak in private so Atticus drags me to a supply closet.

We walk past Luca to get there, his eyes on us as Atticus swings the door open wide and shoves me in, gently but the hand on my arm is firm. It makes me feel as though I'm about to be scolded like a child and I have exactly no interest in submitting for that.

"I have more important things to do tonight than argue with you about some slut you've sold yourself to."

His eyes narrow as he shuts the door behind himself, the room falling into darkness. It takes a second for my eyes to adjust but when they do I find boxes stacked up everywhere and a pissed off man who looks as though he'd like to strangle me.

I know all too well what that looks like.

He steps forward until he's crowding me into the wall and snarls at me, "I need you to stop being a child about this!"

I startle away from him. "A child? You think I'm being a child about the man that I have loved and craved and longed for just giving up on me and for what? For some misguided sense of self-sacrifice?"

His eyes narrow and he stalks forward. "Self-sacrifice? Really, Floss, you know better than that."

I let out a deep breath and ignore the burning in the back of my eyes. I will *never* cry in front of this man again. "I don't want a man who will give me up the second things get hard. My life has been nothing but difficult so far, Crow. I don't expect that to change anytime soon and I only accept people who would kill for me. Every member of my family would bleed and shed blood for me… you've only ever proven you'd leave me for my own good. That's not what I want."

I turn on my heel and stalk towards the door.

Atticus Crawford has never, not once laid a hand on me.

I can count on one hand the amount of times he's hugged me, I have enough fingers to tally up the times he's brushed my hand with his own, so I'm not expecting him to grab me and stop me from leaving.

I'm certainly not expecting his hand to clamp down on my neck, spinning me around and forcing me into his arms before I even realize he's touching me. His hand stays on my neck, holding me still as he leans down with fire in his

eyes and breathes the words against my lips.

"I killed for you long before your brother did. I was bleeding out the buyers your father auctioned you off to before you made it to middle school. You think I walked into the Game clean? My hands were dripping with the blood of men who wanted to destroy you, Avery. Don't you ever tell me I gave you up, I have never given you up. I've tried to give you a good life, if you don't want that then you're mine. No more coming to meetings with the Butcher draped all over you, no more dancing in the Bay with the Stag. You have my full attention. What are you going to do with it?"

I stare him down and it occurs to me that now he's finally saying to me exactly what I always wanted.

That's not what I want anymore.

I do want him… but I'm not going to give up Aodhan for him. I'm not going to stop being who I am just to have him.

I want more than that.

"It's too late, Atticus. You should've taken me when you had the chance."

His hand tightens around the back of my neck and I think if it were anyone else I'd be panicking but I know Atticus Crawford, the Crow of Mounts Bay, better than I know any other man. He might have lied to me but I've always known who he is at his core.

I'm safe with him.

Too fucking safe, too protected, too far removed from the real world by his obsessive need to keep me breathing.

I don't want *safe* anymore.

He sees it too, finally looks into my eyes and sees the real shift that's happened between us. I think that scares him a little. I think he was always so sure of me and that bubble that both he and Ash put me in that he never really thought through what would happen if I wanted out.

I tip my head back slowly to stare him down.

His restraint just disappears, as if the tether holding it to him was cut and now I'm faced with nothing but the beast who hides in the luxurious suits. His hand finally moves away from my neck to clamp down on my shoulder and push me to my knees.

I refuse to let myself think about the state of my dress on this dirty floor.

He reaches for the zip of his pants slowly, like he's waiting for me to punch him in the dick and run off screaming, "Is this want you want, Avery? I thought you didn't kneel for anyone?"

I roll my eyes and hope he can see it. "Either do it or let go of me, Atticus, I have a gala to attend."

He unzips and frees his cock, stroking his hand up and down right in front of my face.

I swallow roughly, deep breath, this is only what I've

desperately wanted from him since I was old enough to know what the hell a blow job was. Now I just have to make sure it's the best damn blow job of his life so he'll never be able to have anyone else touch what's mine.

"I'll be gentle if you're scared."

I scoff at him but his words cut a little too close to home. "This isn't the first dick I've sucked, Crawford, like I'd be scared of you."

His eyes turn to slits, a hand clamps over my face and tilting my head back until he can look into my eyes as he fists his dick again, slapping it against my cheek. I look up at him and the cold steely gray of his eyes cuts into my soul.

I still want him.

Just as bad as I've always wanted him.

I guess I'm going to be doomed to be in love with a man who can't give me what I want, no matter how hard I try to plead with him to accept who I am.

At least I'll give him up knowing what he tastes like.

I open my mouth for him, my pussy drenched as he groans and moves his hand to cup my chin as he guides himself between my lips.

I suck him down until he moves his hand away and lets me do what I want. I push further and further until he's hitting the back of my throat, sucking and humming until he grunts and starts to move his hips subconsciously,

driving his cock into me until I'm getting wet at the thought of him driving into my pussy the same way.

There's a knock at the door.

"Fuck. Off." Atticus snarls as I push at his hips, just enough that his cock pops out of my mouth and I can breathe.

My eyes slide over to the door, the sounds of the other guests talking out there a distraction. I don't want anyone walking in and seeing me like this, down on my knees at Atticus's feet, his zipper down and his dick still wet from my mouth.

I swallow but the voices get louder, and when I hear Luca's voice join the mix I try to stand up only for Atticus's hand to clamp down on my shoulder.

"The door is unlocked." I snap, but his mouth stretches into a smirk.

"Do you want it or not?"

He's calling my bluff.

He still thinks I'm going to stand up and bitch him out, slap him and storm out of here so that he can go back to pretending that ignoring me is for my own safety.

Well he's not expecting me to stand up and he's definitely not expecting me to lean back on the wall behind me, slipping a hand into the high slit of my dress and dipping two fingers into my own pussy. My eyelids drop until I can barely see him but at this point I'm an expert

at getting myself off so there's no helping the reaction my body has.

When I look up through my eyelashes at him, his dick is throbbing as his hand slowly strokes over the length, and the way he's holding his breath speaks to just how little control he really has.

"Well? Do you want it or not?" I echo his own words back to him on a low moan, and I watch as the tethers of his restraint snap. He surges towards me, trapping my body against the wall with his, one hand on the either side of my head as his chest starts to heave.

He speaks between gritted teeth, "You really want to do this in a dirty storage room? You really want your first time to be here? You're better than this, Avery."

I almost choke on the words but there's no hiding it from him and I can tell myself I'm just trembling from the way his hips are grinding my own hand into my clit until I'm desperate for more. "This isn't my first time. Fuck me."

His eyes flare out, and in the blink of an eye his hand is back on my neck squeezing a little as he presses me into the wall with the bulk of his body. It's been years since I've seen him out of a suit and it's not until he's pinning me here that I realize just how *big* he really is.

I realize the restraint he must be showing every time Ash takes a swing at him.

Even with my heels I'm nowhere near tall enough so he has to lean down to snarl in my face, "Who the fuck touched you? You told me you broke up with Rory and never said a word about anyone else? Tell me."

I'd rather die than tell him about Aodhan.

There's the tiniest bit of guilt in the pit of my stomach but I'm selfish and ignore it. At some point I need to stop doing what's best for everyone else and just do exactly what I want to do.

Aodhan and I haven't even talked about what we're doing and I've wanted this for longer than I can remember so I'm not going to let anything risk this moment.

I lean up the little bit I can until my lips brush against his, an echo of my own trauma that I'm going to replace in my mind, and whisper, "Fuck *me* or fuck *off*. I'm over this little bout of foreplay you're so intent on having."

A very not-Atticus-like snarl rips out of his throat and the hand at my throat tightens a little before it drops away and my heart drops.

Of course he's going to stop.

Of course he was the one bluffing.

He moves back and right when stupid, useless tears start to fill my eyes he bends down to grab the long panels of my dress that fall to the ground and he rips until the split tears open all the way up to my stomach.

I'm too shocked to move my hands but he's too focussed

on taking what he wants to notice my jaw dropping as he grabs my wrists and yanks my hands away from my pussy. He doesn't hesitate to replace my fingers with his own and when there's no resistance or so much as a flinch for me another snarl rips out of his throat.

I wasn't lying to him about my virginity.

Again I think that he might just turn around and leave but he doesn't, he swoops down to kiss me deep and raw, biting at my lip like he's trying to punish me. I can count on one hand the amount of times he's kissed me too and none of those times were like this, this feels like a claiming and a branding, like he's desperate to burn the touch of any other man right out of my body.

His fingers are just a little too skilled for me, jealousy flooding me as he crooks his fingers inside me to find my g spot with the type of ease that only comes from practice but the pleasure flooding through me is too distracting to think about that stuff right now.

I might just hunt those women down though, destroy their lives in a fit of rage.

My pussy is weeping by the time I come, squeezing down on his fingers as my legs threaten to give out.

Before I come down from the high he bends down again to hook his arms around my legs and lift me up into his arms, slamming my back into the wall as he finally pushes his thick cock into me, my pussy gripping him like

it never wants to let him go.

It's not painful like the last time but it's tight, like I'm too full of him, and my legs tense around him as I wait for it to start to hurt when he moves.

It doesn't hurt. Not at all, not even when he slams into me like he's trying to punish us both for this entire mess of a night. His pelvis keeps grinding against my oversensitive clit and it doesn't take much to push me over the edge again, a scream ripping out of my throat that he barely manages to muffle with his lips.

He kisses me like we're both dying even as his hips snap into me, not slowing at all when he finally comes, grunting and biting my lips so hard we both taste blood.

He holds me there for a second as he catches his breath, his forehead pressed against mine, then he slowly lets my legs drop back down to the ground, the drop is even further thanks to my hells being kicked God knows where in this tiny room.

He steps away from me to fix his pants, my skirt dropping be to place and if it weren't for the stream of his cum dripping down my legs you'd barely be able to tell that the love of my life just fucked me raw while his men stood outside and listened.

Oh God.

It'll be the second time Luca will know all of the sordid details of my sex life.

"Tell me who the fuck touched you."

My neat freak ways come in handy and I make a mental note to stop having unprotected sex with men in public as I use a wet wipe from my purse to clean myself up. Oh God.

"It's none of your business. You didn't want me, what does it matter?"

He grabs my wrist and pulls me until I'm pressed against his chest again. "I will find him and I will kill him, Avery. I…"

I arch an eyebrow at him. "I thought you didn't care? I thought you were protecting me, not saving me for yourself? If you have regrets then it's your responsibility to live with them. I have *none*."

I snap the door open and find Luca leaning against the far wall, a blank look on his face but his eyes still trace over the state of me. I glance down and find two very obvious patches on my knees.

God *fucking* dammit.

I need to find Illi and get out of here.

Illi doesn't say a word to me the entire drive home but I'm sure it must be killing him to keep quiet.

I don't know why he's kept his mouth shut for me but I appreciate it. I feel just as spaced out and weird as the last time I had sex, like something major has happened

in my life and I've lost another of the tethers keeping me from floating away. When I catch myself thinking that I desperately want to slam my head into the dash of Illi's car.

Have I lost my mind?

When we stop at the last set of stoplights before the gated community my ranch is in, Illi turns to me and says in a low tone, "O'Cronin is waiting for you back at your place. Is that okay or should I call him and tell him to leave?"

Well, that settles it.

Illi knows exactly what happened in that storage room with Atticus and he could potentially call Lips and tell her right now. Lips could tell Ash and then everything is going to blow the hell up.

"Avery, stop looking at me like a guilty teenager. I'm not fucking saying a word, I'm just asking if you need me to cut O'Cronin loose because I will. I'd rather do that then break his fucking neck if he decides to be stupid about this."

It's sweet but I'm not one to dance around something like this. Besides, Aodhan has become my safe place for this sort of thing and if he wants to get angry at me for having sex with Atticus when we're not even technically dating then I don't want to be friends with him... or whatever the hell it is that we're doing.

Dating maybe?

Does it count as dating if you never really do anything or ever talk about what is going on but there's a heap of touching and sexual tension?

I need Lips and I need some girl talk, even if she is the worst at it.

I shake my head at him and he looks like he wants to talk about it some more but the car behind us starts blaring their horn and he has to focus on the road some more.

I argue with him about walking me into my house but Illi is nothing but a gentleman with me, opening the car door and unlocking my front door for me. He calls out to Aodhan too but I hightail it for the staircase, intent on scrubbing the night away from me.

I'm not ashamed… except for the part where it still wasn't enough for Atticus to really accept me and want me for who I am, not the perfect image of a girl he has in his head.

I empty my purse out on the bed and then I stalk into the bathroom, throwing it in the bin, followed by my shoes.

There's no way I could wear them again after this.

I don't even want to look at them.

I'm too busy in my own head to even notice that Aodhan has followed me up here, that whatever Illi said to him didn't make him run out of here screaming into the night never to look back again, until he gently takes my wrist and turns me around to face him.

I'm not sure if I'm relieved he's still here or pissed that I now have to deal with the consequences of my night.

He doesn't say a word, just slowly looks over every inch of me, takes everything in until my skin begins to crawl.

My voice sounds strange even to my own ears as I say, "Why are you looking at me like that?"

His hand reaches out and touches the top of the thigh split on my dress and I look down. There are threads loose there from where Atticus tore it up my body and out of the way, and suddenly I feel dirty.

I will not cry.

Aodhan doesn't speak either, he just follows me up the staircase and into my bedroom. I don't even think about what's right or wrong, I just strip out of the dress and throw it into the bin in the bathroom. The mirror there isn't kind to me but I stare at every inch of my skin on show, assessing and finding myself wanting. The silicone bra is a fucking nightmare to get off and my feet feel as though I've been standing in glass all day.

I stumble into the shower and let the scalding water drench my skin.

"If that motherfucker hurt you I'm calling Illi and taking his fucking fortress on. I'm sure we could take the suits out."

I choke on a sob. "He didn't. We had sex but I wanted

to… even if that's not a smart thing to do and now here I am, telling you about it so I'll lose you too."

It just slips out of me, that little bit of hope that I have that all of this touching and flirting and cheek kissing means something so I tense up while I wait for him to cut me down. God, even if he did want me I've just given him the best opportunity to walk out of her and forget about me.

He opens the shower door and reaches in to turn the heat of the water down with a scowl. "Just because you're hurting doesn't mean you should boil to fucking death in there."

I glance down and find my skin way past rosy red and into that bright lobster shade that my OCD tendencies loves so much. "I need to get clean."

His eyebrows draw together and his voice dips low. "Then grab some fucking soap. Stop hurting yourself over some motherfucker who doesn't deserve you and don't worry about something as stupid as me leaving. You think I don't know you love him? You think that shit will scare me off? Queenie, nothing affects you and me except you and me. He's not going to ruin this for us, get that through that gorgeous head of yours."

# Twelve

I wake up to my phone ringing.

I turn on the lamp beside my bed and then almost have a heart attack at the sight of Aodhan sleeping in the bed next to me. After I'd scrubbed myself raw, ignoring his growling and grumbling about how rough I was being, Aodhan had tucked me into my bed and laid with me to listen to everything that had happened for the night. I glossed over the sex with Atticus part but I was honest that it happened.

It didn't seem to bother him, he just laid back beside me and took everything in, asking more than a few questions about that *Amanda Donnelley* woman that I don't yet have the answers to. I fell     asleep long before he did and I forgot he was even here. My phone doesn't wake him and I try to keep my voice down as I answer.

"Are you hungover? Should I be whispering too?"

I huff at the smug tone Illi is throwing at me. "That's not necessary. Is there a reason you're up so early on a

Monday morning? I thought you were nocturnal, this changes everything I thought I knew about Mounts Bay."

He chuckles down the line at me and I can hear the sounds of the street behind him, some grunting and the rattling sounds of chains… or maybe handcuffs? Handcuffs and a chain?

"Where the hell are you?" I murmur, trying and failing to not wake Aodhan up. He grunts and stretches, rubbing a hand over his face and groaning.

"Who the fuck is that? Fuck, it had better be O'Cronin because if it's the Crow I might have to come around for a visit."

I slide out of the bed and try not to look at all of the skin Aodhan is showing. I shouldn't care about abs, I should care about tattoos and scars and very nice biceps and yet here I am… enjoying the sight of the very wolfish looking grin on his face as he stretches out on my pristine linens.

"It's Aodhan, not that it's any of your business who I spend my time with. If you're attempting to keep tabs for my brother I should warn you that no matter what you might think I'm the danger in my family, not the snarling asshole traipsing around the country with his little foursome of debauchery."

That was a great dig, I'll have to remember it for next time Ash calls me to rant.

Illi grumbles at me down the line for a second but then

he finally cuts to the chase. "I've sourced a dealer for us to question. A couple of my friends dragged him over, he was selling at the docks and tried to outrun them so he's a little worse for wear. Do you think you could head down here? Get O'Cronin to drive you down."

Bossy men.

I agree but only because I want to know about this dealer and who the hell is pushing the Jackal's product. When I hang up from him I find Aodhan grinning up at me with a rumpled sort of look on his face, his hair curling around his head in a mess that should not be as attractive as it is.

"I've never slept in a bed with six dozen pillows before. Very comfortable."

I scoff at him and throw one of them at him. This all feels too… casual for me, the joking manner he treats me with is disarming and with my defenses down he keeps slipping through to that ice heart of mine.

I'm not sure I ever want him to stop.

"We need to get over to the Bay, Illi has a dealer in his workroom for us to question."

Aodhan grumbles and nods, pulling himself up and out of my bed so I get a full body shot of him standing there in only a pair of charcoal boxer briefs.

He has a great ass.

I make the bed while he uses the bathroom. He's quick

and I find one of Harley's shirts for him to wear under his jacket. It's a little big thanks to all of Harley's time in the gym but where the neck sits a little lower shows off the edges of his tattoos. I want to know what they all look like. I'd seen them back when he gave me his shirt at the Jackal's lair but I'd been too out of it to really take them in.

Once he's ready he kisses my cheek and heads downstairs, muttering about trying to work out how to operate my coffee machine.

My hands shake the whole way through my shower and I try to take a very short one, knowing that I'd scrubbed myself raw the night before. I choose my clothing with less care this time around but I make a very bold choice and go with a pair of black jeans and a deep, forest green silk camisole.

I put it out of my mind until I walk downstairs, a pair of Choo's on my feet and a matching clutch packed and ready to go. When Aodhan sees me he grins, handing me a coffee in my favorite takeaway cup. It's not exactly to my taste but it's a solid first attempt and when I tell him that he grabs my hand, kissing my cheek and leading me back out to his car. He waits with me while I arm the security and then he helps me into the Impala.

It's still very clean in here and I wonder if he's doing that for me because he knows just how badly mess and clutter upsets me?

"Is the green a statement today or a coincidence? Don't break my heart here, Queenie."

He starts the car with a roar and when I huff he grins at me, grabbing my hand and kissing the back of it.

Are we dating?

Is that what's happening here? I would say yes but he didn't care about me having sex with another man in the back rooms of a gala last night so that kind of feels like mixed signals.

I should just talk to him about what the hell it is that we're doing, find out for sure what is happening right now, but for once I don't want to quantify this. I don't really want to have to face everything that's going on and for now it isn't hurting anyone to just enjoy his company. To wake up next to him, to have my sheets smell like him, and to drink slightly sub-par coffee that he made me.

I think I need to call Lips and talk this out, bestie-to-bestie.

I clear my throat carefully and play around on my phone as I answer him. "You slept in my bed, I can wear your color today if I want to."

We hit the highway and he waits until we're cruising at a steady clip before he runs a finger down the side seam of my jeans. "Not just my color. The shoes are a little worrying though, I'll need to kill whoever takes the Jackal's colors over just to make sure there isn't anymore competition."

I smile at my phone. "There's no competition here. I'm not a prize to be won."

He mumbles nonsense under his breath but I get to texting Lips, keeping her up to date about everything going on.

*If Roxas tries to flirt with you, shut him down fast. Don't mention anything about Atticus because he'll only get a hard-on about pissing a member of the Twelve off. Harbin is good though, he'll be solid.*

Right.

We'd very briefly encountered Illi's closest confidants at the biker bar Lips had taken us to back in high school after Ash had fought at the Dive, the night Lips had met with the Viper over his allegiances. We had spoken to them though, Lips had just acknowledged them after Illi had warned them to keep an eye on us in case someone tried to jump us.

They'd come to take out the Jackal and his men too with the rest of the Unseen MC but from what Lips has told me they aren't the blind followers that the Boar normally fills him MC with. She doesn't know the specifics of why they don't fully trust the Boar but it's something to keep in mind.

Everything about Mounts Bay is a twisted web of betrayals and loyalties.

The only way to be sure you're not going to be stabbed

in the back is by keeping a hell of a lot of tabs, which is why my murder board in the basement of my mansion takes up an entire wall already.

"Do you know Harbin and Roxas?" I murmur and Aodhan grumbles again.

"Illi's biker friends? Yeah. They're good guys… loyal as fuck to him and both of them have a reputation of being good men to have at your back. They once took out an entire building of armed bodyguards with Illi and the Wolf. The four of them just walked in and massacred the entire place like it was nothing. Anyone who can keep up with two is solid in my books."

I make a note to ask Lips about that rumor later but if I had to guess, my money is on the killing being a part of Odie's rescue.

Lips would have been fourteen at most.

A shiver runs down my spine, the same one I have every time I think about all of the bad shit that happened to her before I ever knew her.

All of the shit that would have happened if we hadn't met.

Aodhan stares around the outside of Illi's warehouse like he's expecting it to blow up.

I've only been here a handful of times but one of the

joys of being a member of Lips' family is that I've never felt unwelcome here. I'm sure growing up in the Bay and hearing the stories of what Illi does to people makes Aodhan feel very differently about being here, no matter how friendly Illi has been to him lately.

"When I was a kid, my grandfather used to tell me stories about the things that would happen to people down at the docks here. It was always just boogieman stories, made up shit to stop us running off and causing trouble, but then one day people started whispering about the Butcher… and suddenly it wasn't just a story anymore."

I look up at him and smile. "There's bodies hanging from the walls in there. Blood spatters everywhere, the staircase is made out of bones."

He scoffs at me, threading our fingers together and then waving me forward like he's going to follow my lead. "We both know you wouldn't willingly step foot in there if it was really like that. I'm a little terrified to meet his wife though, I heard he's dangerously overprotective of her."

I roll my eyes at him and step forward to key in the passcode. Lips and I are the only ones who have it and Aodhan is good about looking away when I mention that to him.

"Just don't try to flirt with her and you'll be safe. He's not a complete psychopath."

The door clicks open and I usher him in, keying the

code into the alarm and waiting until it beeps a clearance for us. The security here is insane but Illi had a lot of conditions about staying here after the Jackal went after Odie again.

I'm not sure if it can get any safer here and if it can, I'm sure it'll happen before the baby arrives.

"I'm not worried about me flirting, Queenie, but I'm irresistible. What if she falls for my good Irish charms and I get killed for it?" He whispers, and I roll my eyes at him but when I glance up at him he's grinning at me, teasing.

He's so completely different to Atticus that it doesn't actually feel all that wrong to be standing here holding his hand while my heart is still torn open from my childhood love.

I wonder if this is how Lips feels about her guys?

I give myself a little shake because our situations are very different. Ash, Harley, and Blaise are all as codependent on each other as they are in love with her. There was never a question if they could share someone, only if they could find someone who would want to and who would love them all equally.

I still can't think about that filthy fucking excuse for a human Annabelle without wanting to scream and destroy something but the real reason she would have never worked out is because she had a preference for Harley and, not at all surprisingly, the sneaky ways she tried to cover that

preference up was part of the reason Harley always kept her at arms length.

He'll never have to pick between Lips and his family because she *is* family.

He'll never have to worry about anything happening to her like it did to his mom.

"Fuck, you didn't say she was bringing a fucking member of the Twelve! We don't like your type around here."

We both turn to find a huge, tattooed biker looking fierce at the top of the staircase that leads down into Illi's workroom. Aodhan subtlety shifts so his body covers me but I huff at the newcomer.

"Roxas, if you don't like members of the Twelve then why do you follow Lips around the Bay when she's home keeping tabs for Illi? I'm pretty sure you have a Boar tramp stamp on your body somewhere, I'm just not invested enough to go looking."

His eyes narrow at me and it's all an act because he's trying to psych Aodhan out. He only lasts ten seconds before a grin splits across his face, all teeth and savagery. "Well, well, if it isn't the Queen of Mounts Bay. You're looking all grown up these days. If you're looking for a little taste of rough—"

Illi's voice calls out from his workroom, "She's had enough rough, shut your fucking mouth before I have to

kill you. Same rules for Queenie as my girl and the kid, I'll fucking gut you."

Roxas rolls his eyes and pushes away from the wall. "Fine, spoil my fucking fun. I've had a long week of hunting down fucking dealers in the Bay for you, the very least you could do is flirt a little."

I squeeze Aodhan's hand before dropping it, stalking forward towards the staircase. "I don't take on charity cases and you were working for Illi, not me. If you want payment I'll write a cheque."

Roxas shrugs and flips the bird at Aodhan behind my back. "I don't take rich bitch money, you might wanna get that stick outta your ass—"

Illi snarls, "Shut your fucking mouth about her before I come up there and shut it for you."

I brush past the biker like he's nothing because I know exactly how to deal with egos like this. No one ever mentions money if they're secure in themselves, obviously he's got a chip on his shoulder about the 'easy' life I must have had.

I hate that type of asshole.

I miss Ash and Harley being here to snarl at anyone who treats me like that but missing them doesn't help me now so I leave the biker behind as I walk down to the workroom.

There's a small landing at the bottom of the stairs before

the workroom where Illi leaves his jacket and cleans off before he goes upstairs to his wife. Odie once told me he's meticulous about never going home to her dirty and he'll always have a long shower before he'll so much as hold her hand after a bloody night of work.

It's very sweet and entirely the reason I think their relationship works.

Illi ducks his head out of the workroom and huffs at me. "No wonder he started his shit, you're wearing designer shoes down here. Grad some of the plastic covers, there's blood all over the floor."

I roll my eyes and Aodhan grabs my purse while I get dressed. He really is too much of a gentleman to have grown up here in the Bay. Roxas snarks at him as he walks past and I consider asking Lips if we can kill him.

That would be nice after this week of mine.

Once I've kitted up I follow Illi back into his murder room and find the dealer already strapped to a chair there, bleeding profusely from several different wounds. He looks as though he's been beaten with a baseball bat, though it only takes a glance at the state of Harbin's knuckles to know it was his meaty fists that did the damage.

"Did you get anything out of him?"

Harbin shrugs. "A whole lotta shit that doesn't concern us. Like we give a fuck about what move the Ox is making. He's fucking pathetic."

I shrug and bend at the waist until I'm staring the dealer in the face. "Still, could be useful for other things. Are you dealing for the Fox? He's the most likely choice for taking over the Jackal's drugs, what with their relationships for the parties they threw together."

The dealer looks so offended at having me speak to him. I can read it on his face. A woman in heels and red lipstick, standing here talking about 'men's business'. I've seen that look a million times before, it's not hard to pick out.

He spits out blood, aiming and hitting my shoe.

I stare down at it with enough panic at the thought of what diseases he might be carrying that I think the whole room takes a deep breath, waiting for me to scream and lose my shit.

Illi has been around for my reactions to the heads arriving in boxes so I expect it to be him coming to my rescue but Aodhan beats him to it, dragging the dealer from his chair and throwing him to the ground at my feet. When the dealer tried to struggle his way to his knees Aodhan uses the sole of his boot on the back of his neck to the ground.

"Say the word and I'll snap his fucking neck, Queenie."

I take a wet wipe out of my purse and wipe down my shoe, just to get the blood off for long enough to finish the interrogation but I will be burning these shoes the moment

I can. My skin is crawling and I want to vomit but I keep the panic from my face.

The dealer takes my silence as a death "I don't know who the fuck the boss is! No one does, he stays in his fucking castle! All I know is we were told to cross the eyes out, the Jackal is dead and they want the message out that there's a new player taking over."

I glance over at Illi and he stalks over to me, crouching over to where the guy is gasping for air under Aodhan's boot. "Gimme the exact orders. Tell me exactly what you were told."

The guy hacks out a breath, wheezing out, "That's it man! Take a black fucking marker and cross the eyes out."

Aodhan's eyes collide with mine.

Illi snarls, "They specified a color? Or are you ad-libbing that shit? We want specifics or you're gonna be sold to cannibals by the pound, they enjoy skinny crackheads. Something about the tenderness of the meat."

Disgusting but effective, the dealer almost shits himself right there on the ground at our feet. "Yes! Yes, he said black. He was specific about it."

# Thirteen

Odie is the sweetest woman alive but if she doesn't give me the secret to her macaron recipe I might strangle her in her sleep.

I'm wise enough not to say this to her but Illi reads it on my face all the same, smirking at me and popping an entire chocolate macaron in his mouth in one go because he's a total savage.

I realize my mind is very disordered right now, I know what's going on, but that doesn't stop the fixation from happening. Nothing can stop it, not after years of Ash and Harley and Blaise all trying to calm me down, not even Lips' quiet acceptance of this problem of mine, nothing can stop it except letting it burn out of my system, destroying everything around me.

Ash does the same thing.

The perks of our childhood locked in a mansion with Joseph Beaumont Sr.

So I try to lock it down just enough that Aodhan doesn't

realize I'm crazy and Illi doesn't call Ash home to me, and it kind of works a little because it doesn't matter how many times I try to make the macarons, they never turn out right, and that's a real issue.

The most important issue of the night, one might say… if they're utterly detached from reality.

*"Tell me what goes wrong with them and I will help solve the problem, la Reine."* Odie murmurs, setting a cup of coffee in front of me. It's too sweet, I can smell it from here, but I don't have the heart to tell her.

Roxas snickers at me under his breath like it's hilarious that I'm thumbing through a cookbook muttering in French with her but Aodhan keeps shifting in his chair. I've grown up almost exclusively around men and I know exactly what that shifting means.

If Aodhan ever makes a move, I can try whispering some French in his ear and see where that takes us. It would have been handy to know back when—

No.

I'm going to stop thinking about that place.

I'm not going to let it ruin my life or the chance of this relationship with Aodhan and I'm already on the edge of doing that for myself.

I fucked Atticus in a storage room.

What I did to Aodhan in that interrogation  room, it doesn't matter that I was doing it to save his life, I didn't

give him a choice. I was doing it whether he agreed to or not and that's on me.

I'm the monster.

Illi clears his throat and says, "Queenie, we need to talk about what the dealer said. Stop worrying about the biscuits, you can fuck around with them later."

Clearly he knows nothing of how my mind works because I definitely do not want to think about what the dealer said.

Everyone in the Bay knows about the color system.

There's no way anyone would choose a color that carefully without wanting it to mean something which means the dealer is trying to frame the Crow for something.

Or that the Crow has taken on the drug empire.

"The Crow would never do it. He would never deal drugs." I say, keeping my eyes on the recipe book but it says all the same things as mine does at home.

Maybe I should come over for a cooking class with Odie? Maybe that would fix the macaron problem? Maybe I should go home and cook twelve dozen batches until they come out right?

Odie's hand slowly slips into mine on the page in front of us both, stopping the flipping. I glance up at her and she murmurs to me, quiet enough that even Illi won't be able to catch the words, *"Do you need me to call la Loup? Or Ash?"*

I realize my hands are trembling.

I look over at Illi and he's staring at me like he's expecting me to start screaming and breaking his plates. I mean… they are the worst shade of red I've ever seen. It's as though Illi wants everyone to think he's serving food in bowls of blood. There's a whole plethora of reds he could choose from and he goes with that shade?

Unacceptable.

"O'Cronin, take her home and leave her alone. If she starts smashing shit, don't stop her." Illi says, and I roll my eyes at him.

Aodhan looks mildly confused but he gets up.

"I'm fine." My voice doesn't sound right even to my own ears.

Illi huffs. "No woman who has ever said she's fine in the history of women was actually fine. Between the spit on your shoes and the idea of the Crow stooping to that level you're done for the day. I'll call the kid, let her know to call you later."

I very carefully straighten up and shake my hands out but nothing stops the shaking.

Joey was bad before he started taking drugs.

He was vicious and violent, he was petty and jealous of Ash and I. Mom loved us both a lot more than she loved him, even though it upset her to feel that way. She knew there was something wrong with him but nothing she ever

did would fix him. He was jealous that Ash loved me too. He was jealous that he wasn't going to have a partner in crime, that Ash would rather walk into my father's rooms of pain and death and die for me than ever let that horror touch me.

The drugs just made everything worse.

The fights Ash and I would have when he and Blaise first started smoking weed together, I was so angry at him for daring to touch it. What if he changed? What if the drugs made him hate me too?

What if the violence in him suddenly shifted and became like the violence in Joey?

I only let it go because it helped with his anxiety and insomnia, but I would never have accepted him taking anything stronger. The handful of times Blaise had tried harder drugs I threatened him with rehab.

How could Atticus do this?

"Fucking Christ, that's why you don't let little rich bitches come play with the big hitters. Can't even handle a little bit of blood, why the fuck the Wolf would keep you around is beyond me. Unless she's fucking you too, what's one more in her bed?"

The fog of my panic lifts just enough for me to notice the room get very quiet, very quickly.

I run my hands down my legs as a very dangerous calm settles over me.

Harbin lets out a breath. "I'm not gonna dig you outta this. I'm just gonna watch you bleed."

Roxas scoffs at him. "And who the fuck is gonna make me bleed?"

Illi glances over at me and then smirks. Aodhan's eyes haven't left me but I look back over to him and shake my head a little.

I'm over this bullshit.

I kiss Odie's cheek and murmur a quiet 'au revoir' to her. I grab my purse and walk past the table, stopping at Roxas and then I lean down until I'm in his face and smirk.

I use the same tone I always do when I'm dealing with some piece of Mounty trash that means *nothing* to me as I tear the little illusion Roxas has built for himself to pieces, "You think you're tough because you ride a bike? Hang out with your little friends? Or is it because your body count is so high? I wonder what would happen to you if some of those skeletons came back to bite you because you weren't always as smart as you are now, were you? No, back before you lit your old identity on fire and started again in the Bay you were nothing but a little crackhead baby in the slums of New York. You thought I wouldn't recognize the accent, you thought I wouldn't make sure I knew everything about every last ally of my family? Please. You're a worthless, poser biker who thinks killing a few men makes you brave. What happened to you as a child broke you and now you're

making it all with that patch of yours. Still, you're trapped because you signed your life away to *the Boar* of all men. Pathetic. And how is your brother doing these days? Can he walk yet?"

His eyes narrow at me, the shock wearing off enough that he thinks about putting his hands on me but I'm not scared.

Not with Illi and Aodhan here. Not with Ash and Harley and Blaise only a phone call away.

Not while I wear the Wolf of Mounts Bay's insignia on my body and her love and loyalty in my heart.

If he touched me he wouldn't be breathing for much longer and for the first time that doesn't make me feel powerless, like some precious thing to be protected and a burden on my loved ones.

Sometimes I guess I need to be reminded that I'm strong by myself but with my family I'm unstoppable.

I pat his cheek like he's a simpleton and then I glance back up at an impressed Aodhan. "I'd like to go home now."

Aodhan watches me carefully as he drives me home but I'm too busy trying to contain the mess my head is in to call him out for it.

"Do you have a file about me somewhere? Do you

already know all about the skeletons in my closet?" He murmurs and I sigh, staring out at the city around us. He's taking a different way home but I know all of the possible routes and I still feel safe here.

"I do. I've had a file on you from the moment I found out about Harley, I've known about you long before you even knew I existed."

He nods, frowning just a little. "And if you wanted to destroy me, what would you say?"

I frown. "I don't want to destroy you Aodhan, but I think I'm already doing a great job of it. Maybe I should fuck someone else, someone other than Atticus just to really fuck my life up. Jesus Christ, why do I keep saying his name? Can we go a little faster? I need to get home."

Aodhan takes a turn and it's definitely not the way home now. "Tell me. What's in my file that'll break me?"

I shift in my seat so I'm staring at him like he's lost his mind because I think he has. "I need to go home, Aodhan. I need a shower and a new kitchen or maybe I'll bake. Can we stop at the store on the way? Never mind, I'll get a delivery."

He pulls into a large parking lot at the fishing docks. There's only one boat here being loaded up and men shouting out orders that I can hear through the closed car doors once Aodhan kills the engine.

"My dad beat my mom every day of their marriage.

Was that in the file?"

I keep my eyes glued on what's happening on the boat. "Yes. Your mum died from it and then he started beating your sister. You're the only one left now you put a bullet in Domnhall. You have cousins though, dozens of them. I don't really know how you keep making all of this time to come see me when you're busy being the head of your family over there."

He pulls the keys out of the ignition and settles back in his seat.

I get the feeling we're not going home and I really don't want to explain to him just how badly I need to break some things. To scour my skin until it bleeds, to strip everything away until the barren void and new beginning settles the panic in my chest.

"My sister killed my mom."

My eyes widen a little and the chaos in my head settles down enough that I can listen to him… for now. I don't know how long it will last.

"My dad did beat my mom and me but he left Cara alone. He beat my mom because he saw her as property and he beat me because that's how you learn to be a man. He always said Éibhear spoiled Harley you know… always said that he was going to turn out soft because he actually loved his son. I think Éibhear was too different for the family, that's the real reason they fucking destroyed

Iris and then killed him. They never liked it when people did things different."

I look over at him but his eyes are focussing on the boat, to where they're getting ready to leave for another long day of fishing.

He continues. "So my dad never laid a hand on Cara but mom did. She was a mean old bitch but she knew better than to hit her around me or dad. Jack and I did what we could to keep the kids all safe but I didn't see what was happening to my own sister… not until I came home to find Ma dead and Cara sobbing over it. She'd slit her own wrists over it, told me she didn't want to go to prison over it. I cleaned her up, got Ma dealt with, and then I told Cara I wouldn't let Domnhall hurt her. I told her we were done with that shit now and I'd keep her safe."

He scratches at the shadow on his cheek from where he hasn't been able to shave. I should really get some supplies for him if he's going to be staying at my house.

Is he going to be staying at my house?

My mind is still struggling to focus on the important issues and not just my issues when he continues, "Cara felt so guilty about Ma. She attempted three times before she finally killed herself over it. So your file is good… but not a hundred percent."

I tilt my head and shrug. "I can live with that… in your case. I have Roxas's history down perfectly though, I made

sure of that. I don't trust anyone who sold themselves to a member of the Twelve without a good reason. Harbin I can see… Roxas not so much."

Aodhan shrugs. "They're best friends. Blaise would follow Ash into anything right?"

I snort, totally unlike me and his eyebrows just about hit his hairline. "Blaise committed murder for Ash as a stupid teenager. Helped him hide a body too, he'd follow Ash into the gates of Hell if I left them both unattended… there's a reason I was only comfortable leaving them now that Lips is around to rein them in a bit."

He grins and looks out of the window again. He's waiting for that boat to be gone but I don't know why.

I reach out and hold his hand. "I'm sorry about your sister. I'm sorry your family is just as broken as mine."

He squeezes my hand and lifts it up to my lips to press a kiss on my palm, the move I'm sure he knows melts me. "You're building a much stronger family. I'm glad you've let me be in it. Cara died years ago but it still hurts the same to know I failed her. I'm not going to fail anyone close to me like that again, Queenie. I'm not going to let men live who hurt my family."

I smile again but my skin is still tingling in the worst way, like electricity is trapped in my veins and I'm being burned alive. "This has been… lovely, but I need to go home. Illi wasn't joking about—"

Aodhan reaches across to grab my chin and kisses me, slow and deep until maybe the electricity settles down for a second.

It won't leave though.

Not even for him.

"You need to break something, right? That's what Illi said, you need to destroy something. How about a little vengeance, Queenie? Would that calm your nerves down?"

My eyes flutter open and I find the clear green of his irises shining down at me as he watches me closely for my reaction. I have to clear my throat to get my words to come out, "There's nothing better than destroying someone's life, especially if they've hurt my family. You should probably know that I'm ruthless by now, Aodhan. There's not a whole lot that I wouldn't do to keep my family safe and whole."

A soft smile stretches over his lips. "Oh, I know Queenie. I think your blood running down my thighs proved that to me. This isn't about your family though, this is about you. This is about getting vengeance for someone daring to touch you."

He glances back at the boat but it's still in sight. So he slides past the steering wheel and across the bench seat until he's in the middle, tugging me up and over until I'm straddling him.

There's a tiny bit of panic in me at the position, but he

tugs me down to his lips again and chases away the guilt with his tongue. I can't help but bite his lip, desperate to break something, to destroy everything around me until the chaos in my chest dissipates.

He grunts and yanks me into his chest tighter, one hand slipping down to grab my ass and pulling at my hips until he can grind on me like we're a pair of normal teenagers making out past our curfew.

I could forget myself in his arms. I think I could even forget the panic, but I can't forget his words and I pull away from his lips to say, "Tell me what we're doing here, I don't like secrets."

He smirks at me. "You love secrets, you just want to collect them for yourself. We're here because I have a shipping container in storage in the warehouse over there and I just need the coast to be clear before we go over there. Lots of eyes down this way, lots of old loyalties we don't want to fuck with."

I nod slowly and he grins at me. "I have my uncle chained to a chair in the shipping container. I can kill him for you or you can do it for yourself, either way he dies today for what he did to you."

# Fourteen

## AODHAN

I pull the door to the warehouse open and the light streams into the space in a wedge that only touches a pair of scuffed up boots.

I was very careful about keeping Diarmuid in a dark little hole that he couldn't climb out of. I hold Avery's hand as her eyes adjust to the darkness but I know the moment she can make out the outline of my uncle in the dark.

He looks a little worse for wear.

Jack and a couple of our other cousins went after him when we finally got word of where he'd been hiding and they'd taken a sadistic sort of pleasure at being able to bring him in. He was already profusely bleeding by the time I laid eyes on him.

Plugging those wounds up hurt me.

I wanted nothing more than to just sit there and watch him bleed out but this isn't about me. This is about Avery

getting some fucking closure because Diarmuid is the reason the Jackal got her in that room. Without that two-timing asshole there was no way the Jackal would have gotten past the Wolf and her family.

No fucking way.

Harley would die for Avery without hesitation. It's the reason I was always so curious about the Beaumont's because one day he got out of juvie and Liam was served with court papers saying he no longer had custody. It was only after he paid off a judge and got a few weeks over the summer holidays that we found out he had billionaire cousins. I'd thought there had to be money motivators for them to want him because Iris never saw her sister, Éibhear never had anything good to say about them either, and who the fuck would want to take on the angry little Mounty boy who spent half his time stealing cars and beating anyone that looked sideways at him?

Jack and I followed him up to that big school of his out of curiosity and one look at the Beaumonts was all it took to see they loved him. He walked through the gates and every kid there standing around with their parents stared at him like he was a god. It made no fucking sense to us until the twins showed up with their friend tagging alone and then accepted him into the fold, Avery hanging off of his neck for a hug in a pair of heels no fourteen year old girl had any right wearing so easily.

From that moment on I knew he'd be okay.

I just had to get rid of Liam and Domnhall and all of the other toxic men in our family to break the cycle of abuse and keep the kids safe from the evils of their fathers.

A few of the women too.

The integrity and loyalty in Avery Beaumont is second to none and I don't know what the hell I did to get her attention but I'll do fucking anything to keep it.

I reach over and very carefully push a strand of hair away from her face, tucking it behind her ear securely.

"Have you danced since your feet healed?" I pitch my voice low but even if Diarmuid hears me he can't interrupt with the gag in his mouth.

She shakes her head. "Not— not properly. I've done practice and some warm ups but I haven't really pushed myself, I've been too busy with my work."

I nod and thread my fingers through hers, not even the slightest tremble in her as she takes in the mangled sight of our prisoner. "Dance for me? When we're done here, I want to watch you."

She startles and then nods, a small smile curling up the edges of her mouth. "I have a studio back at my house. With the gym, down by the pool house. I haven't shown you down there… I don't think you've made it past the fridge?"

The little sly grin on her face while she snarks playfully

at me is fucking perfect and I can't help but play back at her, even with Diarmuid sitting there waiting to die. "Forgive me, Queenie, you'll have to draw me a map to get down there."

The smirk on her face grows, her eyes glowing up at me even in the dark and it strikes me again just how fucking gorgeous she really is. How the fuck someone like her might be interested in someone like me… fucking confusing but I'm not a man to let a good thing go and she might just be the fucking best thing.

Even with her obsession with that fucking asshole the Crow, she's still going to be the best fucking thing that ever happened to me and I don't give a fuck who I have to kill for her.

It's going to hurt a whole lot to give this kill over to her but I will.

"So how are you going to do this, Queenie? Do you want a knife, baseball bat? I'd offer you a gun but that's not all that smart in this tiny room."

She blinks at me. And then she blinks some more. Finally she finds her voice, "There is absolutely no fucking way that I'm swinging a bat at that man. I've managed to go nineteen years without knowing what that looks like and I'd like to keep that streak going, thank you very much."

I shrug. "Knife it is. Did you bring yours or do you want to borrow one of mine? I don't usually let people

touch much shit but I'll make an exception for you."

She rolls her eyes at me but it's a fucking cute gesture. "No, idiot, I'm not going to be doing this killing at all. I'm glad you tracked him down but I want to smash some plates and tear the carpet in my bedroom up… not crack a skull open and be covered in blood. I have people for that kind of thing, I don't do it myself."

Huh.

I wasn't expecting that. I mean, I know she hates blood and anything gross but there's always been a ruthless edge to her, a cut throat nature about her that I always thought she'd need his death for herself.

I totally misjudged bringing her here but he has to die today. "The longer I leave him tied up like this the more chances there are for shit to go wrong. I need to take care of it if you don't want to. I didn't want to take this away from you after what he did."

She reaches out to squeeze my hand. "I don't need to kill him. That's very sweet of you but knowing that he's dead is more than enough for me. I can go wait out in the car."

I smirk and grab her elbow as she turns away from me. "Queenie, there's no way you can go wait out in the car for me down here. You'll get fucking kidnapped and ransomed and then the Wolf would come down here breathing fire like she wants to burn the entire fucking city

to the ground."

She smirks and shrugs because I'm saying nothing but solid truth. "So you want me to just… stand here and watch? I'm not going to do that. I honestly can't think of anything worse, do you have any idea how rare these shoes are? Hand crafted by artisans with only the finest leather, there's no way I'm going to let you get blood all over them. No way, O'Cronin."

I shrug and walk over to the far side of the container, enjoying the snarl that Diarmuid forced out of his mouth around the gag. There's a small collection of weapons and some supplies for cleaning up. I'd made sure to have a full plastic body suit for Avery in case she wanted to do the kill herself but was worried about the mess.

Who am I kidding?

Of course she'd be worried about the mess.

I grab the spare folding chair and one of the plastic sheets because I doubt she's going to be all that happy to sit on the seat without one. I get it set up for her as close to the door as I can, waiting until she sits down and gets as comfortable as she can on the cold metal, and then I kiss her again, one last time before I get to work.

"If you get blood on me I will murder you in your sleep, O'Cronin. The Wolf isn't the only one hiding in the shadows." She murmurs with that same playful smirk.

I lean down and kiss her, ignoring Diarmuid's grunts

behind us both at the display. "You can kill me anytime, Queenie, you know that."

# Fifteen

## AVERY

I sit on the small chair and text Lips back while Aodhan deals with Diarmuid.

The sounds aren't so bad now I'm more accustomed to this sort of thing and I don't watch him work, my eyes and attention staying focused entirely on my phone as I give her the details of everything happening here.

She's very impressed with Aodhan's work ethic and the way he kept to his word.

*Tell him I want the fingers. It'll be a good companion to Annabelle's hand.*

I gag at the reminder that she even has that disgusting jar stashed in her bag at all times to ward off the panicked feeling she has about Harley's near-miss with that jealous little whore.

*Disgusting. Any specific finger or whichever ones take Aodhan's fancy?*

Diarmuid's boots make a squeaking noise against the steel bottom of the shipping container as he struggles, the grunts of his coming from behind the gag sound frenzied and enraged but that is quite soothing for me.

*Does he have bolt cutters handy? I want both his trigger fingers, Illi can pickle them for me.*

Again, I gag except this time Aodhan hears and takes notice. "How are you doing over there, Queenie? We can go get some air if you want."

I shake my head but keep my eyes where they are. "Lips is being gross, she wants his trigger fingers and she wants him to feel them come off. Apparently bolt cutters are the most efficient method of removal, do we have any spare or should I call Illi?"

The squeaking of the boots comes to an abrupt halt.

Clearly the Irish shooter still thought there was a chance of his making it out of here alive but there's no way he'd be able to function without being able to work.

No fingers, no sniper.

"I've got it covered. Don't you worry about it, Queenie, just keep your eyes on your work."

I nod my head and thumb my way through some of Amanda Donnelley's financial records that I've been sent by one of my contacts. He's not as good as the Coyote but I'm conscious of the fact that Jackson lied to us all about Nate and I don't want to start relying on him for

absolutely everything.

I zone out as I read the files over and over again to find something, *anything*, that is a clue for what the hell her deal is… where she gets her power, what it is about her that makes Atticus sweat.

I'll admit his reaction to her has made the entire endeavor personal.

I hear the muffled screaming and the crunching noise of the bolt cutters but, after swallowing the bile back down my throat, I push it all away and use the time wisely. I have a phone full of pressing issues that need my attention and there are never enough hours in the day to get through it all.

I'm so focussed on what I'm doing, and so trusting of Aodhan, that I don't know exactly when Diarmuid dies, only that the thumping sound his body makes when Aodhan unties it from the chair startles me out of my focussed work.

"Sorry, Queenie, I didn't mean to scare you. Rigor mortis makes it a bitch to move them if I left him up there while I got you home." He murmurs and I shrug.

I carefully repack my purse and stand up, keeping my back to what I'm sure is a blood-soaked mess behind me.

There's some movement and grunting behind me and then Aodhan walks up beside me with his jacket zipped all the way up. His hands are a little bloody and his jeans but

the jacket is clean.

"I'll get you home and then I'll call Illi to help me get rid of the body… he had some suggestions for the disposal."

I roll my eyes because *of course* the Butcher wants to get creative with Diarmuid's finally resting place, just to make sure it isn't all that restful. It's exactly what the traitor deserves too, after what he did to betray Lips and Harley, but I don't really need to know about it.

I just need to know he got the job done. "He's definitely dead? Where are the fingers? If you say you have them on you I'm probably going to need at least a month before you attempt to touch me again. How do you feel about sitting in a bathtub of bleach for an hour or so?"

He smirks at me and gestures for me to follow him out. I appreciate the distance he puts between us both because there is no fucking way I want to touch him right now.

I've hit my limit.

I'm confident enough in myself and the value I bring to any table to admit that. I don't need to kill things just to stay relevant and keep my place as *the Queen* Aodhan and Illi keep insisting I am.

Aodhan seals the shipping container back up, snapping on a series of padlocks just to be sure we don't get a missing body on our books, and then I follow him out into the sunlight.

I know as soon as we see the car that something is wrong. Aodhan pauses, his back stiff, and then he growls out a stream of vicious curses under his breath. I glance around him to find another photo of me with my eyes crossed out pinned to the side of the Impala with a knife sticking out from between my eyes in a clear threat.

Jesus H. Christ.

I glance around at the docks but there isn't any security cameras in sight and Aodhan had been careful to make sure that we didn't go in there until there was no one around so I can't remember having seen any cars or homeless people.

Aodhan grabs the knife by the handle and yanks it out with a terrible screeching noise that only lasts a second but sends shivers down my spine regardless. He hands me the photo and then opens the card door, pausing for a second and then says, "Step back, Queenie. Lemme check there is a fucking bomb on board before you get in."

A bomb.

*For fuck's sake.* I should have thought of that, especially after what happened to Harley's Mustang back in junior year at Hannaford, but it's as though my brain is still rattled from the entire mess of a day and I'm not thinking how I normally would be.

Aodhan crawls around the car on his belly until he's sure there's nothing there and then he checks every possible crevice and corner of the interior before he lets me take my

seat, a grim look on his face.

"I'll call Illi once I've got you home safe. Are you sure the security there is legit? Nothing getting through it? Because this asshole is persistent, I'll give the creepy fuck that." He murmurs as he pulls out of the parking lot and cuts through the slums to get me home through the quickest route.

I nod and pick the photo back up to look it over, swallowing down the bile in my throat. "Jackson redid the entire property this time, there's no way anyone can get through it. Aodhan… this photo is from the gala."

His jaw in tense like he's grinding his teeth. "I know, Queenie. Whoever is doing is fucking stalking you and I'm not gonna let that shit fly. I'll check over that mansion of yours and then I'll go hunting. There's a few leads I can try and I'm sure Illi will have an idea of where to go next. Have you told the Wolf about this yet?"

It's strange that he always reverts to calling her by her street name but I nod. "I've been keeping her updated. I… gloss over it a bit more with the guys. Harley has already commented on how hard it's been to keep Ash on the tour and if he found out that the photos are new ones and not just high school?"

Aodhan nods. "You'd be wrapped up in bubble wrap the moment he got back."

I nod and fuss with my purse, just little soothing

movements that settle my nerves down enough that the need to scream doesn't overwhelm me. "The whole point of me staying behind was to find myself… and to prove to myself that I don't need to hide behind my brother. If he comes running back here now then it's all been for nothing."

When we get back to the mansion Aodhan pulls up outside the front gate while I call the Coyote to review the security cameras before we go in. We're both being extra cautious because the Jackal certainly taught us that lesson in the worst way and there's no way I'm being kidnapped by some psycho again.

Once we have the all clear I direct him to park right at the front door in the spot Illi usually uses. With the electric gate shut and the sensors all on I should feel safe but when Aodhan helps me out of the car the hole from the stalker's knife is like a morbid reminder that someone really has set their sights on me.

I just don't know if they want me dead or just scared but neither are happening anytime soon.

Aodhan goes straight upstairs to call Illi and shower in my bathroom to clean his uncles blood from his body.

I don't think about it at all.

I know that I'm the only one who hasn't cleaned the blood of my victims off of myself here, Lips and the guys have all cleaned themselves up wherever the last couple

of years, but I've only scrubbed myself raw from my own blood. It makes some kind of cosmic sense that Aodhan would be up there in my ensuite using my soaps and shampoos to scrub away the mess he'd made of Diarmuid on my behalf.

I go down to the studio and get changed into my ballet gear. My leotard and tights are a little looser than they should be and I make a note to get back to eating more regularly now I'm not keeping to the guys eating schedule. Harley never failed to keep me eating every three or so hours thanks to his high metabolism. It takes a lot of calories to be as jacked as he is.

I wince as I put my feet into the pointe shoes, cursing under my breath as useless tears fill my eyes. They hurt more than they should to go in and there's a good chance I'm not going to be able to dance as well as I could before the Jackal burned me.

I stretch out for twice as long as I would normally just to be sure I'm ready to move my body without risking my body any more than necessary. I run through one of my old routines slowly, testing to see which of my muscles feel tight and which are more sore than they were before.

Before the Jackal had taken me and damaged my feet I was working through the routines required to dance as Aurora in 'Sleeping Beauty'. I didn't have any grand plans

of becoming a professional dancer, I don't want to be some pretty thing for rich men to covet, but the idea of never being able to push my body like this again is terrifying.

I need to dance and feel the burning of my muscles the same way that Ash needs to run until he loses feeling in his legs. We need to push our bodies into feeling something so we don't drown in the overwhelmingly crushing doom of our lives.

I take a deep breath and I start.

It hurts but I push on, holding my core and watching my form, counting in my brain to shift my focus away from the pain. Lips taught me all about that and there's three different languages that I can work through if I need to and it's been a while since I had to use Russian.

I make it through the first act before I pause and find Aodhan sitting on the floor, leaning against the mirror there with one leg bent up and his arm resting on top like this is just a regular occurrence for him.

The look in his eyes makes my breath catch in my throat.

Breath control is something a dancer always has to work on and I try to hide the effect he's having on me but the smirk that stretches over his lips is telling.

"No one has ever looked that fucking good in a tutu before, Queenie. That shit should be illegal... I can't believe your brother was okay with you dancing in it."

I roll my eyes and walk over to him, slipping my shoes off before stretching. Okay, slipping isn't the right word for describing the torture of pulling them off of my battered and scarred feet but I'm trying to look effortless and elegant. I don't look down at the state they're in and, thankfully, Aodhan doesn't either.

He's too busy eyeing off every inch of my body in the leotard. It's tight enough that it fits like a second skin and if I weren't wearing the tights with it there wouldn't be all that much covering the apex of my thighs.

"He's not my keeper. I listen to what he says about my safety but he doesn't ever have a say on what I wear. He knows it and you better know it too."

His smirk gets wider and his eyes finally land on mine as he grabs my hand and tugs me over to him until I'm straddling his lap. "Why would I complain? I get to see you in this and that's something I'm not fucking around with."

It was easier back in the Impala to be this close to him because my mind was so chaotic but now that I've burned some of the energy off I don't know what the hell to do. Should I loop my arms around his neck and kiss me until we both forget about the photo and the corpse back in the shipping container and just fuck on the floor of my studio?

Shit.

"Aren't you supposed to be going back to the docks

with Illi? What are you doing back down here?"

He groans and pulls me in close. "I got distracted, I can see your nipples through this thing and fuck if it doesn't make me hungry for you. I haven't been able to stop thinking about how your skin might taste or how sweet your pussy must be. I've never spent so long obsessing over anything in my life and then I come down here to say goodbye and you're twirling around like a wet dream. Game over, if you hadn't stopped when you did I was probably going to get started without you."

His hips lift up and grind into me until I can feel every inch of his very interested dick sliding along my pussy through the layers of fabric between us. I choke back a moan, because I've messed around with guys before but none of them had shown any interest in eating me out and I'm *very* interested in trying it out.

Lips doesn't tell me a thing about her sex life at my own request, because gross, but I've heard the screaming that comes out of her bedroom here and the guys room back at Hannaford and I want that.

I want to forget I'm supposed to be quiet.

I want to come so hard everyone knows it's happening.

I want to feel that smug sort of satisfaction that you get when you're wanted and loved and worshiped by the person you're with.

I haven't had that yet. Sure I came both times I had

sex, even when I wasn't supposed to but there was no afterglow or worship happening. Only fear and jealousy and desperation.

Aodhan groans and pulls me forward more. I assume he's going to kiss me and make good on his words, spread me out and give me the experience I want, but then his hand moves to fish around in his pocket until he has his phone in his fist.

He answers with a snarl, "I'm busy, I'll call you back."

I raise an eyebrow at him when he frowns and huffs down the line, "It can wait… fuck it, I'll do time… this is worth it… fuck, fine. Fine, I'm on my way. I'd kill the cunt all over again if I could."

Great.

I'm still not getting what I want or need. I might as well be a fucking pariah at how this is going. I slump down until my forehead is resting on his shoulder, inhaling low and slow, enjoying the smell of my soap on his skin mixing with the aftershave he uses.

Am I going to have to make it happen for myself? Am I going to have to sit him down and explain exactly what I want just to get a chance at it?

Christ.

I don't have time in my life for that.

"I don't want to go, Queenie, and if it weren't about your safety I wouldn't. Just as soon as I find this fucking

cunt coming after you, I'll never leave again."

I nod and stand up. I can get in some more practice, enough to burn the frustration out of me that I don't want to admit is entirely sexual. He grabs my wrist and pulls me in to kiss me again, his tongue tangling with mine until that frustration is at an all time high.

"Leave now, O'Cronin, before the Butcher comes down here and makes you his problem." I mumble against his lips and he groans at me.

I'm saying it for me because if he doesn't leave now I might just beg and that's not going to happen.

I've never been the type.

# Sixteen

A odhan and Illi find nothing.

No witnesses, no evidence, no signs of foul play except the knife itself. I'm pissed but not at all surprised. Aodhan returns home for the night to check in with Jack and his leads on what the hell is going on and I find myself once again alone in my stunningly empty mansion.

The next morning I'm sitting in the basement staring at the wall of photos and red string lines connecting them when my security alarm is triggered then disabled. I check my phone and find Illi unlocking my front door, wiping his feet on the doormat politely, and then opening the staircase up to stomp down the stairs towards me. He doesn't even try to look elsewhere, he knows that this place has become an obsession for my waking hours.

"I brought coffee and a whole new set of 'what the fuck is going on' for us to figure the hell out." He murmurs, handing a cup over to me and sitting on the chaise next to me.

I murmur a quiet 'thank you' and take a sip.

I fucking miss Lips.

No one makes my coffee like she does.

I smile at him and turn a little so I'm facing him, crossing my ankles and grabbing my phone out of my pocket so it's close by for whatever the hell is going on now.

Illi rubs a hand over scruff on his cheeks and then nods at the photo wall. "How are you feeling about the Graves kids? Anything flag for you yet?"

I groan. "No, nothing. I went through their records and had a contact runs their bloodwork to attempt to find the missing sibling but nothing has come up yet. The entire MC is a mess of old rivalries, betrayals, and business deals gone wrong. The only ones up there who aren't a mess are Wyatt, the cop, and Noah because he's dead and it's hard to be a pain in my ass when you're already in the ground."

Illi chuckles at my snotty attitude, then he sighs and I know I'm not going to like what comes out of his mouth next. "We're going for a drive today. I got a call last night about a job. I've been taking a few little things on now D'Ardo is gone, just so long as they're close to home, and I got a call for something right up our alley."

I sip at the coffee and wave a hand at him. "Please tell me we're meeting with someone about killing Donnelley

because she fucked the wrong governor? I'd really love that."

He chuckles at me. "No. Colt Graves called me for a hit. You wanna meet another one of Lips' brothers, get a read on him for yourself?"

I turn to face him fully. "A hit? Why the hell would he need you to do the killing for him, he's a biker? I'm very intimate with his rap sheet, I can list the whole damn thing to you, he doesn't need you killing for him."

Illi shrugs and points at the wall of photos. "Maybe he needs that brother of his taken out? I dunno, but I doubt this is a trap. I haven't heard from him in years but the last time we saw each other… there wasn't bad blood between us. I wouldn't be inviting you along for the ride if I had doubts about this, Queenie."

I nod, because I know he would never risk my life like that, but this still feels… wrong.

We're missing something here.

Illi glances around. "Is O'Cronin not around here? Did you finally convince him to leave you alone for a minute? If he's annoying you just lemme know. I'll skin him for you."

I shake my head at him, ignore him cackling at my expense. "I thought you only let your friends call you Illi? Should I be worried?"

He grins and shrugs. "You know it's different for you

girls. They might all be family but if one of these dumbass boys steps out on you or does something else fucking stupid? I'll kill them, no questions asked."

It's psychotic and very sweet and after growing up with Ash, that my favorite mix.

I do feel compelled to reply, "I can kill them for myself but thank you. I'm glad the dumbass boys that Lips is with are all obsessed with her."

He scoffs at me and stands up, stretching his back out until it pops. "The Irishman who keeps coming around here is just as obsessed. The Crow too, he just has his head too far up his own ass to go about it the right way."

I shrug and stand up with him, finishing the last of my coffee off. "I don't care about any of that. I just want to fill my black book and sort out Lips' twisted family tree. Let's go meet with Graves and decide if the executioners block is calling his name."

Illi waits for me to change clothes quickly. I'm conscious about wearing a white blazer over the navy dress, a beautiful pair of Manolo's I'd happily have sold my soul for if I wasn't able to cover the cost without even feeling it. I'm taking my role as the Wolf's representative very seriously and as Lips always says, half of being a crime lord is reputation.

Mine is going to be impeccable.

Illi has brought his Mustang over for a change and

he opens the door for me like always. I settle back in the passenger seat and text Lips to keep her updated. I can tell from her replies that she's worried about this meeting, worried that Colt is going to be an asshole or, worse, a problem for us.

Ash and I had an entire childhood with Joey to know he deserved to die, that there was never going to be redemption for him. Lips has only had a couple of months even knowing that she has siblings, let only navigating whether they're decent people.

If they're shit and they leave us alone then they can live.

If they pose a threat to any of us they have to die.

I blow out a breath as Illi gets onto the highway and ask, "What's your take on Colt? I know I've asked before but every time I ask you about him you remember something else. I don't want to miss anything."

Illi shrugs and curses under his breath at how bad the traffic is at this time of the day. "Well, the first time I met him was because I grabbed him off of the road. Actually it's the same place we're meeting him today. I tortured him for a few days for information, he didn't give anything up, but he did manage to break out of my workroom and find Odie."

I hum under my breath. "So he's resourceful... I doubt you left him much to work with down there."

Illi shrugs. "Honestly, I was a fucking mess back then. I'd only just gotten Odie back from the cartel, my mind wasn't fucking good. I was probably sloppy about it but even after days of being carved up he got out and up into my apartment. Came face-to-face with Odie and instead of killing her or just fucking leaving he offered to get her out. He took a look at how messed up she was and thought I was hurting her. I decided he wasn't so bad when he tried to help her."

Without being there I can't say for sure if I also think he was trying to rescue Odie.

Ash once told me of the games that Joey would play with the girls Senior would give him. He would tell them he was trying to rescue them from our father and then he'd help them run away to the guest house where he'd rape and murder them.

Senior only gave him girls when he did something 'good' so it'll only happened a handful of times but it was fucking awful.

Ash still has nightmares that it's me or Lips trapped in that guesthouse with Joey.

Illi runs through the other short meetings with me. There's nothing new to pick over but now that they're fresh in my mind again I feel more ready to meet Colt. There's less chance of me missing things now I have a little more of his background fresh in my mind.

We drive for over an hour until finally Illi pulls into a rest bay off of the highway. There's no one else around and it looks as though not many people stop here. I move to get out but Illi shakes his head at me, slipping a tablet into my lap.

"Stay there. I've told him to get in the back seat, there's a camera set up so you see his face and review the footage."

I raise my eyebrows at him and he chuckles at me. "I've been taking your ideas on board! I got Jackson to rig it up for me, nearly fucking killed me to let the little cretin in my car but I know you like to obsess over the details."

It's sweet and the tablet is easy enough to work. We sit in silence together as we wait for Colt to arrive and the roar of his motorcycle is impossible to miss.

I feel the flutters of nerves in my belly, at meeting this brother of Lips' that no matter what will change things. No matter what, Lips will want to deal with him.

The door opens and then the car bounces a little as it takes on the extra weight of another person sitting there.

I glance at the screen in front of me to find Lips' brother in the backseat.

Heir of the Chaos Demons and eyes as fiercely unsettling as the Devil himself.

Colt Graves.

"Things have changed since I was last here." He has the same southern accent as Poe does, that rough way of speaking that's so different to the Cali girl of my own.

He scowls at Illi as he looks me over. "Who the fuck is this?"

Illi smirks at him. "Calm the fuck down, she's a friend. She's good friends with my girl."

Colt glares at the back of Illi's head. "Which girl? The one you married or the one you sold your soul to?"

Huh.

I wasn't sure how much of the Bay's politics is talked about outside of California but apparently the news of the Butcher's induction made it to Texas.

Illi shrugs. "Both, actually. We run a tight ship. Queenie here is just along for the ride today, keeping her out of trouble."

I roll my eyes but his words work like a charm, the scowl on Colt's face eases off until he only looks mildly irritated at being here and no longer outright suspicious.

"So, what's the job? I wasn't expecting a call from you."

Colt eyes my seat off as he scratches at the scruff on his chin. "I need someone taken out, no questions asked and no ties back to me. You think you can do that?"

Illi huffs. "I'm definitely gonna ask some questions but I can kill whoever you need. Name, identifiers, a photo and

a reason, Demon."

Colt pulls out his phone and clicks through his photos, handing it over to Illi to look at. When I glance down at his hand, there's a little diamond tattooed to his ring finger… that's a sign of something. I don't know the specifics but I make a mental note.

He huffs as he sits back in his chair, looking out over the barren desert outside the car window. "Is there an unlisted number I can send that through to? I don't want anyone tracing this shit."

Illi tilts the screen just a little so I can see.

It's a Chaos Demon.

Georgie, the Vice President of his own MC, it looks like Colt Graves is trying to work his way up in his father's club by any means necessary.

Illi shrugs and waves a hand at him. "I know who he is. Gimme the reason, you could take him out yourself on a drug run. Stray bullets happen all the time on the road."

He stares at me for another second and then says, "He doesn't fucking go on them and… fuck, not many people know about this. I keep it quiet for a reason."

Illi nods his head slowly. "I trust Queenie with my life, she's a vault. I wouldn't have brought her along otherwise."

Colt stares at me for a second longer but whatever the reason is that he needs Illi to do the killing for him is urgent enough that he finally takes a deep breath and says,

"I have a sister."

Illi doesn't move a muscle.

Neither do I, but that isn't what I'm expecting.

Colt doesn't notice our new, statue-like states and continues. "Grimm's a fucking cunt about her, has it in his head that she's a risk to the club so he's told the brother's that he's making a game outta her."

What the fuck?

I glance at Illi but he's completely expressionless for now. "Are you close to this sister? Don't want her getting hurt?"

Colt grimaces. "Fuck, she's been outta my life more than she's been in it but she's only a fucking kid. Lives with the Unseen down in Mississippi, got a cop for a half brother, and she doesn't remember a thing about me… but I remember her. I've done what I can to keep my club the hell away from her… to give her a chance of getting clear of Grimm. Now that he's painted a target on her back? I can't keep up with that shit, I need some help. Whatever the cost, I'll pay it. I'll figure it the fuck out, just take Georgie out for me."

I shouldn't attempt to speak to him, not after his reaction to me being here, but I have to. "What exactly is the game Grimm has started?"

Colt stares at me and my heart clenches a little at the intensity of his eyes. There's a little of all of the siblings

staring back at me and it hits me right in the chest just how badly I miss my best friend.

"He's told the club that the only way on the council is to be a Graves or to have one. The whole fucking club is gunning after a fifteen year old little girl to get a spot at that table. No doubt the second one of them manages to get her and drag her back Grimm'll slit her fucking throat. He doesn't like the idea of daughters. Says having pussy in the family is fucking useless."

God.

If only that piece of shit knew.

If only he knew about the pussy in the family who walked into the Game and killed her way into the Twelve. Who became the most infamous assassin the Bay had ever seen, the fear she strikes into the hearts of any Mounty looking into the shadows at night. If only he knew about how she took on the Jackal and Senior and walked out of it alive.

I want to break something.

Illi looks as though he's trying not to put his fist through the car window.

Colt nods. "Like I said, he's a real piece of shit."

I shouldn't say a word.

I really shouldn't, and the look Illi gives me is disapproving, but I turn in my chair and stare at Colt for a second.

"Why do you care about your sister? If you don't know her… why pay all of this money to keep her safe?"

He frowns at me and glances over at Illi like he's trying to figure out my angle. I don't care, I'm asking for Lips. When I call her the moment I get home I want answers to every question she's going to have for me.

He shrugs. "It's not her fault that Grimm is a cunt. She got the worst mom outta the lot of us too. Chance is… Chance is fucked up but his mom fought Grimm on everything she could for him. Mine overdosed years back but she kept me fed. Posey's mom auctioned her off for a hit. Left her behind to fend for herself when the acid dropped in her system. I'm the oldest, it's my job to look out for the other two and I've done what I can but Georgie will be fucking impossible for me to take out without Grimm catching wind. Believe me, I've tried."

I pull my phone out and start running through all I know about the Vice President and his whereabouts. He's in Texas, I know this for sure because he barely leaves the compound and he certainly never goes out on jobs. "You want the Butcher to head to Texas?"

Colt nods. "Georgie doesn't leave his crack whores there. He's either high or balls deep at all times. Fucking useless cunt."

Illi scowls. "Why him? Where is his death gonna help the kid if he's not going after her?"

Colt glances between the two of us slowly and says, "Two birds, one stone. Grimm'll call everyone home for a vote, nonnegotiable, and they'll vote me into the Council to replace Georgie. I'll have more of say on what happens from there... I'll make sure I only send halfwits anywhere close to Mississippi. Men dumb enough that they won't make it past the Unseen to get to Posey."

It looks as though Colt Graves won't just live, he'll find his own way into the family.

There's no way that Lips won't seek him out knowing what he's willing to do for Poe, no way that she'd ever let him deal with his father without her support, and honestly? It's only taken one conversation for me to feel the same way about him. He's not only got a soul but a soft spot for Poe... I wonder what Nate would do if he knew? If he knew just how far Colt would go to protect his little sister?

"We heading to Texas, Queenie?" Illi murmurs, a smirk already over his lips.

I shake my head. "No. The Wolf will take care of this one for us. You know as well as I do that she's the right choice for this one."

Colt stares at us both in shock from the back, finally croaking out, "What's this gonna cost me?"

Illi shrugs. "Nothing. The Wolf doesn't take cash. You'll owe her a favor."

Colt blinks at him, scratching at his chin. "I'm not

sure what I could possibly do that would be of use to the infamous Wolf of Mounts Bay but if it saves me green then sure. I'll owe her a favor. What could it hurt?"

A hell of a lot more than he thinks.

But that's for later.

# Seventeen

I wait until I'm home and in bed before I call Lips.

They're in Kansas for a sold out show so I wait until I'm sure they'll be back on the bus before I call. I'd text my Mounty to tell her we needed to speak and she'd promised to go straight back to the bus after the show so I wasn't waiting around for whatever debauchery they decided to get up to together.

It's a little after two in the morning when she finally calls and she whispers down the phone to me, "I'm sorry it's so fucking late. The venue was a nightmare to get out of and security has been a problem the whole trip. I'm about to fight the guy in charge of the tour so you might have to bail me out for that shit."

I laugh at her, the grumpy and savage tone is just so her. "Ash can bail you out except I guess he'd be sitting in the cell next to yours. Is Harley managing to keep his head a little better now you're out of the Bay or is he still being an overprotective dick?"

She giggles and I hear the sounds of traffic down the line even at this hour. They must be parked up close enough to the venue that people are still leaving. "He's been so freaking relaxed it's kind of freaking me out. He only threatens Finn every hour, practically civilized. Ash has been better… mostly because Blaise has been keeping his either half-cut or high the majority of the time so he's mellowed a little. It's like fucking babysitting toddlers, I swear to God."

I giggle along with her. "I haven't heard you this happy since… ever. I don't think you're having that bad of a time. That's really great. I'm so relieved for you."

She sighs and then mumbles down the line. "I feel guilty for how much fun we're having. You should be here having this fun too but I know you wouldn't be with everything going on. Fuck. I just miss you, okay? I miss you a lot and it's fucking weird living with this many guys and being the only girl. I got my period last week and Harley was the only one sober enough to take me to the store for supplies. Literally no one had a fucking tampon, not the bus or the venue… it's like uteruses aren't a thing on tour and I was pissed. I raged out a bit and then Finn said it was hormones. Avery, he almost fucking died."

I almost die… of laughter, the seriousness in her voice kills me. "Did Harley take the knife off of you? What a dick."

She snorts. "I walked away. Ash was the one who almost killed him. Told him never to talk about my body again and when Finn said he wasn't Ash knocked him out. He still has a bruise under his eye. That shit was hilarious."

Kudos to Ash, I'll have to buy him something nice for treating our Mounty so well. He's been eyeing off the newest Ferrari, that'll do.

I fill her in on the entire conversation with Colt and she's quiet through the entire thing, not making a single sound until I tell her about the little game her sperm donor has made around Posey.

"Are you fucking kidding me? Fuck. Fuck! Nate's gonna lose his shit."

I hum under my breath. "Yeah, he will. If he doesn't already know, he's got pretty close tabs on her, doesn't he?"

She grumbles under her breath. "Yeah, he does but I'm not sure he has someone in the club itself or just watching it."

I stretch back against the pillows in my bed and switch the light off. Some things are better discussed in the dark. "Honestly? I think Colt might be our person on the inside. He does not like his father, that much was clear as day Lips. I have the recording, I can show it to you whenever you're ready."

She hums, a habit she's picked up from me, and says,

"I will. I'll watch it when I get home, for now I'm happy to just kill the VP and deal with the rest when this tour is over. Anything else? How is Aodhan? And Atticus, Illi has been telling me he's been a dick but that's kind of his deal these days."

God.

That's the perfect opener and I take a deep, deep breath. She's my best friend, my ride or die, and if I can't tell her this absolute mess I'm in then there's something fucking wrong with me.

One last breath. "I think I need a girl chat about the entire situation and it's killing me that you're not home for it."

She huffs out her trademark laugh at me, the throaty one my brother would bleed men out for the rest of his life to hear. "I'm surprised you didn't just climb onto your private jet to come find me for the night."

I sit up in the bed, restless now, and prop my chin up on my fist. "I thought about it but Ash would throw a tantrum about it and we wouldn't get a second alone. How is he? He only ever gives me safety reports when I call him."

"He's... good, I guess. This trip has been kind of— I mean, it's been great, but I think we're all still just in a weird place."

I don't like the sound of this. "What does that mean?

Has something happened? You just told me things were great."

She sighs. "No, nothing has actually happened but its like we're all holding our breaths waiting for the bus to fucking blow up or something. Like, we can't possibly be lucky enough to be alive and happy. It's just... weird."

I get it. That's exactly how I was feeling before I found myself busy with men and politics and dead threats. "I have something I want to tell you but I need two things from you first."

"Anything, you know that."

I've *really* missed the hell out of her. "I need to know that you're completely alone and there's no chance of any of the guys hearing this conversation and I need you to hear me out... to hear the entire story before you say anything. You can't hang up on me to call... anyone else and order a hit."

There's complete silence on the other end of the line, then she takes a deep breath and says, "Okay. Okay, I'm definitely alone and I promise I'll hear you out. I also promise I won't order a hit because from the sounds of it I'll be coming home to do the killing myself."

It's sweet and blood-soaked and entirely a Lips thing to say.

I move to lay back down, it's impossible to get comfortable, and stare up at my ceiling.

And then I tell her everything.

I tell her exactly what happened in the Jackal's lair, I tell her about Luca finding us there and keeping my secret, I tell her about the deep ache in my chest that I still feel for Atticus but the butterflies that Aodhan has somehow buried deep in my gut and the way that I'm now desperate for them *both* to love me. How maybe now it's impossible to decide between the two of them. I tell her about the dead end I've hit with her other siblings and the file that Atticus handed over to me about Nate's murders. I tell her about the new photo-mapping of connections I've started in my basement that I've been losing more hours than I'd like to admit just staring at and getting lost in all of the possible plays that are happening at once.

I tell her about how scared I am of how Ash and Harley will react if they find out about what the Jackal forced me to do to Aodhan and the fact that no matter how much people will try to play it off as his fault… I made the choice, not him.

Then I sit there in silence and just think about it all until she finally speaks.

"If I could go back in time and do things over, I'd be the one cutting the Jackal's head off. Fuck, I think I would have just fucking blown the entire shithole up and been done with it."

I laugh at her but the fact she hasn't immediately started

asking questions is soothing to me.

How do I describe the trauma?

Because I don't regret what I did. I don't hate Aodhan or what happened just maybe how it happened. I'm worried that he only really wants me because of my virginity and some weird sort of obligation he's feeling. Even now that he's been affectionate with me, I've had this awful feeling in the back of my mind that all of this is some joke on me… like I'd never actually get to have someone that loves me for me.

God, what a mess.

"Aves, if he still wanted you after you and Atticus fucked at the gala then I think it's safe to say that he wants you. Fuck, he could've just moved on with his life after we rescued you from the Jackal. He's a member of the Twelve, he's in our inner circle, he doesn't need to date you to have influence. He's already got it. I saw the photos of the aftermath of his fight with Atticus after Luca came and got you, Illi gave me the details. A man doesn't react like that unless he has skin in the game."

I huff and then groan as my eyes close and I can see so clearly that wall three floors down of all of the faces of the people who might just want us dead. I've stared at it for some long that it's etched into my mind now, no chance of ever forgetting a single detail.

"So you're saying I should pursue Aodhan? Forget

about Atticus and just go after the man I raped? Jesus. It's so fucking bad when I say it out loud."

She huffs at me. "Avery, it sounds bad because it's not what happened. You gave something up to save him, he could have argued with you, he could have said no."

My eyes well up just a little but I blink until they clear. "He did. He—"

She interrupts me. "No, you just said he told you that you didn't have to. That's no a man saying no, that's a good man giving you an out. Look, I'd be the first person to tell you if I thought something bad happened in that room and it did but that was all on Matteo. Fucking nothing is on you, Aves."

I sigh. I want so badly to believe her but I can't until I speak to Aodhan.

What a fucking mess. "So I'm just supposed to invite him over and say, 'oh, about that night, did I assault you? Is this all Stockholm syndrome or are you good for round two? A girl has needs you know?' Because I may *die* if I have to say that to him, Lips. No, I'd rather die than say it."

She scoffs at me. "At least invite him over for dinner. You know guys do better with a steak in front of them. He's a Mounty though, so don't go crazy with all the trimmings. Just a steak and beers and call it good."

I try to do simple.

And for my standards the four course dinner with two options for dessert that I cook entirely from scratch is simple but I'm sure it's not what Lips was trying to get through to me. When I send her the menu for critiques she replies something snarky back and I switch my phone to silent so I don't have to listen to her laugh at me over my obsessive freakout.

I need everything to be *perfect* and I don't have time to remind her that she was an absolute idiot about the three guys who were desperately trying to get her attention but when this dinner is over you better believe I'm going to call her and rehash the facts.

I time everything perfectly so I'm out of the shower, dressed perfectly with makeup and my favorite pair of Louboutin's on by the time the doorbell rings.

Aodhan had used his own code to get through the gate which means that I got an alert but I didn't have to actually buzz him in which is a nice extra feature. I run a hand down the silk of my dress before I open the door, one last calming ritual to help me settle my nerves at whatever this night is going to throw at me.

Aodhan is too attractive for words tonight.

He's wearing dark jeans and a button-down shirt in a charcoal gray that clings to his biceps in a delicious way. His boots are new, definitely not the blood-spattered ones

he'd worn to deal with Diarmuid, and his hair is clean and slicked back away from his face.

I lean forward and kiss his cheek, taking note of the very clean and very male scent of him like he's put a lot of effort into his presentation for me tonight. I like that, I like it a lot and he's already made it to the top of my ongoing list of favorite people for today.

He grins at me with that kind of male satisfaction that doesn't make my teeth clench or my blood boil. No, it gives me flutters in my stomach until I want to climb him and kiss that grin right off of his face. "The Wolf called me today, told me to prepare myself for a Beaumont dinner."

There go the flutters, my stomach drops to me feet. I'll *kill* her. "And you still arrived to my door in jeans and biker boots? Disgraceful."

He shrugs and steps up to me, crowding me against the door. "They're my best pair. If you wanted a suit you would've called someone else."

He doesn't say who but then he doesn't need to. We're both very aware of the other man who lingers around me even when he's snarling about how much he doesn't want me.

"Stop think about him, Queenie, I shouldn't have brought him up. Dinner smells good, did you go with steaks or are we having lobster. Harley always fucking brags about your stew, if you made that I might move the

hell in."

I roll my eyes at him but he just keeps on grinning, swopping down to kiss me. There's no mistaking the interest there. No mistaking it so whatever Lips said to him it wasn't that bad.

I still want to call her and bitch her out.

He takes my hand as we walk into the dining room where I've already set out all of the food. His eyes widen a little but I squeeze his hand a little. "I like cooking and I'm used to doing it for a crowd so I went a little overboard. You can take some home to Jack and the rest of your family."

He nods and helps me into my chair like a gentleman. Even more points to him, I try to contain myself a little because we still have to get through the conversation.

I avoid having it while we eat but I can't hold it off forever.

Aodhan notices me fussing about with my plate and cutlery and raises an eyebrow as he uses his freshly baked sourdough bread to mop up the gravy on his plate. His enthusiasm at my cooking is also a point in his favor.

I take a deep breath and then stumble over my words anyway, "I— Christ, okay, I need to talk to you about that night. I need to talk to you about what happened and what… exactly we're doing here."

Aodhan takes another swig of his beer and shrugs. "Sure. Whatever you need, Queenie."

Fuck.

Some part of me was hoping he'd say 'no thanks' and I'd get out of this which is so unbelievably unlike me. I'm not a girl who sweeps difficult things under the rug. I'm the girl who ruins lives and arranges to bleed men out for daring to breath in my direction. I don't run or hide so why am I so desperate to do that now?

I take a long sip from my glass of wine and muster up the courage. I'm Avery Beaumont, for God's sake.

"I need to know what exactly to think of me after what happened when the Jackal… forced us. I need to know that this isn't happening out of some kind of… some sort of obligation."

He stares at me like I'm dense. I know the look well, I've had to use it against Lips a lot in the past while she sorted out the mess of her love life. She was being incredibly naive though, and self deprecating, so I'm sure I'm not doing the same here.

"What I think… about you? Queenie, I'm not sure where I've been vague about what I think of you."

I try not to huff and snap at him but I'm pissed he's making me spell it out. "Aodhan, I stabbed you to get the Jackal to stop hurting me and then I forced myself on you at his request. I didn't listen to you when you said no, that makes me a fucking—"

"If the word 'rapist' comes outta your mouth right now

I'm going to break the pretty plate you just threaten me about against the fucking wall. Heads up, don't fucking talk about yourself like that around me or we're gonna have problems. Big ones because you, Beaumont, are fucking perfect. The type of woman any man would crawl through his knees over glass every damn day to get the chance to be with and I won't fucking hear you talking shit about yourself like that. Not at all, so just fucking don't."

He glares down the table at me like he's waiting for me to pick a fight but, while I'm not sure I believe his assessment of the situation, I'm glad relieved he just aired it all out for me to pick over. "If you say no then I should have listened to you. I've thought about it a lot, the Jackal was distracted enough not to even check the live feed… I could have tried something else to get us both free and safe."

He sets down his fork. "I was saying no because why would someone like you wanna fuck a Mounty like me? Fucking you wasn't the problem, in any other situation I would've been a hundred percent down for that, Queenie, but you were fucking terrified. You were hurt and needed help and you still did what you could for me the second you saw that guy die from the collar. If you think any of my anger at what happened is directed at you… no. Fuck no. I'm pissed you were a virgin and had no choices. You're the one who was assaulted."

I cringe. That's not my view of that room at all. I had a choice and I made it. Fine, the options weren't great at the time but being with Aodhan wasn't a terrible thing.

I have felt guilty every second or every day since about just how much I enjoyed it.

I wonder if I had've just fucked him and refused to kiss him or speak to him, if I had've just taken it the way the Jackal had intended, would I still have felt the guilt? If anything, I think that would've felt worse. The way that everything happened meant that I didn't feel *violated* but that was at Aodhan's expense.

When I tell him this he gets really angry… the type of angry I've only seen that once back in that room with the Jackal. "I told you, nothing was at my expense. Whatever choices you made, I was giving them to you. Fuck, if you had've stuck that knife through my heart I still would've been happy with your choice. I went there to help you and if dying for you did that then I'd go to the grave without a fucking complaint. What else do I have to say to you for you to understand that I'm not going anywhere? I've watched you march into every fight with your family with your head held high and your little arsenal of tricks and I knew that you're it for me. Sometimes you just know these things and, Queenie, I'm not fucking this up, no matter how hard you push."

I put my fork back down on the table because suddenly

I know exactly why Lips struggles to eat with her heart in her throat all of the time. Aodhan watches me for a moment and then reaches into his pocket, pulling out a little black jewelers box. It's too big for a ring, *thank God*, and I recognize the stamp on the front as one of the smaller and more exclusive stores in the Bay.

It's somewhere I would actually shop.

"Jewelry? I am notoriously difficult to buy for, Aodhan, you really shouldn't have." I murmur even though my heart has really set up for the time being in my throat no matter how hard I swallow. I wait until I'm sure my fingers aren't trembling before I reach out to take the box.

He smiles at me, radiating smug energy, and says, "I cheated but I know you'll love this."

I open the box and immediately I want to cry. I want to breakdown and weep like a child because there's never been a better gift for me.

It's the necklace Lips gave me for Christmas, the little platinum cage with the blue diamond in there except now there's another diamond in there with it. Dark, brilliant green that's the same shade as his eyes.

A lump forms in my throat.

"You chewed me out for going back in there and getting shot, remember? I couldn't leave the necklace behind… after what happened, I couldn't have you lose that too."

I swallow and slip the chain over my head. It's a little

tight but I make it work until the little cage and the priceless diamonds are hanging over my bare chest.

"You know that Lips gave it to me as a favor? If anything happened to me I could use it on her behalf and no matter the cost, she'd fulfill the favor."

He smiles and nods. "Of course. I'm taking a leaf outta the Wolf's books and I'm not giving out favors… except that one. Just for you, Queenie."

I blink away my tears and swallow around the lump in my throat until I can speak without sobbing. "I would like it if you stayed the night."

# Eighteen

The moment I get our plates into the sink Aodhan pulls me into his arms like he's been waiting all night to do it.

He kisses me like it's the first time and the last time all at once. He kisses me so deeply and desperately that it's as though he wants to consume me and keep me with him forever but he's sure he'll never get to.

He lifts me into his arms without breaking the kiss and once my legs are wrapped around him securely he slides my shoes off and lets them drop to the floor.

I break away from his lips to inform him that I value my shoes more than most people value their lives but he cuts me off with a growl, "Shut it, Queenie, you're lucky I'm not ripping this dress to pieces and fucking you on the kitchen counter. You want a bed then kiss me."

I can't argue with that because I would have to decimate my kitchen and start again at the thought of cooking where my naked ass had been.

Never mind the wet spot.

Oh God.

Aodhan huffs at my panicked look and keeps one hand on my ass to keep me secure and then he cups my cheek to draw me in closer to take over my lips again, kissing me senseless until I forget all about the disgusting aftermath of kitchen sex.

I barely notice he's walking until we get to the staircase but when I attempt to slide down his body and back to the ground he grunts again and snarls, "I was hoping to do this without ropes this time around but if you don't quit overthinking every little thing I will tie you to the bed and edge you all night long. If you're into that then keep pushing because I'm a man of my word."

I stop wriggling.

There's no way I'm going to be okay with delayed orgasms all night, I feel like my entire life has been one big edging session with all of the men I've had any real interest in either not wanting me enough or trying to hurt me.

He chuckles at me and starts up the stairs without any difficultly which speaks to just how strong he really is. It's a deceptive thing because he's not completely jacked up but there's a deceptive strength in him.

I don't want him to trip and break both our necks so I duck my head down to start kissing down his neck. He

already knows they path to my bedroom after following me in there and staying there the last time we were here together so I can focus on marking him up. I want there to be no doubts about this man being taken, I've had enough of other women messing around with what's mine. He groans and gets a move on, hitching me up further in his arms and stalking into my bedroom.

He finally lets me down to hit the lights and I move like I'm going to head into the shower, because that's exactly where I'm heading, and Aodhan's arms loop around my waist, tugging me back into his chest. "No way, Queenie, no way are you scrubbing yourself down again like last time. Get your ass on that big fluffy bed of yours so I can taste you."

A shiver runs down my spine, my nipples pebbling underneath the lace of my bralette and poking through the silk dress until he groans and runs his hands up my belly and over the fabric to seek them out. His mouth trails down my neck, licking and sucking, and when his fingers brush over the peaks the rough feel of his fingers pushing the delicate lace into the sensitive skin has my legs trembling and all of the arguments I have about showering try to fly out of my head.

"I need a shower." I gasp out and he growls at me, his fingers squeezing and pinching at my nipples until my pussy weeps.

"No fucking way. Get the dress off and get on the bed, I want to taste you not your fucking soap."

I want to argue but the pinching gets rougher and more punishing the longer I hesitate until finally I step away from him, pushing his hands away from my body and staggering over to the bed on legs that want to give out. The dress I'm wearing is held together with a sash around the waist and with a single tug it falls away from me. I desperately want to fold it neatly and put it away but there's no way I'll make it past Aodhan to do it so I cringe as I let it fall to the plush carpet.

"Fuck. Fuck me. Take the panties and bra off too, Queenie. I'll be too rough with you if I do it, I want you too fucking bad right now to be gentle about it."

I chuckle at him, low and breathy as I do as he says, glancing back over my shoulder to tease him, "Maybe I want rough. Maybe I want you to need me so badly you forget to treat me right."

He grunts and strips out of his clothing, a no-nonsense series of movements that aren't an attempt to seduce me but do exactly that. The tattoos over his arms are all old ones had long before he became the Stag, but the antlers over his chest are the markings he got for his position in the Bay. It's impressive and fierce, coming to life on him as he moves and flexes unzipping his jeans and kicking them off of his legs.

His cock is hard already, curving up towards his belly, and I don't try to hide my staring from him even when he starts groaning and stroking himself. "You want rough because you think if I'm treating you right that I'm coddling you which I'm definitely not. You're Avery Beaumont, Queen of the Bay and the Wolf's most trusted friend. I'm treating you like the best fucking thing that ever happened to me because you are. Now climb that perfect ass of yours up onto that bad and spread you legs, show me what I want dripping down my chin."

Oh God.

I climb up onto the bed, propping myself up onto my elbows so I can watch as he stalks over to me and climbs up onto the bed. I'm expecting him to come and kiss me some more, but when he climbs up my body he gets as far as my nipples and stops to swoop down and take one into his mouth, licking and sucking and groaning. My hands tangle into his hair and tug, moaning and squirming under his hands when he works his way down my body.

The growl that rips out of his throat as he stares down at my pussy is desperate and hungry, like he's barely holding himself back. "This is mine now, Queenie. Every night you're gonna cook some fancy feast for me and then I'm eating you out for dessert."

I huff at him and slump back in the pillows. "Are you? Because right now you're just talking it up, you're yet to

actually eat *anything*. I'm starting to think it's nothing but words."

It's like waving a red flag at a bull. My challenge lighting up inside him like a flame to kindling and he doesn't ease me into it at all, he just swoops down and pulls my hips down until he really is feasting on me, licking and sucking until I squirm underneath him in pleasure. I don't have time to think about anything, not with his tongue tracing over my clit, flicking and circling over it until I'm so wet that I know I must be dripping down his chin. The orgasm, when it hits, is more intense than any other I've ever had and my hips lift from the bed as I chase his tongue and grind myself against his face like a harlot.

I expect him to stop and strip off, probably slap his dick on my cheek and tell me to reciprocate.

He doesn't.

He settles in against the sheets and makes good on his promises, eating every inch of my pussy until I'm sobbing against my pillows and completely unaware of how many times I've come. My throat hurts from how many screams his tongue has coaxed out of me and I'm not sure I have any feeling left in my legs.

When he finally climbs up my body he's good enough to wipe his face on my sheets before he kisses me, a roguish grin on his face that steals my breath out of my chest. He's fucking *breathtaking* like this and, though I always knew

he was an attractive man, it wasn't until right now that it hit me right in the chest.

Then he pushes up like he's going to get up and leave me.

"Where are you going?" I murmur, keeping my voice low so it doesn't break. I feel so exposed lying here and if he walks away right now I'm done with men. I'll be a celibate old witch and buy a dozen cats to keep me company, just to really keep to the stereotype.

Ash would love it.

He sees the little frown and kisses me. "Condom. Unless you have some under your pillow? How prepared were you for tonight? I'm starting to feel like you planned everything out."

His teasing tone is a little inappropriate because that's exactly what I did. I planned the entire night out and even if it is going far better than I imagined it's still running to the general script.

"I'm on birth control, I have been for years, and I already have your health records. I'm also very impressed that you went and got tested for me."

He blinks at me for a second and then shakes his head. "Of course you do, Queenie."

I smirk and open my mouth to snark back at him but he hooks his arms around my legs and drags me further down my bed, away from the pillows and so I'm completely

trapped underneath him. I feel freaking tiny when he cages me with his arms, his chest close to double the width of mine and when he covers me completely I feel a deep sense of safety there.

He came for me when he didn't have to. He wanted to die for me, not once has he blamed me for any of the choices I've been forced to make and every step of the way he's trusted me to make the right moves against our enemies. He's protected me without locking me in a tower and throwing away the key.

He wants me for more than my money or my connections. He wants *me*, I'm sure of it.

I don't wait for him to kiss me. I grab his face with both of my hands and I kiss him the way he always does, as if my life is ending and he's all I need to die with. My hip lift from the bed without me even thinking about it, desperate for the weight of him and empty without him.

He grunts and leans on one hand to use to other the slip two fingers into me, groaning as I clench around them.

I mumble against his lips, "Fuck me."

It's a relief to only feel a good stretch as he fills me, no pain or guilt or anything, only the delicious full feeling and when he groans and nips at the skin on my neck like he's holding back I hook my legs around his waist to pull him in deeper until his hips are flush with mine.

He holds still for a second and my eyes narrow up at

him until he huffs out a breath at me and says, "Lemme enjoy it this time, you're too fucking tight and I need a second so I don't ruin it."

I scoff at him and he grins at me, kissing me again and when he finally starts to move his hips are relentless, pushing and grinding into me slowly at first but then it's like he loses himself in the feeling and then he really does start to pound into me until I feel like I can't breathe in all of the best ways.

My body writhes under his, it's impossible to stay still, and when his hands slips between our bodies to circle over my clit I shatter, my eye rolling back into my head as I come apart at the seams and clamp down around him like I never want to let him go.

He grunts and bites my lip as he comes, gentle enough that he doesn't break the skin but I feel the sting of it anyway.

He pulls out of me but when he collapses onto the bed beside me he tucks me in close to his chest, completely disregarding the mess I'm in as his cum drips down my leg.

Miraculously, I stay calm about it. Probably because I'm still riding the high of my orgasms and somewhere in my brain I know I'll be able to talk him into sharing a shower with me before we sleep.

"Count me in on your plans of eating me out every

night. It was much better than I thought it would be."

Aodhan scoffs at me. "You thought I'd be shit at it? Thanks, Queenie, you know how to sweet talk your man."

My man, Jesus H. Christ. "No, I meant I didn't expect to enjoy cunnilingus that much. I always thought it'd be too… wet."

Aodhan's arm tenses around me. "There goes my afterglow. You mean to tell me that asshole didn't go down on you? He just fucked you at a gala and didn't even make sure you enjoyed it? What exactly is the history between you two, Queenie? I'm a little fucking confused and I can't exactly ask Harley about your dating life. He'd rage out and break something, probably my face., and I like it too much to have it rearranged."

I sigh and lean back in the bed, trying not to feel so uncomfortable at talking about this because… he just ate me out and fucked me so hard my legs are still shaking, I doubt this is any more revealing than that.

"I dated a bit in high school after Atticus rejected me. I made out with a few guys and… there was one guy I thought about having sex with. I went as far as giving him a blow job but then he cheated on me with the worst fucking whore in the school so I broke up with him."

Aodhan grumbles under his breath, his fingers stroking over the soft skin of my stomach. "What a fucking idiot. Tell me your brother beat the life outta him."

I don't talk about this with anyone… ever. But it feels like that little bubble is around us both again so nothing outside of us exists. "He didn't take the break up well. Ash and Harley tormented him, which he deserved, but in typical asshole fashion he cornered me in the bathroom and tried to rape me. He said I was a tease because he would have never cheated on me if I hadn't led him on."

Aodhan's entire body freezes until he's barely breathing but I continue, better to get the whole story out and into the air so I won't ever have to speak about it again, "So he cornered me in the upperclassmen toilets and there's no way I could fight him off. He was a football player and my brother had done everything in his power to make sure I never had to get physical with anyone. I'm a dancer so I have upper body strength but it was like no matter how hard I pushed against him, he'd push back twice as hard. I was terrified… and then suddenly he was shoved away from me and I was so relieved because I knew only my brother or Harley or Blaise would have come to my rescue like that. I was safe if one of them had found me."

He tugs me over until I'm lying on my side facing him, his arm over my hip keeping me close. "You're lucky they did."

I give him a rueful smile. "They didn't. The scholarship student I'd spent the entire year terrorizing did. See, my psychotic older brother had become obsessed with her

and no matter what I did, this girl wouldn't drop out. I threw everything I had at her and she just dodged it all. Or endured it, the stuff that Joey did to her… she just kept going. She was the last person I would expect to help me but she didn't hesitate. Not once, she took him to the ground and knocked him out like she was some sort of trained killer… we've been best friends ever since and there's nothing I wouldn't do for her."

Aodhan nods and a slow smile stretches over his lips. "The Wolf and the Queen, Mounts Bay doesn't stand a chance."

I hum under my breath quietly as I think, an annoyingly resistant habit of mine. "I've been considering that… about how exactly we're going to keep the Twelve under our control. We already have three members in the family, the Butcher backs us… as well as other big players. Atticus is our ally and, no matter how much Ash hates it, he'll stay an ally because of me. I'm sure of that. The Boar is a wild card. The Tiger has always sided with Atticus and Lips but it's not exactly an alliance. There's too much uncertainty."

Aodhan frowns and pulls me closer. "This sounds like you want to sponsor someone. Whoever it is, I'll put them forward for you. Name it and it's yours, Queenie. No matter what."

I huff at him. "And what if I name myself? What if I want a seat at the table?"

He leans forward to press our lips together, his tongue darting out until the stroke of it over mine has me ready for round two.

He pulls away and murmurs to me, "I'm not going to stop you from doing anything, Queenie. If you're sure you can walk into the Game and take your opponents out then go ahead. I doubt Ash will be so happy about that, or Harley. Fuck, Illi will probably throw down over it too."

I giggle at him. "So you're fine with it because everyone else will stop me and do your dirty work for you?"

He smirks at me, biting my lip before sucking on it like he wants to distract me. His fingers trail up to my necklace and he pulls back to look at it again where it hangs on my naked chest. "There's room in there for another diamond you know. If he ever gets his head out of his ass."

I startle and blink away tears as I look him over. "Please tell me you're joking? You're giving me up for the Crow?"

He huffs and grabs my wrists, pulling me until I'm straddling his waist. My heart thumps a little but it's different here, the room is dark and clean and mine. There's no place here for the ghosts of the Jackal.

"I'm not giving you up for fucking anything, Queenie. Nothing would make me let you go… but if you want him as well then I can live with that. I want your heart to be whole, not torn in half."

I clutch at the necklace in my hand. My words come out

thready, "Atticus won't share. I'm surprised you would."

He shrugs. "I've watched Harley share for months… he doesn't look like he's suffering. I think he found someone worth it and, Aves, you're fucking worth it. If Atticus doesn't see it that way then that's his loss."

# Nineteen

$F$alling asleep in clean sheets after a shower with Aodhan is just as perfect as I thought it would be.

Waking up to him eating me out again is even better.

I want nothing more than to spend the day in bed with him and to just enjoy being together. While forgetting about everything that's happening around us is the dream it's also almost impossible to do with my phone buzzing constantly with a slew of messages from informants and Illi checking in on me.

I had text Lips before falling asleep last night and the smugness in her was radiating through the three word sentences she replied to me with.

Aodhan kisses me and heads to the shower while I start sorting through all of the information that came through while we slept. There's nothing really interesting until I get to the guest list of birthday dinner the Ford sisters are throwing for their decrepit ninety-something-year-old father.

There's a lot of names there that will be useful to me on that list but I have my sights set on Olivia Bromburg specifically.

Her husband is in the DEA and with the Jackal's product flooding the streets of the Bay that makes him very useful to me. I've never met him, I only know him from the gossip, and there's no time like the present to go looking for some more leads.

I decide to go with my strengths and I tell Illi that Aodhan will be escorting me to the high society dinner.

It's a very murky truth.

Technically he is escorting my there… and then he's going to wait for me outside the building where he can come and rescue me if something goes terribly wrong.

When I tell him about my plans he gives me the same crooked smile he always does and says, "Good thing I would rather drink bleach than eat snails with rich dicks or I'd be a pretty fucking offended that you don't wanna be seen at parties with me."

I roll my eyes at him and stalk out of my closet in my lingerie and heels. The dress I'm wearing for the night is tricky to get on by yourself and I had called Aodhan up to my bedroom early so he could help me into it.

The problem there is that the moment he sees me in the strapless and very tiny lingerie it's very clear that he has other ideas for how we should be spending the night.

"I don't have time for whatever you're thinking about and I definitely don't have time to reassure you that the real reason I don't want you to attend the dinner is because the women there are like vultures and they'll be all over you the moment you walk in."

He doesn't move from where he's sitting on the chaise lounge at the end of my bed, his elbows on his knees and his eyes eating every inch of my skin up.

I continue like he's replied to me, fussing with my curls in the mirror like I ever have the chance of being happy with them. "I don't mind taking Illi in there with me because the women seem to be able to smell the 'happily married serial killer' on him and leave him alone. Well, they still stare at him like they want to fuck his brains out but none of them actually approach him to do it."

I step back into my closet to grab the dress and when I walk back out into the bedroom Aodhan is still sitting there staring at me.

I roll my eyes at him. "My tits aren't that great, can we focus?"

He scowls at me and when I hand him the hanger with the dress he stares at it like I handed him a ticking bomb. "What the fuck even is this? Where are the sleeves?"

I roll my eyes and then spend ten minutes explaining to him how we're getting the thin sheets of fabric not only on my body but securing them there so I don't accidentally

flash anyone my tits.

He gets very scowly at the thought. "Are you sure you're not willing to take Illi with you. I'd feel better knowing he'd stab anyone that gets flashed if I do a shit job of getting this thing to stay the fuck on you. Don't you have any like… normal shit to wear? Something with straps and zips and shit?"

I huff at him and then I lift my arms for him to slide the pieces of lace where they need to go. By the time I'm slipping my shoes on I'm confident the couture gown is going to stay put. White lace is difficult to pull of without looking like a wedding gown but this piece is very obviously a statement piece of art draped over my body like it was made for me.

It was.

I have spent many hours discussing my fashion needs with Vera myself.

Aodhan drives me over in my Bentley, bitching and biting his lip at me the whole way when I have to slide the dress right up to be able to sit until the tiny triangle of my panties is on full display to him the entire drive over.

"Rich parties might sound as boring as fuck but the dress code has me tempted to go." He mumble and I pinch his thigh playfully.

"And which socialite are you hoping to see?"

He smirks. "There's this gorgeous one who wears a lot

of white. On anyone else it would probably look like they were aiming for innocent but of this girl? Fuck, she looks like she's about to take you the hell out, Black Widow style, and I'm ready to die whatever death she's giving out."

He's laying it on a little thick but I'll take it, really anything to get me through the drive over there without dissolving into my nerves. I can tell he's just trying to distract me and I appreciate it.

When we finally pull up and I maneuver myself out of the car without his help, though he tries and I shut him down pretty fast, he huffs as he stares up at the building.

"Are you sure I can leave you here? If something happens to you I'll be fucking furious, Queenie."

I roll my eyes and lean down to give him the barest of pecks on the cheek. "I'll call you every hour I'm in there but I'm only planning on being there for one… two at the most. I promise."

He nods and when I straighten up he drives over to park up and wait for me. It's very sweet.

The party is being held at a gentleman's club out in the middle of nowhere.

It's a terrible venue and chosen because of the Ford family's close ties to the place but there's only one section of the building women are even allowed to enter so I'm escorted to the elevator by one of the valet's and he waits there with me until the doors open, seeing me inside and

then pushing the buttons to the right floor for me like I'm unable to do it myself.

When the doors open I roll my shoulders back and walk into the room with the same confidence I do everything in my life. There are whispers around the room but nothing too terrible and after I find myself a drink I slowly work my way around the room greeting the women and men in attendance until I find who I'm looking for.

My mark for the night, Olivia is flirting with Samual Washington, another doctor who was on my father's roster for the prescription drugs he would use sometimes in his torture. I give him a disapproving glance before turning my body to him in a move that is very clearly a dismissal and he stalks off without a word. We've interacted a handful of times in the past so he knows exactly what I'm capable of.

Olivia blinks at me and then glances around like she's trying to find away from me but there's not a single person in this room who is dumb enough to try. Atticus isn't here tonight and the Amanda nightmare of a woman is nowhere in sight.

"Avery, what a lovely surprise to see you here tonight. It's been some time since I've seen a Beaumont attending a party in this circuit."

I force a smile onto my face at her, honey sweet and with none of my usual cutting ice. "I admit I haven't found much reason to attend lately but I've had some openings in

my schedule and thought I should pop my head in. There's still the same boring women gossiping about nothing, not really my style. And you? Have you been loyal to your lovely little *friends*."

Olivia herself is an oil magnates daughter and his sole heir. This in itself should ensure that the women here are nice to her because nothing gets you higher up the ladder quite like an impending inheritance, but ten years ago when she married her high school sweetheart she'd taken a tumble down the socialite ladder.

Christopher Bromburg's family are rich, successful, and very new money.

The type of new money that wears flashy labels and talks about their salaries over the dinner table. I heard his father bought a yacht and named it Mo' Money Mo' Problems which, besides being fucking stupid, is the cringey type of bragging that the upper society hates to see.

Christoper is an agent in the DEA Office of National Security Intelligence and though he loves his family, he is nothing like them. He married for love and having the very docile Olivia in his bed is exactly what that very intelligent and, frankly, boring agent wanted.

She's the key to getting that man on my roster.

Olivia cringes a little and glances over at the other women but they're all watching us with a sort of horror,

like there isn't anything quite as terrifying as me taking an interest in her.

I think it's hilarious and the desperation wafting off them all is enough to choke on. Every last one of them is trapped in an unhappy marriage with men who need a bucketload of viagra to fuck them and really they're just jealous that Olivia is married to a man who doesn't stray from her after every little bleach blonde whore that crosses his path.

It's pathetic.

"Richard Ford is an old friend of my father, it was important to him that I attend. I don't intend on staying long." Olivia says, taking a sip of the champagne in her hand.

It's a very diplomatic answer, one that I don't have it in me to give back to her. "Why would anyone stay here for longer than it takes to down a drink? What the hell is Jessamine wearing? She looks abhorrent. Did Christopher attend with you?"

Olivia shakes her head a little. "He's been very busy with a big case. The narcotics issues in this country are only getting worse. It's good for keeping his position secure but makes the hours a nightmare."

Dammit. I nod sedately and take another sip of my drink. When I turn to find a refill I see Luca and Atticus walk in together and I curse under my breath because

of course they're here. Of course despite Atticus being perpetually busy with his own empire he found time to be here tonight.

*Of fucking course.*

Atticus's lip curls the second he sees me and he starts towards me. Olivia glances between us both and then scurries away. It's fine, I only really wanted to get a feel of her which I have.

I have a plan for her and Christopher now.

"What are you doing here? Are you trying to piss me off because that's *exactly* what you're doing." Atticus hisses at me and I grab that fresh glass of Champagne to get through this without pulling a knife on him.

"I was invited. Why should I be forced to stay home just because you've got issues with me?"

He lets out a breath and looks around the room. Ah, so that fucking bitch is here too because she's the only person I've seen him get this twitchy over.

He finally turns back to me and says, "I don't have issues with you, Avery, I just want you—"

"If the words 'to be safe' come next you can swallow them because I'm over this narrative. So beyond over it that I might go find a drug den in the Bay to spend a few hours in just to ram it home to you that I will do whatever the fuck I want, whenever the fuck I want. I belong to the Wolf of Mounts Bay, not you. My safety is *not* your concern."

He grabs my arm to spin me around and chew me out I'm sure when a hush takes over the room and I just about scream.

What the hell is it about this woman that has everyone running scared?

I'm the danger here, not this fucking flirty bitch with sub-par fashion choices and a murky past at best.

I'm Joseph Beaumont's daughter. I am the descendant of Russian royalty and I have the ear of the Wolf herself, what the hell does she have?

I sound jealous but really I'm just pissed that while I was off surviving a war between the most dangerous crime lords in the country this bitch was sinking her claws into the pawns of my board, the one I was born to rule.

She's eating at my fucking table and shitting all over my space.

I won't have it.

Naturally, she makes a beeline over to me, her hips swinging in the garishly cutout gown that shows enough skin that the entire room knows she's not wearing underwear. Not my style at all, too much going on, and the shoes are terrible. Nude and too pointed for the look.

She smiles up at Luca and when he doesn't return it she pouts.

I scoff at her, barely stopping myself from stalking away from her but Atticus's hand is still firmly wrapped

around my arm.

She sidles up beside me and says with a sing-song voice, "I heard you're looking to start a collection of your own? That's interesting and quite a silly thing to do here. Everyone in attendance is already mine. You should plan these things out a little more thoroughly."

I turn around to face her fully, tugging a little on Atticus's hand but he doesn't let me go. "I highly doubt that. At least half of the people here were on the Beaumont payroll until my father died and we both know he would never answer to a woman… no matter what your *charms* may be."

She cocks her head to one side and giggles. "Joseph has been dead for weeks, you're a little late to secure them for yourself. You should listen to me, Beaumont, because maybe you're a little young to be playing here."

The condescension in her tone make my jaw ache from the clenching of my teeth. The moment I know what her deal is I'm going to have her killed. Whether it's Illi or Lips or Ash, I'll plead my case and have her throat slit for daring to speak to me like this.

Maybe I'll have her tortured a little first.

She smirks at me. "You're not as good at hiding your feelings as you think. If you want me to die for my sins shouldn't you know whose anger you're risking first? Take a walk with me."

Atticus's hand tightens around my arm and when I shoot him a cool look his eyes burn back at me with rage. Deep breath, I ignore him as I turn to her and smirk. "Sure. I can make some time."

# Twenty

There's an old service elevator that goes down to the lower levels of the manor that is in perfectly maintained condition but is still creepy to climb into. The moment we got up from the table Atticus had found his way over to me and the skill that he has to do that without being obvious in something that can't be taught. He's lived in this world for so long that it's as easy as breathing to move all of the pieces to where he wants them to be without any of the smiling and laughing patrons noticing him going in for the kill.

I notice.

Amanda does too.

She smiles at me like this is all going according to her plans and I have to smile my way through the frustration of knowing that and accepting it. I can't win if I can't see the board we're all on. I can't win if I don't know the game and the stakes to what we're playing.

Atticus stands close to me as we get into the elevator

with Amanda, Luca walking in behind us and pushing all of the buttons. He's furious, the stiff lines of his shoulders tell me as much, but I really don't care. He could have told me what is going on but he chose not to so he can keep his fury to himself and burn in it.

"You look like a little bird in here, Beaumont. A little, fine-boned bird in a cage. You might want to make sure you don't get stuck here." Amanda murmurs to me, leaning in close to my ear and I force myself not to move away from her, no matter how badly I want to get away from the feel of her breath rolling down my neck.

It's disgusting.

I keep my mouth shut and that just makes her laugh. "Oh, little bird. Of course you're not worried! So surrounded by men willing to kill for you, where is that delicious Butcher of yours? Did he finally choose his wife over you? Was it the baby that swayed him?"

Atticus tenses, I presume he was unaware of Odie's pregnancy, but there's no way I'm letting this woman threaten Illi's unborn child. I have no doubt that's what she's doing.

"Dynasties are built on the strong foundation of a family. Loose, moralless women like you wouldn't understand such a thing."

She giggles under her breath at me. "Loose and moralless? Ah. I was unaware that fucking a man in the

back rooms at a gala was such a pious thing to do. Fucking another down in the docks of Mounts Bay? At least the Crow has good breeding, the other one is nothing but a gutter rat. Was it the rape at school that made you this way? Did it derail you from your dreams of marrying a Crawford and settling down to live out your privileged life?"

Atticus doesn't mask his feelings about this question at all. Instead, he turns to look down at me and I *refuse* to feel guilty about Aodhan. I refuse to feel a goddamn thing about what has happened in my life.

So instead I look over at her and smile. "If you're jealous because I have no intention of fucking you, Donnelley, you should know that you never really stood a chance. If there were any inclination in me to be with a woman I would never stoop to be with someone like you."

There goes that infuriating giggle of hers again, the one that sounds like she's trying to be some psychotic school girl. "No, you'd fuck the legendary Wolf of Mounts Bay. What it must be like to know her… I had a pet assassin once. He was ex-army and came highly recommended, you know. There was never a death too difficult for him to execute and he never asked questions. Great in bed too, his dick never went down."

My lip curls at her because for one I don't give a fuck about her sex life and for two she's equating Lips to a fucking animal to keep and that is beyond insulting.

The elevator finally dings like it's going to open and she leans into me again. "Your Wolf killed him. I've never seen anything like it and I knew then that I'd like to find her and keep her too."

The doors open before I can answer but I'm very glad that Lips went away with the guys and there's no chance of this woman getting her claws into her. I need to figure her the hell out and then have Illi gut her before she tries to go after my Mounty.

Hell.

I'll call Nate if I have to.

Luca steps out of the elevator and Amanda follows him, tucking her hand into his elbow like they're the best of friends even though I can see him cringing away from her touch.

Interesting.

Atticus holds out his arm for me to take and, though I'm shocked he's doing it, I take it. We walk behind the other two and it occurs to me that I have a gun in my purse. Not a single person has attempted to search me or even ask if Im carrying a weapon, soit would be easy to just aim it at her head and take the woman out.

I wonder if Atticus would stop me?

I think he would but I'd like to think it was for my own safety and not just because he has such an weird reaction around her. It's not exactly fear but he knows something

about her that clearly I don't.

The foyer the elevator opens up to is empty and decorated completely differently to the rooms upstairs. The open and bright rooms up there were luxurious and inviting, the type of spaces that people will gossip about and covet but down here is a very different feel.

The carpets are a deep, dark red and the plush for of thread count that only comes from an unlimited budget. Millionaires don't get this sort of thing, hand woven and thousands of hours of work for something that you only walk on. The walls are all covered in the finest silk wallpapers and show gory scenes of battles and orgies, brothels and boneyards.

No, this room as unassuming as it is was put together with the intention to impress and terrify. I take stock of it all but I'm not concerned. I'm a Beaumont, I don't feel fear at this kind of showy bullshit.

If anything, I'm impressed that Amanda really wants to worry me this much. To bring me down here means that she knows that her snide comments and flirting mean nothing to me and now she's pulling out the bigger tricks that she's hidden up her sleeves.

We finally make it over to the large wall of cherry wood paneling, the door almost invisible to the eye. There's a man standing beside it with the same sort of microphone pinning to his lapel as Atticus's men have. He nods at

Amanda and murmurs into it as we approach but his face stays strangely blank.

"Your father will be so happy to see you, Atticus." Amanda murmurs, and my eyebrows creep up.

That's who's waiting behind this door? It's been years since I last saw Randall Crawford but I'm not scared of the asshole. He's disgusting and he buys girls the same way that Senior did but he's not a man I've ever worried about.

His taste is for poor girls. Girls who have no hope in their lives, girls who will grovel at the men who bought them if they think it will save them. Girls who don't give a fuck that he's a disgusting fucking creep once they find out he's worth billions.

Of course Amanda is into him.

The door finally swings open and the bodyguard steps aside to usher us through. Atticus's arm tenses but he leads me through.

It's only the fact that I've spent my entire life hiding all of my reactions that I don't jump out of my skin when the doors open and we find a naked girl chained to the floor by her throat. She's younger than I am, trembling, and her eyes are wide with terror.

Atticus' shoulders roll back as he straightens up but other than that he doesn't react, just directs me past the girl as if she's not even there. It only gets worse the further into the room we get.

The girls are all either naked or wearing some form of latex bondage suits, some of them in masks with only breathing holes so they're completely blind and faceless.

These ones all look empty, broken, and lifeless. Atticus doesn't look surprised at the rest of them, no reactions, and I wonder how long he's known about this little party room.

I wonder how many of these girls belong to his father.

Randall Crawford smirks at me from the table, a cigar in one hand and a glass of bourbon in the other. He looks nothing like his son, his russet hair slicked back and his nose slightly crooked at the end. He's wearing a suit but it fits to his thick body in a way that looks off, like everything was cut on the bias and now it's warped. He's looks just as evil and sadistic as I've always known him to be so that isn't the surprise.

The surprise is Lauren Drummond kneeling at his feet.

The missing daughter of the MBPD Chief is completely naked except for a shibari rope looping around her and binding her. The art form itself is usually exactly that, an art, but the way it's been done to her is disgusting to look at and I imagine extremely painful to her.

The ropes are wrapped around her breasts are so tight that her skin is purple, her nipples barely discernible from the rest of her skin thanks to the coloring and mottling.

Tears run down her blank face but she isn't sobbing or even really crying, it's like her body is going through the motions but her mind is completely gone.

It's the most horrifying thing I've ever seen.

"Amanda! What are you doing down here so early? I thought you were too busy rounding up the sheep to come and play with us."

She smiles at him like he hung the moon and it's a struggle to keep the repulsion off of my face. Atticus is locked down hard and fast, not a single twitch or flinch to be seen in his face. Even his arm that I'm holding is relaxed which is good because it means they can't see the tenseness of my own stance.

"I brought your son and one of his little birdies to see you, Randy. She's not to your taste but I think Holden would like her."

Randy? I want to vomit and I keep my face blank but at the mention of Atticus's older and completely vile brother I have to force myself not to run screaming out of the room. Sure enough one of the door behind the table opens and out he walks, tucking his shirt back into his slacks so there's no mistaking what he's been doing out there.

New plan.

I'll call Illi back here to burn the place down to the ground, locking the door first so that we kill everyone in here while we're at it. Just wipe the entire place off of

the map and be done with it because the entire Crawford family is disgusting except for Atticus.

How the hell he ended up decent in that household is a miracle.

"Well, well, little Avery Beaumont. You grew up!" Holden says with a smirk and then he makes a big show of looking around me. "Where's Alexander? I thought the two of you were attached at the hip… honestly I thought he went from your mother's tits to yours but I'm not one to judge."

I loathe this man.

I loathe him almost as much I loathed Joey's existence.

"Lovely, my entire night has been ruined. All we need now is the pedophile drug addict to round things off. Where *is* Bing these days? Thailand? Cambodia?" I snark, and Atticus groans at me under his breath as Holden's eyes light up.

"I always did love a girl with spirit. I could break you nicely, Beaumont, and without your father around there's no one to save you now."

I roll my eyes at him, ignoring the danger I'm in because there's something about him that digs in under my skin. Probably the fact that, unlike Bingley, Holden looks similar to Atticus and Clarissa, their mother. Seeing the same steely gray eyes staring at me like he wants to flay the skin from my body is infuriating to me.

I hate the man.

"There are a lot of people who know that I'm here tonight. If you want to piss them off then go for it, Holden. I dare you to *break me*."

Lauren's eyes flicker at the scathing tone of my voice, like maybe hearing it is triggering some kind of memory in her void-like state and she's remembered who she really is but then it's gone and she's back to being nothing but a naked girl again.

Holden smirks at me and takes a step forward, that smirk turning vicious when Atticus moves to stand fully in front of me. Luca steps in closer to us both but he doesn't have the chance to throw himself at Holden and take the creep down.

Amanda holds up her hand and, shockingly, Holden stops in his tracks. "She belongs to the Wolf of Mounts Bay, has a diamond around her neck and everything. If you touch her you'll have half of the most dangerous crime lords of the state after you."

Randall glances up at me as well, and I keep my face blank. I'm shocked that she even noticed the diamonds tucked into my dress but from the moment Aodhan gave it back to me there's no way I'm taking them off again.

"The Wolf... so you know the Butcher too, then? Was it because of you that he took out your father? I should've known, you were always too good at corrupting the men

around you." Holden sneers at me, all of the joking wiped away from him now he knows where my protection comes from.

I'm intensely curious about how they know about Lips and which one of her jobs made them so cautious of her. Was it Amanda's military sniper or something else? I know she doesn't know any of the Crawfords, her reaction to finding out about Atticus's link to me was genuine and she would have told me if she'd met any of the other men, but there are plenty of people she could have taken out that would impress these men.

Also, I find it hilarious that they've assumed the Butcher took Senior out.

Nate is a very useful ally to keep a secret from anyone, especially this family if they're going to become a problem.

"What are you doing down here, Beaumont? Come to see my collection? Joseph wasn't one to keep trinkets but I'm more sentimental than he ever was." Randall says, and then he bends down to put his cigar out on the exposed skin on Lauren's shoulder.

Still, she doesn't react.

I step up until I'm standing at Atticus's side again and raise an eyebrow at him. "I'm here because your little friend thought this would scare me enough to stay out of your parties. I don't think she likes the reputation I have, petty jealousies of poor breeding, and she thought this

would scare me off."

I ignore her entirely and look back over to Holden. "I watched the Butcher carve a man to pieces last week. I watched the best shooter in the Bay lose his fingers thanks to my family, and I took delivery of the Wolf's enemies heads during the warfare of the Jackal's lost campaign to be the biggest name in the Bay. If you think same naked women will scare me… well that just speaks to just how little you really know, Crawford."

Holden straightens abruptly and I mentally give myself a point for that jab hitting the mark. It might be a teeny weeny lie but he doesn't need to know that I've done everything in my power not to watch any of the gruesome shit that my family is involved in.

Amanda watches the reactions on each and every one of the men, including Atticus and Luca. I wonder if that's what I look like to everyone around me, robotic and assessing as I take in all of the data and run calculations on the risks.

The door into this sadist's playground opens again and a slew of men walk in, all of them holding cigars and whiskey glasses as they laugh and joke amongst themselves. None of them are worried about the girls, not the one crying at the door or the others who have already been hollowed out to nothing but pretty, broken shells.

I memorize each and every one of their faces, searing

the names I do know into my memory forever because even in they don't fall in whatever warfare is about to break out I'll be coming after them and leaving nothing behind.

The Butcher doesn't let rapists live.

Neither does the Wolf or Ash Beaumont, hell, the entire family has a 'no forgiveness' policy.

Randall flicks a hand at us both. "I don't care for speaking to children who don't know their place. Show them out, Amanda."

She smiles and waves a hand at us. I'm about to tell her exactly what she can do with that hand because I'm done with this farce when Atticus gets ahold of my elbow again and steers me out.

When we get back into the elevator Amanda turns to me and says, "How close are you to the Wolf? I've been meaning to arrange a meeting with her but she's notoriously difficult to see."

I would rather throw myself into a vat of rotting corpses than make that introduction. No, I'd rather arrange for Lips to climb through this bitch's window and slit her throat while she slept but I play it coy, always extracting information, "Atticus could have brought you the Wolf if you wanted him to, why go through me?"

Amanda's head cocks to one side. "Could he? He always told his father that she sided with the Jackal. If he lied, well... Randy would be most displeased."

I glance over my shoulder at her, covering for him because I always will. My loyalty has always been unshakable. "Alliances change and evolve. When did you last ask him? She might be more favorable now that the Jackal's been dealt with."

She tilts her head and nods, staring at Atticus with a hunger that pisses me off even if he ignores it entirely. Why is she looking at him like that if she's very clearly in bed with his disgusting father and, very possibly, his brother too?

Finally she moves away from us both and back through the front door, smiling at Luca even while he stares her down in that very Mounty way he has.

I wonder where he came from?

Atticus grabs my arm while I'm distracted and walks me down the front steps, cursing under his breath about the entire night but I personally thought it went well.

I have a lot of leads to chase up now.

"Why did the girl at the front door upset you?"

He frowns when Aodhan's Impala pulls up to the curb. "She was new. They usually keep the girls in the back rooms until they've been broken in. I wasn't expecting someone still terrified at what's going on to be right there at the front door."

I open my mouth to reply but he leans down to open the door for me, snarling at Aodhan, "Take Avery home

and make sure she stays there. This is no fucking place for someone like her."

When he shuts the door behind me I watch him get smaller in the mirror and wonder exactly when we stopped respecting each other at the very least.

# Twenty One

## ATTICUS

The Mounts Bay Juvenile Detention Facility is highly overcrowded and underfunded.

It makes my job for the day much easier, not that I would ever tell Avery that, she looks at me like I've hung the moon when I pick her and Ash up to head over to meet this mobster cousin of hers.

I've known about him all along.

Alice had told Mother about him. Just once, she slipped up and mentioned him without meaning to and the horror on her face when she realized her mistake is still so clear in my mind that I don't think I'll ever forget it. Mother hadn't ever told Father about it, she enjoyed having that little card up her sleeve, but I know exactly why Alice was so horrified.

There were too many monsters in her world, lying in wait for an opportunity to strike, and the little O'Cronin

boy was born with a target on his back.

Avery is calm and steady when she climbs into the back of the limosine but Ash is in a foul mood. He barely spares me a glance, sitting close to her side and ignoring me the entire trip over. To anyone else he would look like an entitled rich brat but I know everything that goes on in the Beaumont manor.

I notice the stiff way he's moving and I'd bet every last dollar of the fortune I've amassed so far that he's covered in bruises.

The weight of the timeline I'm being forced into lays heavy over my shoulders but to strike too soon is to risk everything. If I pull them out of that house and Joseph Beaumont starts using his resources to come after us? He's old money, older than the Crawford's and even older than this country. His reach goes beyond that of the institution of the Twelve and I can't just rush into it.

If Ash dies at his brother's hands I will bear some of the responsibility.

Avery would never forgive me and I know I'd never forgive myself.

"Can he leave with us today?"

I look over at Avery and find her with her phone out, like always. She's cunning and calculating, all of the intellect of her father but none of the psychopathic tendencies. "You can meet him and see if he's open to your help. If

everything goes well we can get him out by the end of the week."

Ash scoffs and Avery tenses, her eyes sharp as she shoots him a look. He ignores me still as he speaks only to his twin. "What are you going to do when we see him and he's nothing but a mobster Mounty? You really want to take on a charity case from the Bay? This isn't a smart idea, Floss. We should have just gone to Morrison's and been done with it."

*Floss.*

The name I gave her all those years ago stuck.

My father's obsession with Roman gods and ancient warfare had filtered down to me until I knew the mythology well enough that even as a child I recognized the little girl I spent so much time around had to be a goddess reborn.

Not that I'd tell her that's where it came from.

Ash has been careful to never be in my company, not ever alone and he never speaks around me so I haven't heard him call her that before. It's hard because I wish I could speak to him more openly and find more ways to help him but he trusts no one.

No one but his one friend, the Morrison's unloved heir, and his beloved sister.

Avery shrugs at him and gives me a little smile, one she only ever sends my way. "I'm not going to leave him behind, not without meeting him first. I'm doing this for

Mom as much as I'm doing it for us. If she wrote him into her will then obviously she felt something for him… even if it was just obligation."

Ash looks ready to argue with her so I cut in. "I've arranged for him to be taken into an interrogation room, the type with a two-way mirror. You can see him first and then decide if you want to talk to him. There's no expectations here, if you decide you don't want to speak to him then we can just leave."

Avery nods and then slips her hand in Ash's. It's just a little movement, something I wouldn't have noticed if I wasn't watching her so carefully, but it settles him down enough that he's silent for the rest of the drive in.

When the car finally stops Ash climbs out and holds out a hand to help Avery out, all of the old world curtesy and charm that isn't readily found anymore but it's not just an act. He handles her like she's made out of glass when I'm sure he's the one covered in cracks.

He stays close to her side, like a guard expecting an attack, and I stay a full step away from them as if that will help settle him down a bit. He waits until Avery is busy signing into the visitors log before he speaks again.

"I don't know why you're helping us but I'd rather you fucking didn't." He hisses and I straighten my tie, acting as though I didn't hear him. He doesn't like having his own tricks used against him but, again, my hands are tied.

Thanks to my connections we don't have to wait, one of the guards takes us straight through to the observation room with a curious glance. It makes sense. We're in the worse institution in the country, the place all of the worst child offenders end up, and Avery has a Birkin bag in the crook of her arm.

She's definitely out of place here.

The guard leaves us in there alone and Ash looks around the room like he's waiting for the explosion to happen, all irritation and agitation.

"This is a bad idea, Floss." He murmurs, and she shrugs.

"I don't care. I have to know."

The moment the door to the interview room opens his face falls, the change in him so abrupt I almost get whiplash.

We all watch in silence as the one of the guards bring their cousin into the room.

"He looks just like Mom." Ash says, swallowing a little at the rasp in his tone.

Avery looks close to tears but her eyes are still sharp as the roam over his figure. "He's been fighting, the black eye and messed up knuckles give it away."

I shrugs at her. "It's a juvie in the worst city in the country, I'm sure he's been in a lot of fights."

Avery nods and steps closer to the glass, her gaze never

moving away from the O'Cronin boy. It doesn't matter that he's big for his age or the sour look on his face, he looks too fucking young sitting there in an orange jumpsuit on.

The tattoo on his jaw is grotesque.

The guard in there with him snaps, "Sit your ass down, O'Cronin."

The kid turns his head and smirks back at him, bravado he wears with ease. "You know how this goes, I'm not answering to that name."

The guard grimaces and snaps again, "Fine, *Arbour*, sit your ass down."

Avery jolts away from the glass.

I know the decision but I'm still shocked that Ash is the one to voice it out loud.

"Get him out."

# Twenty Two

## AVERY

Aodhan spends the night with me after the failed attempt to add to my roster. I barely sleep, the pent up rage and disgust at the entire Crawford family and that bitch Donnelley eats away at me until I end up down in my basement looking at the murder wall again.

I should really stop calling it that but after Illi had declared his intentions to wipe half of them from the face of the earth to clear up our schedules a little the name had stuck.

I'm completely on board with killing the Crawfords.

Holden always was a creep but seeing him last night confirmed that he needs to die whether Atticus likes it or not. He'd always told me how much he hated his family… well, he hinted to it. He was never vocal about them enough to actually say that he despised them but his disapproval of their… lifestyle was always clear.

Maybe I read that wrong.

He wasn't happy about me being in that room but Senior always lied to my mother about what he spent his days doing as well. She found out about his true depravity the day she died and tried to leave.

Has my love and obsession with Atticus blinded me in the same way?

Sometime after the sun comes up Aodhan finds me in the kitchen, baking out my rage and frustration with French Patisserie goods. He wisely doesn't comment, just takes the freshly brewed cup of coffee from me and takes a seat at the breakfast bar to dig into the fruits of my insanity.

"I'm gonna get fat spending all this time around here. How the fuck is Harley jacked up and not a fucking beach ball?"

I scoff at him and push the tray of jams in his direction. "Maybe because he spends half his life either working out or chasing his Mounty around like a little lost and very horny puppy? I'm sure that in itself burns a lot of calories, he could probably afford to ease up on the weights."

Aodhan chuckles at me and I try not to preen under his predatory gaze. He watches me like he's coveting me, planning out everything that he's going to do to me the moment he can, and after the pleasures I've had with him I'm not going to stop him.

Except if he tries anything in my kitchen.

I'm not a savage.

I'm rolling out pastry for three dozen croissants when he gets a call from Jack about a job they're doing for the Boar and he has to head out for the day. He doesn't look happy about it but honestly, I'm planning a quiet day of planning and assessing before I call Lips and discuss what the hell we're going to do about everything.

She's on her way to Texas to kill a biker for her half-brother.

I don't want to distract her from that job but I'm also very aware that she works best under pressure and with all of the facts. There's too many blank spaces on that wall of mine and if I want to fill them in I'm going to have to talk it through with both her and Illi. I need to know what they've heard of the Crawford family. Lips has other contacts, I'm sure we'll find out more of their story and know how best to strike them.

She could call Nate and ask him to look into it.

I brush that idea off the moment it enters my head. If Atticus is looking into Nate and what it is that he does when he's not killing for his sisters, then we don't want the self-aware psychopath coming back to the Bay or digging around in our delicate politics.

Aodhan presses me into the kitchen counter to kiss me senseless before he leaves, my head cradled in one of his big hands and the other on my hip to draw me in closer.

"Call me if anything happens. If Crawford shows up here I wanna know about it. I have a few things to say to him."

I roll my eyes at him but he doesn't back down, holding my gaze until I give him a halfhearted nod. I'll call him but I highly doubt Atticus will be back here.

He didn't even attempt to call me after the gala, why would he bother now?

If it weren't for Aodhan, the idea to give up on men altogether would be too tempting right now.

After I've filled my freezer with my baked good and scrubbed my kitchen completely I spend an hour on the phone with Ash to talk him down from running after Lips while she's on a recon trip at the Chaos Demon MC.

Harley went with her, leaving Ash to babysit Blaise because of the groupie problem he's been having, but my brother is not a man to sit around while the love of his life is in danger. If I were there with them it would be different, he could convince himself that watching me was a greater priority and Harley is more than capable to watch after Lips, but Blaise can take care of his own… we all know it.

Then I spend a few hours working on my dancing again because now that I stepped over that threshold with Aodhan's prodding I'm craving the burn again.

I go to bed that night with a text from Aodhan that he's still working the shipment and not to wait up. I'm grumpy

about it, who wouldn't be when orgasms that good are on the line, but the fact that he's letting me know where he is without ignoring me or making me feel guilty about wanting to know is another big point for him.

I'm woken by a phone call from Aodhan at stupid-o-clock. I haven't been woken up at this time since school finished and I'll admit I'm not in the best mood about it, especially because I went to bed alone.

"Someone had better be dying. If this is a booty call I swear I will *never* touch your dick again."

He huffs at my mood and then there's a little pause before he speaks, just long enough that I sit up in my bed as I prepare myself for the worst. "Listen to me, Queenie, I don't wanna do this. I really fucking don't, but I need you to go with the Crow back to his place for a few days."

I freeze and my tone goes icy cold without thought, "And why exactly would I want to do that? You know—"

He interrupts me, "I know exactly what that asshole did and I promise you, I'm not fucking happy about this. Something happened over here and I just need you safe for a few days while Illi and I sort it out. I called him before I called you but only because… fuck."

There's a beeping noise done the line and when I check my phone I find Illi trying to call me too. My insecurities might make me doubt Aodhan's intentions but I know Illi would rather bleed Atticus out than send me over there

without backup so whatever is happening, it's serious.

"Tell me everything while I pack a bag. You'd better promise me you'll be back to pick me up the second you can, O'Cronin, or I'll send the Wolf after you with a knife in the dark. We both know she'd do it for me."

He huffs and I can hear talking in the background of the call, lots of female voices, young and old. He's home, I can catch a few Gaelic words but I have no idea what they mean, I only recognize the intonation.

"I know she would and if it were for you, Queenie, I'd let her but… my house was shot up while I was working down at the docks. A spray of bullets over half the compound and no one saw a thing. The security cameras were cut so I have no fucking clue who was behind it. I assumed it was payback for Diarmuid because he did have a lot of friends but when I made it home to check out the damage I found a photo tacked to my front door from your little stalker… you and me with our eyes crossed out."

I curse under my breath and pull out one of my overnight bags, carefully folding my pajamas and underwear in there. Once it's full I pull out another and pack away jeans, shirts, yoga pants, and a few light sweaters.

I pack a third with dresses.

You never know how many outfit choices you might need and I'm angry enough to want a lot of options here.

"So we're being stalked and threatened together.

Lovely. Did you tell Atticus about this yet or shall I call ahead to warn him I'm coming to stay? He'll love this, you know? He's going to chain me up, lock the doors, and never let me see sunlight again. Call Ash and Harley sooner rather than later about coming to rescue me."

He doesn't laugh about my dramatics like I expect. That's more worrying than anything else he's said so far tonight. "What else? What aren't you telling me?"

I hear the crunching of his boots and the sounds of his family quieten down as he walks away from them. "The Crow is going to have a lot of questions about the photos. He's had a guy snooping around after me for weeks and he got down here not long after I did. I'd taken down the photos and I was vague about them because… I needed to warn you first and find out what we're going to say about them, to make sure our stories were the same."

I sit back on my heels in my closet and stare at the dozens of shelves, all of them filled with shoes, as the dread pools in my gut. "Where was the photo taken?"

He heaves out a sigh. "Don't panic. I've gotten all of the photos and I have them with me. If you don't want anyone to see them, then I'll burn them right now before Illi gets here but Avery… they're from the Jackal's lair. They're screenshots from the video recording. Someone has a copy."

I gag.

I need to vomit, I can't contain the deep sense of shame that overtakes me and triggers my stomach to empty, but I choke it down. Aodhan grunts like he's taken a hit and murmurs down the line to me all of the things he'd like to do to whoever the fuck has found that tape.

It doesn't matter though.

If it's out there it's only a matter of time before it becomes our problem.

It takes me a minute to get myself under control but when I do there's tears in my eyes and my voice comes out as a croak, "I told… I told Lips about it. She knows. Show Illi and tell him about what happened because I need that video gone, Aodhan. If Ash sees it… we can't let that happen."

Aodhan curses under his breath. "He's just gotten here. I'll take care of it, Queenie, just stay safe and I'll check in when I have something. You know we won't stop until this asshole is dead."

That's not as comforting as it should be because the fact of the matter is that Illi is going to know what happened now too. It's a necessary evil, I'd rather it be him than Ash or Harley, but it's just going to be another person picking over my decisions and seeing me in a different light.

I send Lips a text and for the first time since they left, I ask her to come home.

I immediately text her again and tell her not to, because

if she comes home then so will Ash and also for the first time I'm pissed my best friend is dating my brother because I need her but I can't risk him coming home and seeing something.

She texts me back and those five little words give me the strength to get up, take a shower, and be the woman I need to be to face Atticus right now because the Wolf of Mounts Bay has never let me down, not once in our entire friendship.

*I've called in a favor.*

I'm waiting on my front steps with my bags when the Rolls Royce arrives.

I'm shocked to see Atticus in the driver's seat and no Luca in the car, and when I start picking up my bags he gets out and frowns at me until I leave them for him to pack away in the trunk. It's still dark out, no signs in the sky yet of the sun coming up, and I pull the coat I'm wearing a littler tighter around my body.

"Thank you for picking me up. I could have driven myself but I appreciate you taking the time for me." I've collected myself enough to speak without choking on the words but my stomach is still a riot of panicked *what if's*.

He stares at me like I'm testing him and says in a low voice, "You shouldn't be driving if there's someone

threatening you. You shouldn't be alone."

I shrug and brush past him to open my own car door, ignoring the huffing he does in my direction. "You drove here alone. I imagine there are always threats on your life… especially when you consider the way you go about business. Why are you any different, Crow?"

He really doesn't like it when I call him that.

I *really* don't care.

"I wanted to have the opportunity to speak with you privately. Your recent… distaste for Luca meant that I thought it was a good idea to leave him back at my place until we've had this discussion."

I slide into my seat and let him shut the car door behind me. The car is stunning, everything that you could possibly want in a luxury car, and I look around at every little one of the details while he gets in and starts the engine.

I might get one of my own.

"I need to apologize—"

I cut him off, "Don't. I don't want or need it. Thank you for letting me stay with you, I'll stay out of your way if you stay out of mine."

He sighs at me and I take a better look over at him. His sleeves are rolled up on the dress shirt he's wearing and one of his arms has a trail of feathers down one side. I haven't seen him in less than a three piece suit for years… since he was nothing more than a child and I had no idea

he even had tattoos.

I mean, obviously I knew he had to have his markings for being a member of the Twelve somewhere in my mind but to see it for myself is another thing.

I want to know if he has any more.

"Avery, I'm trying to fix things between us. This is the first chance I've had to speak to you privately in months… years, even. Other than at the gala, I lost my head."

I look out of the window so I don't obsess over the tattoos enough that he notices my interest. "What you do with your head is none of my concern. You had every opportunity to do the right thing, Atticus, you chose not to."

My phone buzzes in my pocket and I think about ignoring it but when he glares down at it I can't help but pull it out and scroll through my messages slowly just to piss him off some more.

"I need your full attention, Avery. I'm willing to discuss some things with you now if it will repair what is happening between us."

I speak without looking up from my screen, "Is this because you know I'm seeing Aodhan? Is this your jealousy speaking?"

His jaw clamps shut and he speaks between his teeth. "If you want to play with Mounty trash then that's your own issue to deal with. I'm talking about what happened

with my family. I'm talking about the game you're playing with Amanda Donnelly that is more dangerous than you know."

My eyes narrow in his direction at his comment about Aodhan but I focus on the other issues for now. I can chew him out later about the absolute hypocrisy of talking down about Mounties when he himself is a member of the Twelve… a Mounts Bay institution.

"Give me one good reason to listen to you because everything you've given me so far has been veiled lies and half-truths for no reason other than keeping me out of your world. This isn't about the sex, Atticus. I think I'm ready to walk away from you if this continues because I'm not going to be treated like this… not even by you."

His hands tighten on the steering wheel until the leather creaks. I settle back in my seat, expecting that to be the conversation over with. There was a moment, after Luca had found me and Aodhan and walked me back out of the old and dilapidated bank, that I thought Atticus was going to finally open up to me. The look on his face when I walked out of there, covered in burns and bruises, wearing Aodhan's shirt and Luca's jacket… he looked at me like I was sun. Like everything in his world revolved around me, like I was the most precious thing he's ever encountered and he would live and die for me.

Something changed.

I don't know what happened after that day, but his carefully surveillance of my life went into overdrive and it was as though he no longer trusts me to keep myself safe. Something very obviously has happened but I don't know what is it.

If he can't trust me with it then I'm done.

"Your father has sold you at auction four times."

I freeze, only my head moving slowly so I can stare over at him. He keeps his eyes on the road, his hands still tightly wrapped around the steering wheel and his jaw is working as he grinds his teeth. I always knew he'd been protecting me but he'd never told me the finer details.

He doesn't sound tense though, he's just firmly laying down the facts that I was completely unaware of. "The Devil was only the last time he auctioned you off at those skin markets. The buyer before him collected women for the pleasure of owning them, the one before that was one of his business associates. The type of man that enjoyed slapping women around and belittling them, and he enjoyed them a little too young. I took care of both of them and so your father just kept using you as a threat to Ash until he would grow bored and attempt to sell you again."

"What about the first buyer?" I whisper, and he pulls into the driveway of his fortress-like mansion, the gates opening for him automatically.

"I bought you first. I bought you and I made

arrangements for you to move into my apartments in Mounts Bay. You could live there happily, and safely, without ever having to see Joey or your father again. I would have taken care of you until you were eighteen and made your own decisions."

My heart is beating too hard in my chest, loud in my ears. "You bought me… to keep me safe from Senior? Why didn't you tell me? Why didn't I get to stay with you?"

He stares at the gates but he doesn't make a move to direct the car down the driveway. "Ash. I was very aware that there was no way to get you and him both out. If I had've just taken you both your father would have thrown everything at me and I wasn't a match for him at eighteen years old. I needed this empire to be able to get you both out and… I knew you'd never leave your twin behind. I knew you'd never be whole without him. It was always my back-up plan, to just take you and run, but until Joey attacked you I thought you were safe enough in the house as long as I kept you from being bought."

I take a deep breath. "Did you know they were hurting Ash?"

He sighs and the leather on the steering wheel creaks again under the pressure of his hands. "I did. There was nothing I could do about it without risking everything. It is not a choice I would wish on anyone Avery but you know how far your father's net reached… there's still a lot of

clean up going on thanks to his death. It's never as simple as just killing an evil man. Dozens spring up in their place."

It's the answer I suspected but not exactly one I want to hear. "Tell me, then. Tell me who I need to neutralize and I'll do it. He was my father, my problem, and his death was for me. Why shouldn't I be the one cleaning up the mess?"

He straightens back up and finally moves the car forward. "I became the Crow for you, Avery. None of this will be worth it if anything happens to you."

I don't get the chance to argue with him, that same argument we always have, because the moment the car pulls up three men coming stalking over to empty my bags out from the trunk, two more opening the car doors for us both and taking care of our every need before I have the chance to answer Atticus.

I feel instantly smothered.

This is exactly what life in the Beaumont Manor felt like. Dozens of faceless, emotionless maids and butlers who saw nothing and everything. Who would take care of everything to the point that life was unbearably boring. I didn't even dress myself, bathe myself, I was thirteen and still had someone to buckle my shoes every day because to bend over and do it myself was unacceptable.

I didn't realize just how much I hated it until I had my own house with no one but myself wandering around the spaces, cooking for myself and cleaning everything

whenever I feel like it.

I don't know how Atticus can stand it either.

"Have dinner with me. We can finish this discussion over good food." Atticus says as he helps me out of the car.

I shrug at him. "I'm not sure there's much more to say."

He pulls me into his body, ignoring his people around us shifting away from the display. "There's always more, Avery. Between us, there will always be more."

# Twenty Three

I spend the day in the rooms Atticus has put aside for me planning out my next moves.

The first thing I do is call Lips and try not to lose my mind at her about what we're going to do.

"Stop worrying about Ash, he's distracted with trying to convince Harley to sneak off into the night and murdering Grimm Graves while we're here just to be for-fucking-sure he never comes after us… he's taken a very anti-father's stance on the tour. Blaise's dickhead father is on borrowed time."

I roll my eyes at her but I'm also secretly hoping Harley caves and they kill the biker asshole. "Have you heard from Illi? Aodhan just keeps telling me they've found someone and taking care of it but that tells me exactly *nothing*, Mounty."

She scoffs down the line at me and I can hear the murmuring of voices outside of the tiny bathroom she's locked herself in for this conversation. "Illi has been

keeping me up-to-date. Look, you probably don't wanna hear what they found down there until we have more details because… well, it looks like someone is trying to set Atticus up. Everything just keeps pointing to the photos and the drugs being him."

What?

That makes no sense to me and when I say exactly that to Lips she agrees with me. "Men don't look at women the way he looks at you if they're not fucking stupid about them. Now, sending death threats to Aodhan I understand but to you? No way. We know enough about him to know that he's not that guy."

I hum under my breath. "Well, who would be setting him up? We're looking into the wrong person because if this is about him then why are we trying to sift through my past for answers?"

Lips groans softly, an echo of my own frustration with the whole situation. "I fucking hate politics. All of these veiled threats and shit… if I want someone dead, I fucking kill them. Other people should do the same."

I chuckle at her, stretching out on the very nice bed Atticus has given me for the night. "If they did that then I'd probably be dead by now. We're lucky they're giving us time to find them and kill them."

She sighs at me. "You have a gun and a knife and I know I've taught you how to kill any asshole that tries to

touch you. Illi is your backup. Aodhan too now, I guess. You're not some weak damsel in distress, I wouldn't have left you if I didn't think you could hold your own. If Atticus starts making you feel weak then stab him, I'm fucking done with him making you feel this way."

I smile through the ache in my chest. "I love you, Mounty. Hurry up and finish that tour so we can plot our global domination and grow old together."

She giggles back at me, always sounding her age when does. Her throaty chuckles are all the streetwise kid older than her years but when I manage to get the giddy laughs out of her she sounds like the fifteen year old girl she should have been.

If her father wasn't biker trash and her mother wasn't a junkie bitch.

"I love you too, Aves. I'll be back before you know it."

She hangs up and I try to rest but my mind is too busy processing information and connecting dots to switch off. The information my hacker has for me on the Graves siblings is infuriatingly sparse and no matter how many times I read it, the eighth siblings name doesn't magically appear.

I'll have to seek other sources for help, as much as I don't want to.

A maid interrupts me around midday to ask if I want to go down to lunch but I'm too engrossed in my work and

she brings me a tray of foods to eat at the small table in my room. The salad is good, the dressing is clearly made fresh and lifts the whole meal, but it's served with fresh bread and a platter of meats that are to die for. If I ever consider getting a live in chef I think I'll steal whoever it is that Atticus employs.

I'm pouring over the Chaos Demons clubhouse blueprints, finding the best routes in and out for Lips, when Atticus knocks at the door and lets himself into the room. I frown at him, not at all expecting him to be dropping by for a casual chat, and he frowns right back at me.

"Are you really not going to come to dinner? I asked the chef to cook the stuffed lobster you love."

Damn him.

I didn't realize all that time had passed and there's absolutely no way I can say no to an offer of that dish. It's my favorite, which he well knows, and I haven't eaten it in *years*.

"I've been busy, I assumed one of your poorly tailored men would come and fetch me for you when you were ready for my presence." I say as I tap through the images on my phone, encrypting them and saving them away for closer inspection after we've eaten.

The frown looks as though it's permanently etched into Atticus's face and when I slip my feet back into my shoes he hands out an arm for me to take. "I wouldn't send up

someone to get you if I thought you would be happy to see me. Every time I see you these days it seems I'm waiting for you to pull a knife on me… or yourself."

I roll my eyes at his dramatics as he leads me down the stairs, his men stationed around every corner. It feels smothering, like I can't breath with all of their eyes on my every move, but I keep my head held high and my gaze icy. I don't want to show any sort of discomfort or weakness here.

I know they all report back to their boss and I don't want Atticus having anything to use against me.

As we walk into the elaborate dining room, with the most exquisite artworks that my mother would have loved, I glance over at the paneling and make a note of the lines on the wood there that aren't a feature the builder wants your eye to follow. He's blended them well but my eye is too good for that kind of trickery.

Useful information for later.

Atticus pulls out a chair for me and we eat dinner together as if nothing has ever come between us. I want desperately to believe it.

But I know it's a lie.

"I told you I don't want to argue with you, Floss. Please can we just eat dinner and talk like we used to?" He murmurs to me, his lips brushing against my ear and I have to hold in a shiver at the feeling.

I nod and take the seat, letting him fuss over me before he take the seat next to mine at the head of the table. His manners are absolutely impeccable, the type you have to be born into because no one taught at a later age can run through them quite as smoothly, and as soon as he's relaxed into his seat the door at the end of the room opens.

Within seconds there are dozens of dishes laid out on the table for us to choose from, not unlike the dinner I had cooked for Aodhan. The room feels different though, the intimate feel completely missing, but still there's some part of me that craves this moment with my childhood crush.

He really has *crushed* me.

"Tell me about Amanda Donnelley."

His eyes snap over to mine as he passes me a plate loaded to the brim with vegetables sautéed in garlic butter. "We're having dinner together, isn't there something else you'd rather talk about?"

I take a glass of wine from one of the butlers. "You told me I only have family and pawns, and you've chosen not to be my family so I'm not sure there is much else to speak about."

He takes a sip of his own glass of bourbon, the same that Ash prefers, and then he reaches over to take my hand.

I hate myself for the way my stomach fills with flutters for him.

I hate it.

"I will tell you about her if you promise to stop acting like you hate me. You're breaking my heart, Floss."

Fuck. "You don't have one... or maybe it's just impossible to reach. How about you tell me about her and I'll take your information into consideration next time I see the bitch in public?"

He scowls at me but nods anyway. "Amanda Donnelley, on paper, is the only daughter to a very old family from the West Coast. Her mother was an heiress from Europe and her father was from a long line of successful businessmen but he never migrated to the states with his family, preferring to stay where his business is."

I shrug. "And on paper I'm a graduate of the finest school in the country taking a gap year to find myself after four boring years of dance and study. Paper doesn't mean shit to me, Atticus."

He shrugs and takes a napkin to wipe at his mouth like he's finished his meal even though he's barely touched it. "She's the bastard daughter of a Columbian drug lord... and she's the only woman your father ever had a relationship with who didn't die at his hands."

I very slowly set my cutlery down.

That is probably the single most horrifying thing Atticus should have said about her because to bed my father... willingly? The man who enjoyed the most violent and sadistic torture? No, he needed it to be able to get off

and now, *now* I know for sure that Amanda isn't just a fucking bitch.

She's clearly fucking deranged and she needs to die.

After dinner Atticus offers to walk me up to my room to get changed before we leave for the Twelve meeting together.

I narrow my eyes at him, because I'm not an idiot and he's being just a little too accommodating after the nightmare of a conversation over the main course. I make sure to walk with him slightly in front of me but after we get to the stairs it's clear that none of his men are following us and there are none of them to be found on the third floor where my rooms are.

"What are you doing, Atticus? What are you playing at, because I don't have time for games tonight." I say with a sigh, suddenly so tired of playing these games with him.

There's nothing I love more than moving the pieces across the chessboard but we've been playing together for years and I'd like it to be over.

I'd like to have him or just leave him.

We get to my room and Atticus opens the door for me, gesturing into the room like he's being nothing but a well-bred gentleman exactly how his bloodline intended for him except that Luca is sitting on the lounge chair in my room.

I turn to face Atticus but he grabs my arm and pulls

me the rest of the way in, snapping the door shut behind us both.

"What the hell do you think you're doing? Get your hands off of me, you have no right to lock me in here!"

I shake his hand off even as he does what I say but he takes a step back until he's physically blocking the door. "You'll be safe here with Luca. These threats have been too specific, too pointed for the stalker not to know about your movements. There's no way we're going to risk you coming to the meeting."

If I were any other member of my family, I'd take a swing at him. I don't know why he's so desperate for me to hate him but he really is shoving me off that cliff and into loathing. "There's no way you can know that! There's no way you could possibly know that tonight is the night that the stalks would do something and it's good to know that you believe your own men to be so inept that they can't keep me safe during the meeting. I, however, have full faith in Illi and the Stag. I'll just call one of them to pick me up."

He doesn't move an inch at my threat and I snap. "If you walk out of that door and leave me here I will—"

His lips are rough against mine as he cuts me off with a kiss and I bite his lip in frustration. It doesn't even slow him down, he just grabs my hips and walks me backwards towards the bed.

I let him for a half second before I remember Luca is sitting there.

I break away from him. "Have you lost your goddamn mind? You can't just kiss me into submission, I'm going to the meeting! Lips named me her representative and I'm going. You're a stickler for the rules, Atticus, you can't break this one."

He lets me go fully and, though his lips are wet from my kiss and his hair is messed up from my hands, his eyes are as cold as ever. "I told you, Floss. I'd rather you be alive and hating me than have you and lose you to death. Luca will keep you safe and he'll keep you here. I'll make sure no big decision are made until the Wolf returns home."

My lip curls but his eyes flick over to Luca and for once the grinning idiot looks somber at his task for the night.

Probably because he knows I'm going to *burn this motherfucker to the ground.*

I pull myself up, roll my shoulders back and then I cross my hands in front of my body, the standing variation of the Avery Beaumont Power Pose.

Atticus doesn't give a shit about it, he just turns on his heel and walks out the door.

The moment it clicks shut I go for my phone only to find the pocket of my dinner jacket empty.

Atticus took it while he distracted me with a kiss.

I have to rein in my rage, hold it back and make a plan because there's no doubt in my mind that I can get out of this room without having to commit murder.

"The door isn't locked Avery, but there's no way I'm letting you out of my sight. The Crow was very clear about keeping you in the house, safe and secure."

I glare over at him and I wait. I wait until I'm sure Atticus has left and is on the road to the meeting. Luca checks his phone a couple of times and I'm careful about being discreet as I take note of where he's keeping his phone. The same pocket has a slight bulge, either a wallet or keys and the main doors of this place will require a swipe card to get through. He also has three guns, one in his boot and two on either side of his hips.

I pout. I pout in a way that I've never pouted before with anyone other than my family. I force my eyes to get a little teary, I huff out a breath a few times like I'm throwing a full mental tantrum and when I see Luca's shoulders slump a little I know I've psyched him out. He thinks I'm lost without my phone and my endless supply of helpers so now is the right time to act.

I feign a slip.

One of the biggest lessons Lips had taught me was to work smart not hard.

Luca is easily three times the size of me. He's tall, taller even than Ash, and he's obviously been working out

even more now that he's not being forced to follow the Jackal around all day. There's no way in a fair fight I'd be able to win against him.

So I'm not going to fight fair.

It's not fair of them to all think that I can't handle myself in this situation. They won't let me make my own decisions about what I can and can't do which is utterly ridiculous because I'm not overestimating what I can handle.

I knew I couldn't kill Diarmuid so I asked Aodhan to do it for me.

I know I would be safest here while Illi and Aodhan went hunting for whoever is sending the photos in the first place so I didn't argue about it.

Not once have I let my ego lead me to my own destruction.

I leave that idiotic bullshit to the men.

So as I pace the floor in front of the bed I wait until I'm out of Luca's reach and I cry out, crumpling to the ground like I've twisted my ankle. My bag is within reach from here and thankfully Lips has given me a list of things to always have on hand.

The number one thing being cable ties.

Luca jumps up from the bed and rushes over to me, crouching down to fuss over me like I'm a damsel in distress.

It's like riding a bike, the amount of times Lips and I worked on the simple maneuver and in under three seconds I have Luca on his back with his hands secured behind his back. I'd asked her about it but she had learnt it from an old Taekwondo teacher she had in the Bay. It's the one thing she's still very closed mouth about, that man who taught her how to disarm people like size doesn't matter at all.

"What the fuck?!" Luca grunts and I lower myself down until we I can whisper in his ear, "Compliments of the Wolf of Mounts Bay. I choose not to kill you on a daily basis. Remember that."

I then pull his phone out of his pocket and dial Illi's number, frisking him for keys or a card swipe in case I need one to get out of here.

"You had better be calling to tell me your boss changed his mind or there's about to be a whole new fucking war in the Bay. Where the *fuck* is she?"

I chuckle under my breath at him, tugging on the zip tie one last time to make sure it's tight. "It's me. I need a pick up, Luca is a little tied up."

There's a pause and then Illi roars with laughter down the line, so loud I have to move the phone away from my ear so he doesn't blow out my ear drum. "Ah, Queenie, you never stop surprising me. I'm already at the door, am I breaking it down or can you walk out?"

I keep the phone at my ear while I strip out of the jacket I'm wearing and I pull one of my white blazers on, grabbing my ghost gun and slipping it into my purse. Luca starts grunting on the ground as he tries to free his hands and I smirk down at his struggling back.

It's good to be on the other side of the equation.

"If any of Atticus's other men try to stop me, I'll shoot them dead."

Illi grunts. "Keep me on the line, kid. I'll come fucking running the second I hear a bullet leave the chamber."

I slip my heels back on and then walk out of the room with my head help high and I smirk on my face. I also have a gun in my hand and I'm not at all the naive girl they think of me.

I don't aim it at any of the men keeping guard in the halls.

No, I press the barrel to my own temple and then I watch them all sweat like a whore in church over it. Not a single one of them approach me, all of them vaguely terrified that I'll accidentally pull the trigger like some inept little girl.

I'm tempted to tell Illi to come in here and gut them all for the insult.

When I reach the door there's a maid standing there in her pristine black uniform with a phone in her hand. When I approach she switches it to speakerphone.

"Avery, do not walk out that door." Atticus snarls down the line, none of his usual cold calm to be heard.

I tilt my head at the woman, ignoring the sounds of Luca being freed from upstairs and raging his way down the flights of stairs. Instead I point the gun at the woman's head and smirk.

"Like I give a fuck about the help. Move or die, the choice is yours."

Unlike every last one of the bodyguards, this woman judges my seething rage correctly and knows I won't just pull the trigger.

I'll do it with glee.

She side steps and I swipe Luca's card to open the door. He yells out my name but the moment it swings open Illi appears in the doorframe and the air gets sucked out of the entire foyer at the rage in him.

I hang up and throw Luca's phone onto the ground, slipping the gun back into my purse with the safety on as Illi crushes the phone under his boot.

"You okay, Queenie? I'm under strict orders from the kid to go full bloodshed and gore on this place if you have so much as a scratch but I didn't need her permission to do it, I'm fucking *itching* for it."

I glance over my shoulder at Luca and let all emotion drain out of my until I'm my usual cold shell. "I'm fine. We're late for a meeting, Illi."

# Twenty Four

The meeting is being held at the Unseen MC clubhouse and the drive there isn't so long that Illi and I can discuss absolutely everything that has occurred since we last saw each other, the debrief we really need, but I do manage to tell him about that bitch Amanda Donnelley and her sexual deviancy… because *of course* you'd have to be fucked up to bed Senior.

My mother was naive and compliant to the match her parents picked out for her, obedient and loyal to a fault.

Amanda doesn't have that excuse.

"I'll kill the bitch, just tell me where she spends her days and I'll carve her the fuck up."

I smirk at him, totally on board for her getting the most blood-soaked and violent death, and murmur, "The moment I know that information, it's yours. I have to give it to her, she's very skilled at staying off of the map."

Illi shrugs. "Isn't that the Coyote's job? Throw it at him and tell the little fuck to earn his spot on the family

protection roster. He called last week about some asshole showing up to his bunker and threatening to blow the place up."

I raise an eyebrow at him. "Who the hell is trying to kill him? Let me guess, he hacked into some guys records for extortion purposes and it's backfired on him? Typical."

"Doesn't matter, the asshole is dead now and the Coyote lives to rifle through someones emails another day."

"How do you go about assassinating someone? Say I needed a man to be taken out without being linked to me, how would I do that?"

He grumbles under his breath, as he weaves through the traffic as we get closer to the slums of the Bay. "You call me or Lips and you ask one of us to do it for you. Your job is the politics bullshit that we hate and all the other evil genius shit that you do. You don't need to become a killer just for fucking credibility. Don't let that piece of shit Crow make you think any differently."

When we arrive at the clubhouse Illi parks up but he doesn't make a move to get out of the car. I wait with him, expecting him to warn me about some new threat or tell me we're waiting on Aodhan, when he blows out a breath and rubs a hand over his face. "Look. O'Cronin told me about what went down thanks to that fucking cunt D'Ardo. I've watched you two together to know he isn't lying about the how of it but I need you to know that you say the word and

he's dead. Fuck, Queenie, you say the word and they're all dead. I knew… fuck, I got one look at you coming out of there and I knew something had happened but I thought it was D'Ardo. I wish I could cut his fucking head off all over again."

It's very sweet and very Illi of him. "I appreciate that but I'm not traumatized by it. It's… it was the lesser of all of the evils and I definitely don't want you to kill Aodhan. He's been… he's been perfect. I'd just rather never talk about it again and I definitely cannot let Ash know about it or see those photos. Illi, he's a lot more like Senior than people think, he's just— he uses those skills for the people he loves, not against us. If he finds out then he will destroy *everything*."

Illi nods and we both watch as Aodhan walks out of the clubhouse and makes a beeline towards the car. "He's a good man… was a good kid too. Did a fucking good job of growing up right with the shit hand you two were dealt. I'm gonna find the asshole who has the tape. I promise you."

I nod and then my car door opens, Aodhan helping me out and pulling me into his arms. "I'll beat the life outta that fuck for trying to lock you down, Queenie. I'll take him the fuck out."

Burrowing into him a little, just for a second, I reply, "It's fine, I proved a point. I doubt his staff will stare at me

like I'm a little defenseless girl anymore."

I pull away from his as he chuckles and Illi stalks past us towards the clubhouse. "I'm assuming if you're out here then they're waiting on us, O'Cronin? I have some words for that fuck Crawford."

We follow him into the building and I thank God that I haven't been forced into this building before and I pray I never have to set foot into it again because the smell… the *smell* is fucking foul.

I gag.

Illi chuckles at me. "Yeah. The sweet stench of stale beer, cigars, and pussy. It's not really your scene, Queenie."

I choke the words out past the sleeve of my blazer that I press over my nose. "We're burning this place to the ground the second Lips is home to help out. I won't be able to sleep tonight knowing it's sitting here, stinking like this, is in the same state as I am."

Aodhan chuckles at me and tucks me into his side a little more securely as we walk past a large table of bikers, gambling and drinking together like this place isn't the pits of hell.

"You wouldn't have survived the Bay. Liam's place was worse than this. Still is, we haven't done a thing with it since we buried the asshole."

Unacceptable. "Illi, add it to the list. We'll take it out as well."

Aodhan and Illi share a look but I ignore them as we get out to the back rooms, a large round table set up there and already half-filled with the other members of the Twelve. The loathing that Atticus throws at Illi and Aodhan is like a physical thing. It's the first time I've seen him show any emotion at one of these meetings and all of the other members are taking note of it too.

I don't give a fuck.

I take a seat and Aodhan sits down next to me. "I'll have my phone back now, Crow."

His eyes barely change when they flick to mine as he slides it across the table. He probably is counting this as another show of weakness at this table of important people but he's putting value in them that they don't deserve.

I could destroy them all right now if I wanted to.

"Coyote, we need to start this or we'll be here all night. We've already been delayed." Atticus snaps.

I look over and find Jackson staring at the wall of mugshots with a smirk. "There was no way I was gonna let you start without her here, like I'd be dumb enough to get on Beaumont's bad side. I like my balls where they are, thanks, and rumor has it she's fully trained with a knife *compliments* of the Wolf herself. No fucking thanks. Hey, where's the guy from this pic, Boar? He looks fucking familiar."

The wording is a little too close for a coincidence so I'd

guess that he was watching the security cams of Atticus's mansion as I took down Luca… which means there's a camera in my bedroom.

Assholes.

The Boar glares at Jackson like he'd enjoy peeling the skin from his body but that might just be his relation to the Devil showing through. "None of your fucking business, asshole. *The Queen* is here so you can sit your ass down and get this over with."

The vitriol that he uses to spit out my name is vicious but I guess he's only decent to his blood and I am definitely not a Graves child.

The meeting is a boring one, full of turf arguments and whining over the Jackal's assets. The Bear wants to take some over, as reparations for his businesses lost, and Atticus shuts that idea down quickly.

"Nothing is stopping you from picking your business back up, stick with what you're good at."

The Bear's lip curls at him and Jackson bursts out laughing. "He can't! No one fucking wants to pledge themselves to the guy who lost everything by choosing the wrong side. Where are all of your men, Bear? Ohhh that's right, rotting in a federal prison."

The Bear snarls back at him, "They wouldn't be fucking there if the Wolf had've stopped being a fucking c—"

I interrupt him, "I'm assuming you're about to say

something that will end in the Butcher hacking your body to pieces and I'm wearing white so let me just stop you there. You lost everything because you got too full of yourself. You're lucky you only lost you business and not your head like the other men and women who crossed us."

The Bear stares at me and then slowly around the table at each of the other members, like he's waiting for one of them to tell me to shut up.

Even in his rage at me being here, Atticus won't say a word against me in this issue.

The Fox, the Tiger, the Ox... every last member remembers all too clearly what happens when you betray the Wolf or speak out against her. The finer details might still be concealed but it's clear that speaking out against the Wolf gets you killed in the worst ways and there's no one here today who is willing to risk that. At least, not so openly here in front of me and the Butcher.

"Let's move on. Are there any other issues that need to be addresses?"

There's silence around the table, mostly because everyone is still looking between the Bear and me, and then the Fox speaks up.

"When are you gonna tell us all that you're the one pushing the Jackal's product, Crow? Isn't that part of his empire that we vote on who gets it? Seems like you have

your own rules for yourself and another set for the rest of us."

It's the most words I've ever heard the man speak. He looks like a washed up rave rat with colorful tattoos over his face and neck. If I saw him at a party I would think he was high and way too old to be out in the Bay but he's the mastermind behind all of the parties on the docks, all of the must-be events that no Mounty would dare miss out on attending.

He's the reason I had to attend in my lingerie junior year, the asshole.

Atticus stares him down with utter disdain. "If I had control of the Jackal's product I would destroy it. Do you have any idea how many people have died from his dirty batches? If I had to guess who was moving it I'd say it's you or the Bear so tread carefully."

The Fox smirks. "Sure, sure. That's the story you're going with. I'm just saying, there's a lotta suits in the Bay these days and all signs are pointing at you. Is the Wolf in on it too? She was always pretty anti drugs so I'd be surprised. Are you a part of her little family or did I miss the memo?"

There's a lot of shifting around in seats, everyone but Atticus and myself are uncomfortable at witnessing this.

Just because I'm sure he isn't the dealer, doesn't mean everyone else has the same conviction.

The Viper grunts under his breath and he spins the rings on the hand that still has all of the fingers. "This is what happens when do-gooders come to the Bay. The Crow fought to keep the skin auctions out of business; why would we believe he's moving the drugs? Fuck, next minute he'll be in my fucking bar tryna shut down my fights. Or will it be the parties, are you pissed enough at losing your girl to the Stag down at the docks that you'll go after the Fox's business?"

I roll my eyes at the snarling and arguing that explodes around the table.

It's going to be a long night.

As much as I want to go home with Aodhan, the O'Cronin compound doesn't have the security that even my mansion has and there's no way he can come home with me tonight. The favor Lips had called in has come up with three new leads on who the hell is stalking me and leaving the photos. Illi is meeting up with one of his contacts about one of the leads while Aodhan will be heading down the coast to meet with another.

Jack will be staying close in case I need anything in the short term which is very helpful now I've planned out the rest of my evening.

We leave the Twelve meeting together where nothing

was achieved except to know that the fractures from the Jackal's betrayal are only getting bigger.

Aodhan climbs into the Butcher's car with us as they drive me back to the Crow's mansion for safe keeping. He's not happy about the plan but I'd discussed it with Illi and we're both sure enough about Atticus' intentions and their ability to get me out of there that I'm fine with taking the security of the mansion for the night.

Atticus will be too angry at me ignoring his demands to skip the meeting to bother me, I'm sure, so it's the perfect time to get some work done.

The only problem is that the moment I slide into the passenger seat, my phone rings with an unknown number.

Illi frowns at me when I turn the music off but the moment the phone reaches my ear the fake honeyed tones of Amanda Donnelley greet me, "A perfect little birdie, playing a game much too far out of her league."

The sound of her voice is like nails on a blackboard to me now, but I'm nothing if not an expert at hiding my irritation from people beneath me. "I'm sure you've built your business up from the ground by passing gossip around from all of your whoring but some of us have more worthwhile things to do than sitting around passing off insults like it's a useful way to spend our time. Is there something of value you have to say or just a general call of idle threats and posturing?"

She's just as good as I am at playing the mind games needed to wage these kinds of war. She giggles down the phone to me, and I know for sure it's a calculated move because of the careful tone of it. She's trying to irritate me into making a wrong move here; I have no doubt she has something up her sleeve from her tryst with Senior.

That's her game plan.

Like it or not, we're women playing in a man's world and one of the reasons I chose not to date a lot in high school is because perceptions of women in our society are deeply rooted in our gender and sex. I hate it, I hate the double standard, but there's only so much that I can do about it.

Does it make me a monster to use those stupid, patriarchal standards to tear this woman down? Probably.

Is that going to stop me?

Absolutely not.

My family relies on me. I'm the fixer; I sort out anything that shows up on our doorstep that might risk our safety. I play the political games in the upper society and Lips handles the criminal underworld.

There's nothing I wouldn't do to keep us all safe.

"I thought you were planning on building your empire out of Crawford's ashes? Every day I see him alive, the more that I know you're a weak-willed little girl, too caught up in her feelings to do what is required to dominate in our

world. You'll end up in chains at his feet like the others."

I scoff at her. "You expect me to believe that Crawford is just like the rest of his family? We've known each other since we were children; you've missed the mark on that one."

She giggles down the line at me again and I start to think that maybe she was dropped on her head as a child or maybe that Colombian father of hers slipped too much coke in her baby bottles to shut her up and it's ruined her brain because there's definitely something unhinged in her.

"You've strayed too far from home, little bird. You might need to call your brother home to rescue you."

She hangs up on me and I slide my phone back into my pocket. The car stays silent for half a breath and then Illi drawls, "What did the slimy cunt want this time? Did she finally muster the courage to ask you out? She's fucking gagging for it."

I shudder and throw him a dirty look. "Don't even joke about it. She's trying to bait me into turning on Atticus; the entire Crawford family ignored him for so long and now they've opened their eyes up to the empire he's built."

Illi shrugs at me. "So they're doing the usual bullshit and hitting him where it hurts him most… typical that you're the one who's gotta hurt for him."

Aodhan leans forward from the backseat and snaps, "Except she isn't gonna get hurt because it's not up to

Atticus to protect Queenie. It's on all of us and I'm not going to sit back and play games with these silver-spoon assholes. I'm fucking finding them and taking them out; we're not waiting around like last time."

Illi grunts in agreement, clearly impressed at his initiative, and says, "Lemme deal with Crawford, Queenie. I have you covered."

When we arrive back at the manor, Atticus and Luca are already there waiting for us. Aodhan gets out first and helps me out of the car, snarling at the first of Atticus' men to approach him to get the fuck away from me. I ignore the looks I get from the entire staff as Aodhan pulls me into his arms.

"Gimme two days to find this guy, Queenie. Two days and I'll have the fucker buried and we can go back to sleeping in that big old princess bed of yours."

I snort at him and pull him down to kiss me, completely unrepentant of our audience… right up until Illi interrupts us.

He opens the car door and climbs out to lean against the roof of the car, looking all sorts of dangerous and at ease. "The Wolf called, she just wanted me to remind you that she's more than happy to use every resource at her disposal to get Avery out of this building if you try your bullshit again. Her brother is in town, y'know. He stopped in to keep an eye on shit for her."

Aodhan's arms tighten around me. With his back to Atticus he mouths to me, "Brother?"

I can't tell him.

We all made the agreement not to speak about him outside of those of us who already know about Nate unless it's absolutely necessary, and I don't think this casual threat is worth freaking Aodhan completely out… not without speaking to Lips about it first.

I trust Aodhan completely, and he might have been voted into the family, but this isn't just about Lips. It's about Poe's safety and she's barely fifteen.

I shake my head just a little bit and murmur, "I'll… I'll have to tell you later."

He frowns a little but nods, giving me one last kiss, and then he pulls away from me to turn and glare at Atticus again.

I'm glad he doesn't try to walk me over, I'm not a possession to be passed between them, and I walk toward the front door. Atticus looks down at me like he wants to strangle me and Luca's lip is still curled at the sight of Illi grinning out on the driveway.

"Thank you for letting me stay even after I assaulted your best bodyguard. Luca, I hope I didn't hurt you," I say, in my sweetest voice that I'm sure is killing them both.

Atticus gestures at his front door with one hand. "My home is always open to you, Avery. I hope this time you

value your life enough to stay here where you're safe."

I straighten my blazer and walk up the front steps, enjoying the looks each of Atticus' staff give me as I pass them. All it took was one little maneuver and they're all now completely aware that I'm not messing around.

As I get to the door, I hear Illi call out behind me, "Oh, and Luca? Make her feel shit about the Jackal again and I'll feed you to the cannibals, piece by piece. Nothing would make me happier than knowing they were digesting you and shitting you out."

J BREE

# Twenty Five

The fortress that Atticus lives in is practically impenetrable.

It was built with that exact purpose thanks to the Jackal's many attempts to assassinate his fellow member of the Twelve and, on paper, it is completely structurally impossible to get in or out of it without being seen and stopped, one way or another.

The problem is that I was raised in the Beaumont Manor.

I know exactly how filthy rich men think and I know a secret passage opening when I see one. Ash and I used to use the servants' passages all the time growing up even though we risked death if Joey or Senior caught us.

Ash slept in my bed more often than his own after Mom died.

He was terrified that Senior would come to kill me next, and even after we moved to boarding school he'd come and sleep in with me just to be sure I was safe.

He calls me most nights he's gone now too.

I thought that the distance would be good for him, that it would help him to fully believe that we're safe now, but he's still borderline neurotic about my safety.

I love him for it and I think if he were traveling with anyone other than Lips Anderson, the Wolf of Mounts Bay and a girl who's been obsessed with him for far longer than she'd ever care to admit, I'd be just as bad.

She walked into Senior's murder room to die for us both.

I'd trust her with so much more than my twin's life at this point. My life would've been so much easier if we'd both been lesbians and I could have married her by now.

I sometimes think we're the real high school sweethearts of the family but I would never say that to any of the guys.

They whine too much.

So even after Atticus leaves me in the formal living room like some fainting, pathetic maiden, I pull my phone out and text the only other person I'm sure would know about the passages.

Jackson.

Which service hall will get me out? I have somewhere I need to be.

I inspect the hemline of my skirt while I wait for the little cretin to get back to me. He's not my favorite tool thanks to his betrayal of Lips to Nate. It doesn't matter to

me at all that Nate was looking for information to protect his sister; Jackson couldn't have really known that he was on our side.

He didn't breathe a word to us until after Nate saved Lips' life.

Not once, even when the heads began cropping up and we'd called all of the meetings with the Twelve.

Lips and I agreed that it didn't get him kicked out of the family, but it definitely has him on my watch list. I'm not sure he realizes he has a strike against his name but all it's going to take is the slightest thing and Illi can carve him to pieces for us.

It would be a shame.

His computer skills are unmatched.

I've got eyes on you. Go to the wood paneling behind you, take two lefts and then straight until you get to the end door. Text me when you're there and I'll override the sensors there so he doesn't get an alert.

I'm quiet and careful to not be seen by any of Atticus' men but in under a minute I'm walking down a pitch-black hallway with the light of my phone, my heels slipped off and in my hands so my feet can be silent on the concrete floor.

Jackson's directions are perfect and I find myself climbing out of a storm bunker onto the next street over from the fortress-like mansion, in a small patch of trees

that hide the exit perfectly.

When I get back out to the road, Jack is already there waiting for me, the engine running and the lights off so he's less visible, and when I slide into the passenger seat, he tips his head at me in greeting before taking off. Watching him drive is like watching Harley behind the wheel, the smooth actions of someone who truly loves the muscle car they're in total control of.

Other than saying hi, he doesn't speak and I get the whole drive over to the Coyote's bunker to work through the information I have. It's a nice change of pace and I'm grateful for it.

Viola looks happier than she ever did at Hannaford.

She opens the door to the bunker with a grin, her eyes squinting a little like she hasn't seen sunlight for months. Her hair is longer, the streaks in it a vibrant pink now and her nose piercing has been changed to a ring. She's wearing one of Jackson's band tees that's hanging down past her knees and a long pair of socks just like Lips does when she's feeling self-conscious about her scars.

"Queenie? What are you doing in our neck of the woods?"

I lean down to put the little plastic booties over my Louboutins and she giggles at me maniacally. "I need some information. This is a family matter but I'm willing to pay for Jackson's time."

She shrugs and pushes the door wider, ushering me in. "Family means family, you don't pay for that shit."

Jackson calls out from deeper in the bunker, "Don't say that! Keeping you fed is fucking expensive!"

I roll my eyes and Viola does the same. A smirk tugs at the corner of my mouth. "Mounties are weird about money and food, something about never having them wires their brains wrong."

Viola shrugs and leads me down the hall. It looks much cleaner in here than Lips warned me and from the look Viola gave me I'll assume she's been cleaning the place up. It's not up to my standards but I think the plastic booties might be overkill.

We get to an open spiral staircase into a large, dark room. There are computers everywhere, dozens of them, and there's code running on the screens of some of them, security footage on others. Jackson is sitting in a gaming chair with a pair of hot-pink bunny ear headphones on that look ridiculous hanging around his neck.

"You didn't mention the place you needed to be was here, annoying me."

I can't come up with an answer to that because I'm too busy staring at the bin overflowing with empty energy drink cans and candy wrappers next to his chair. I look a little closer at the desk and it's clear he's been working too much to take any real care of himself because he looks

faintly… greasy.

Disgusting.

Viola snorts at me. "He's showered, Beaumont, stop wrinkling your nose at him like some stuck-up socialite."

I narrow my eyes at her. "I am a stuck-up socialite, Ayres, and I highly doubt he's actually clean. You might have lowered your standards but I'd rather die."

Jackson chuckles at me derisively and shrugs. "You and Crawford were made for each other."

Unlikely.

If we were made for each other, he would have loved me when he had the chance.

"Can we focus? I'm on a time crunch here and I need to get back to the Crow's mansion before he realizes I've been here."

Viola rolls a chair over and motions for me to sit before stalking off to find another one for herself. Jackson's eyes stay glued to her ass the entire time and I kick his chair.

"Focus. I need this information and I'm not paying you to stare at Ayres' ass."

He huffs and I send him a copy of the DNA profile I need run through the system. I've already had my usual guy on it but when it came back with sealed records, I knew this was a case for Jackson.

"You already know about the fucking Devil, who else is there? I have a file for her daddy, do you want that?"

I shake my head. "The one you gave Atticus? I have it already. I need to know who else flags as a match."

He stares at me and then starts the search. He starts listing off the siblings, and I mentally tick each one off. Colt, Chance, and Noah are in the system thanks to their rap sheets, Lips is in there because of her hospital stays. Poe was also hospitalized as a toddler thanks to her drug addict mother and Wyatt had his tonsils out.

Nate isn't in the system.

No surprises there.

There's a long stretch of silence and then Jackson blinks at the screen for so long I start to wonder if he's had a stroke.

Then he curses under his breath and runs the search again. "This can't be right. What the fuck is in that man's DNA? Is he some sort of super villain or something?"

My stomach drops a little and Viola glances over at me. "What is it Jackson? Stop messing around."

He scowls at the screen and then sighs, hitting print and I fuss with the hem of my skirt as I wait for the files to print out.

He sighs. "Listen… Senator Blakeley is on the Crow's hit list. He's got some pretty big power moves happening at the moment about trafficking and exploitation laws so there's a lotta eyes on him from our neck of the woods, if you catch my drift."

I think I do but he's such a freaking psycho that I have to ask. "Break it down a little more for me. He's against trafficking?"

Jackson cracks his fingers as he talks like the action is unconscious. "Yeah. He's been a big hitter about kids going missing, women being taken and sold, and the string of prostitute deaths they've been having in DC. He's been getting traction on a lot of laws that will make things a lot harder for that kind of crime to happen."

I nod slowly. I'm not sure where he's going with this but I guess he'll get there eventually if I let him ramble on. "Why would the Crow want him dead then? I'd say that's the type of senator this country needs."

Jackson shrugs and his knee starts bouncing. I don't understand how he spends his life down here in the dark if he needs to move so much to focus.

"The Crow offered to back him, give him a whole lotta money for his campaign because he does want that kind of man making decisions. Blakeley said no, told him once he had the trafficking thing under control he was going to focus on breaches of information. Extortion, money laundering, all sorts of shit that he knows the Crow has interests in. Told him he wasn't ever going to be a kept man."

I nod. I think it's naive but noble enough.

Jackson turns the monitor around until I'm staring at a

screen full of data that means nothing to me. "Blakeley's DNA matches. He's the other Graves sibling."

As I walk back through the secret tunnel back up to the house, I use the light on my phone and I almost miss it. I have to turn the light off to make the call but there's no other sounds in the tunnel so I decide it's worth it.

"Jackson… where does the other tunnel lead? Is that the way down to the basement?"

He grumbles down the line, "What do you mean, there isn't a basement."

Even in the dark my eyes narrow at his bullshit. "Second strike, Jackson. One more and you'll be dead."

He chokes on air and sputters out, "There's no fucking basement! I've been through the house blueprints; I know the whole place like the back of my hand. There's service tunnels and that secret exit you used to come see me but there's no basement. I swear! I swear on Viola, there isn't a fucking basement."

Huh.

I actually believe him. The panic is real in his voice which I know for sure because Viola is in the background of the call trying to figure out what the hell is going on.

So this basement is at the same level of security as mine is… I wonder if his murder board is down here too?

He's always handed me physical documents when I've asked for information; he believes in being able to hold photos and files. Well, that and he's been worried about being hacked which makes sense considering we all know the Coyote.

I don't have to think about it anymore, I hang up on Jackson and switch my phone to silent, creeping my way back through Atticus' house to the room he assigned me. I send a message to Illi about finding a possible lead here and then I change into a pair of Lips' flat shoes. She left behind one of her work bags, or murder packs as Blaise so lovingly calls them, and I was smart enough to bring it along. We're close to the same size in shoes and clothes. Close enough that I can make it work and even though I feel stupid, I change into her black clothes from the bag too, just in case. These clothes are what she wears when she doesn't want to be seen so maybe they'll help me stay invisible enough to check the entire basement out before Atticus and his army of suits notice I'm gone.

If not, I'll just go back again tomorrow.

I grab the knife Lips gave me and taught me exactly how to use and a small torch from her bag, and then I tie my hair up. I feel so strange, like I'm playing dress-up in her things, but I'm not sure how long I'm going to be staying here and with Atticus and Luca gone it might be my best chance to go and check it out.

I barely breathe the entire way down there.

I almost get caught by one of his kitchen staff, already up and baking bread for the morning, but I'm small enough to duck into one of the alcoves until he walks past. My heart is hammering in my chest, so stupid because it's not like Atticus will do anything if I'm caught, but I don't want to lose the opportunity to figure out what the hell is really going on with him and a secret basement?

Best place to hide a murder board.

I get through the wood paneling as easy as the last time and the steps down the second, obscured tunnel are so steep that I have to brace myself against the wall to stop myself from pitching forward. It's too dark to even consider going without the torch on my phone to let my eyes adjust. I never really felt like this place was the dark fortress that Lips and the guys always complained about it being but this is the creepiest thing I've ever done by myself.

I really wish Lips was here.

I count a hundred steps down and then stop because it's too depressing to think about having to climb back up them once I'm done down here, but it's only about a dozen more before I finally reach the bottom.

The basement is really hot.

The air down here is so stuffy that I have to take a second to breathe properly so I don't have a panic attack. Then there's a rattling noise and my heart tries to leap out

of my chest.

If there are rats down here, I will die.

I hold my phone out clutched in both hands ready to call Ash, not that he can help me from hundreds of miles away, and then I hear the groaning.

Fucking groaning.

Here I was thinking that if I can grow up in the Beaumont Manor and hang out at the Butcher's workroom and live with the motherfucking Wolf herself, then I wouldn't be scared of Atticus Crawford's basement.

I was wrong.

This is terrifying.

Why the hell did I even think about coming down here by myself? I could have very easily convinced Aodhan or Illi to come over and do this with me. I know where the secret entry is; I could've just snuck them both in through there.

The groaning gets louder and definitely sounds pained. Who the hell does Atticus have locked down here? The rational part of my brain starts coming up with plausible explanations.

This will be his interrogation room.

It'll be where he's keeping someone strapped to a chair.

This isn't some sort of creepy Collector situation, the groan was too low to be a woman, and there's no way Atticus would be keeping someone chained in his basement.

Except then I round the corner and find a man chained to the floor, a filthy mattress and a bucket sitting with him and a small area partitioned off with a glass wall.

Exactly like Illi had described the collector.

The guy has his back to me but he's mumbling under his breath, a string of nonsense and garbled sounds, and although he's emaciated you can tell he was once a big guy. The clothes he's wearing hang from his rail-thin body and as he rocks gently, I can see his bones sticking out all over him.

None of that makes sense with the Atticus Crawford I grew up with. He wasn't ever a violent man, he didn't ever treat me disrespectfully like his brothers did, and he has protected me from anything that ever threatened me.

But my mother once thought the same about Senior.

She never knew the evil things that he did to women; he hid it from her perfectly until she started questioning the way he was raising and interacting with Joey and Ash. His lack of interest in me. The way he very clearly didn't love us and only ever saw us as possessions.

Could Atticus be the same? Am I blinded by my own childhood crush on him that I'm doomed to do the same as my mother and shackle myself to a monster?

I'm panicking now.

The same panic I had when the doors of that elevator were closing and Lips told me she knew him. The moment

the words tumbled out of her lips that he'd built his entire other life that I had no idea of and everything changed. Everything.

My mind is a whirling mess of panic and I need to either vomit or pass out. I turn and find the murder board I was hoping would be down here but it looks nothing like how I expect it to.

I freeze.

Dozens of photos are printed out, all of them connected with black string and thumbtacks just like my board but the photos themselves are not what I was expecting. I thought I'd be seeing my father's associates and friends, I thought there would be the Crawfords all up there with the deviant behaviors and buying habits. I was expecting big players on the political fronts and judges, FBI senior leaders and some foreign diplomats.

Instead, I'm looking at my family.

Ash, Harley, Blaise, Illi, and Odie are only the beginning. The entire O'Cronin clan is there and every last one of the Graves siblings.

He even has a photo of Nate.

In the center is a photo of Lips from school, a grin on her face and her eyes crossed out with blood.

# SIGN UP FOR MY NEWSLETTER TO HEAR ABOUT UPCOMING RELEASES

# ALSO BY J BREE

## The Bonds That Tie Series

*Broken Bonds*
*Savage Bonds*
*Blood Bonds*
*Forced Bonds*
*Tragic Bonds*
*Unbroken Bonds*

## The Mortal Fates Series

Novellas
*The Scepter*
*The Sword*
*The Helm*

The Trilogy
*The Crown of Oaths and Curses*
*The Throne of Blood and Honor*

**The Mounts Bay Saga**

**The Butcher Duet**
*The Butcher of the Bay: Part I*
*The Butcher of the Bay: Part II*

**Hannaford Prep**
*Just Drop Out: Hannaford Prep Year One*
*Make Your Move: Hannaford Prep Year Two*
*Play the Game: Hannaford Prep Year Three*
*To the End: Hannaford Prep Year Four*
*Make My Move: Alternate POV of Year Two*

**The Queen Crow Trilogy**
*All Hail*
*The Ruthless*
*Queen Crow*

**The Unseen MC**
*Angel Unseen*

# ABOUT J BREE

J Bree is a dreamer, writer, mother, and cat-wrangler. The order of priorities changes daily.

She lives on the coast of Western Australia in a city where it rains too much. She spends her days dreaming about all of her book boyfriends, listening to her partner moan about how the lawns are looking, and being a snack bitch to her three kids.

Visit her website at http://www.jbreeauthor.com to sign up for the newsletter or find her on social media through the links below.

**Also by J Bree**

**The Mounts Bay Saga**

The Butcher Duet
*The Butcher of the Bay: Part I*
*The Butcher of the Bay: Part II*

Hannaford Prep
*Just Drop Out: Hannaford Prep Year One*
*Make Your Move: Hannaford Prep Year Two*
*Play the Game: Hannaford Prep Year Three*
*To the End: Hannaford Prep Year Four*
*Make My Move: Alternate POV of Year Two*

The Queen Crow Trilogy
*All Hail*
*The Ruthless*
*Queen Crow*

The Unseen MC
*Angel Unseen*

# QUEEN CROW

# All Hail